PRAISE FOR *CH...*

"*Pam writes with the warmth...
so characteristic of her. And F...
those church halls where I've h...ed at jumble sales, tried to keep
fit, gone along to local meetings, and danced the night away at
family wedding receptions. Pam introduces us to all those familiar
characters we know so well – although the vicar's not a bit like me!*"

Revd Kate Bottley, broadcaster

"*What a fantastic book! Instantly likeable with wonderful
characters who draw you into the delightful mix of joy, poignancy
and warm familiarity. HOPE HALL at Christmas is well worth
diving into.*"

Lou Fellingham, singer and songwriter

PRAISE FOR THE *HOPE HALL* SERIES

"*Brilliant, witty, and full of down-to-earth humour... Enjoy!*"

JB Gill, TV presenter

"*A delightful read.*" **Revd Cindy Kent MBE, broadcaster**

"*Pam Rhodes has given us a story of warmth, humour, and hope
about lives shared and burdens carried.*"

**Sheridan Voysey, BBC Radio 2 presenter and author of
*Reflect with Sheridan***

"*Written in Pam's characteristic gentle and humorous manner...
powerfully demonstrates the strength of community and the
importance of faith.*"

**Debbie Duncan, author of *Brave: Showing Courage in All
Seasons of Life***

"*Oh, the hours I've spent over the years in halls just like this one!
All of life is there... Pam's storytelling captures it in a brilliant way!*"

Aled Jones, singer and broadcaster

"*A heart-warming story of small town life, beautifully written.*"

Jack Sheffield, author of the *Teacher* series

By the same author

With Hymns and Hearts and Voices
Fisher of Men
Casting the Net
If You Follow Me
Saints and Sailors

In this series

Christmas at Hope Hall

PAM RHODES

LION FICTION

Published by Lion Fiction
www.lionhudson.com
Part of the SPCK Group
SPCK, 36 Causton Street, London, SW1P 4ST

ISBN 978 1 78264 289 3
e-ISBN 978 1 78264 290 9

First edition 2021

Acknowledgments
p. 255: Common Worship: Pastoral Services, material from which is included
here, is copyright © The Archbishops' Council 2000, 2005 and published by
Church House Publishing. Used by permission.

A catalogue record for this book is available from the British Library

Printed and bound in the United Kingdom, June 2021, LH26

*With thanks to Dr Anna Zahorski, who digs out facts before
I even realize I need them, provides encouragement when
I'm waning, and is always the most wonderful friend*

Editor's note

The Hope Hall series was commissioned before COVID-19 reared its ugly head, and Kath Sutton's community and its environs have been fortunate enough to escape any trace of the virus. You won't find any masks, vaccines or hand sanitizer between these pages, but you will enjoy the warmth, humour and human touch so many of us have missed since the pandemic began.

Chapter 1

He was there again!

It was Monday morning – the first in September – and the moment Ray Brown pulled back the bedroom curtains, he spotted the intruder.

That same little dog was sitting on his front lawn, looking for all the world as if he were smiling up at Ray's window. Ray snapped the curtains shut again, deciding he would come back to open them once the uninvited visitor had gone on his way.

Before leaving the room, he tidied the bed and reorganized the bits and pieces on his bedside cabinet and chest of drawers, so that everything looked exactly as it should. With a nod of satisfaction, he pulled the door closed behind him before making his way downstairs.

The house was completely silent. That was the one thing he still hadn't managed to come to terms with. The radio had always been on when Sara was there, and she would hum along with whatever song was playing as she got out the crockery, toast rack and a selection of cereals for the breakfast table. Sometimes he would come downstairs with his nose twitching at the aroma of grilled bacon, heralding the arrival of the full English breakfast his wife had allowed him a couple of times a week.

He hadn't had a breakfast like that for months. In fact, he hadn't had a breakfast like that for more than a year, because that was when Sara's cancer had first taken hold, robbing his beloved wife of any optimism that she could beat this challenge with her usual dogged determination. She couldn't. She had lost that cruel battle a little over five months ago, though it felt like only five days. She had lost her life and he had lost the love of his life. Although he kept going, still working diligently in his role as caretaker at Hope Hall, telling anyone who asked he was fine, he knew that he wasn't really. He was just going through the motions until he could be with her again.

Habit dictated that he sit at the dining-room table to eat his bowl of cereal. He knew Sara would expect that. But even with the radio on, loneliness engulfed him. Mornings always seemed to be the worst. He knew he would feel better once he was on his way to Hope Hall, ready for a busy day at work.

He climbed the stairs again to clean his teeth, then headed into the bedroom, where he gingerly pulled back the curtains to check that the dog had gone. He had. The coast was clear.

Pulling on his favourite anorak, Ray let himself out by the back door so he could collect his pushbike from the garage for the journey to work. He had just climbed on, and was about to set off, when a small furry bundle threw itself at him, barking with excitement, practically knocking Ray and his bike into the flower bed.

"What the devil are *you* doing here?" shouted Ray. "Go home, you mutt! Go back and bark at your own door! I hope you haven't left any unpleasant presents in my garden. Just push off!"

The dog simply sat down on his haunches with his head cocked to one side. His long, pink tongue was lolling out, and one of his ears was completely flat while the other was pointing up at a jaunty angle. His expression was one of sheer delight, as if he couldn't be more pleased to see Ray.

"What sort of a dog are you, anyway?" grumbled Ray, staring at the animal as he considered the question. He was probably some sort of terrier judging by his wiry ginger and white coat. His slight frame suggested he was speedy, agile and small enough to squeeze through seemingly impossible gaps in fences and hedges with ease – as he had obviously done to gain access to Ray's garden. "Well, you've got no breeding, that's for sure," he commented. "Or perhaps you've got too much… a little bit of this, a definite touch of that and far too much of everything else! But you don't live here, so scram! Go on, get off home!"

The dog gave a friendly bark that sounded almost like a farewell salute, then obligingly trotted off. He slipped through the bottom of Ray's hedge before heading down the road.

Ten minutes later, Ray found himself chaining his bike to one of the hooks at the side of the old school building that was part of the Hope Hall complex. The hall stood at right angles to the school, as it had for exactly one hundred years. Just a few weeks earlier, the whole town had gathered there for the centenary celebration of the much-loved memorial hall, during which its old foundation stone had been relaid, and a new plaque had been placed proudly alongside it for future generations to see.

Ray was often the first to arrive, especially on a Monday, but this morning Management Assistant Shirley Wells had plainly beaten him to it. There had been a large christening party at the hall the day before, and Shirley was always keen to get everything completely clean and sparkling before any other use was made of the rooms. Ray smiled to himself. He had been a caretaker and maintenance man for most of his working life – always ready to fix, decorate, manage or mend anything to do with the fabric of a building – but he could never match Shirley's passion for cleaning. She was like a whirling dervish, swooping into every nook and cranny with her mop, duster and squeegee bottle. No spider, smear or speck of dust was safe once she was in action.

"Morning!" Shirley's voice echoed around the empty hall. "Just thought I'd get a head start. Apparently, the Red Cross team who are organizing their first-aid courses for next week are coming in today to have a look around. They'll be wanting absolute cleanliness, and I'm going to make sure they get it!"

"I can see that," grinned Ray. "You're scrubbing that poor windowsill to within an inch of its life!"

"Well, the christening crowd from yesterday left a bit of a mess – and you should see the state of the balcony lounge, where they had their buffet. I'm heading up there next."

"I'll dig out the road safety cones from the store cupboard ready for the cycling proficiency session in the playground this morning," said Ray. "The children will be arriving at about ten o'clock."

"The teacher's already here. He popped his head round the door to say that he'd be sorting out the high-vis jackets in the back of his car if you were looking for him."

"I'll go and meet him then, and make sure he's got everything they need."

"And I'll make us all a cuppa in about fifteen minutes," suggested Shirley, "as soon as I've given that balcony lounge a good seeing to." Her head dropped as she peered down at a minuscule mark on the hall floor and instantly fell to her knees with a cloth and can of spray polish at the ready.

For years, the local junior school had held cycling proficiency classes for all of its pupils during this first academic term of the school year. The children were aged between nine and eleven, some with their own bikes, while others borrowed from the school's own collection, which comprised ones of various ages and states of efficiency. PE teacher Bill Evans had been responsible for these classes from the very start, so Ray knew him well. He liked the friendly, encouraging way Bill had with his pupils, especially those who were plainly terrified of riding a bike, even in the safety of the playground – let alone facing the appalling prospect of venturing on to a road, where there would be cars and lorries to take into account. As a keen cyclist himself, Ray usually remained on hand during these classes, steadying the less certain students and congratulating those whose technique was coming along.

By half past nine, the two men had a route clearly marked out around the old school playground, all prepared for the onslaught of junior-school children, who would come through the Hope Hall gate at exactly ten o'clock. Ray was so engrossed in the class that followed, it was eleven thirty before he knew it, and the children were ready to head back to school for their lunch. Chatting to Bill as he helped carry the jackets and road markings over to the PE teacher's car, Ray suddenly stopped dead in his tracks.

The intruder dog was sitting on the steps of Hope Hall, as bold as brass! He had the same idiotic smile on his face and was staring directly at Ray, fully expecting his own excitement to be matched by his new best friend.

"Your dog?" asked Bill. "He looks like a nice little chap."

"He is *not* my dog!" snapped Ray. "And I'd like to give his owner a piece of my mind! He's been in my garden three mornings in a row now. I've tried to get rid of him, but this is the first time he's actually followed me to work."

"Is he chipped?"

Ray looked at Bill blankly. "*Chipped?*"

"Most dogs and cats have a chip inserted just under the skin at the back of their neck when they are registered with a vet. If this dog has an owner who cares for him, he'll probably be chipped. That'll give you his name, address and the details of whoever owns him."

"How do I find out if he's got a chip?"

"Where's the nearest vet? Probably Smith's on the High Street, I reckon. Why don't you take him down there?"

"Because I have neither the time nor the inclination to have anything to do with that darned dog. He's not mine!"

"Well," said Bill, kneeling down to stroke the soft fur around the dog's ears, "he hasn't taken his eyes off you. *You* might not think he belongs to you, but it seems he does!"

Ray sighed with exasperation. "I'm going to ignore him, go inside and get on with my work. He's sure to get bored and head off to annoy someone else."

Bill stood up with a knowing grin. "Good luck with that. I'll see you – or maybe *both* of you – next Monday. Bye now!"

Within the hour, Ray had come face to face with the dog again, this time inside Hope Hall, where it seemed he had followed a visitor into the Call-in Café. As Ray arrived, the intruder was just finishing off the remains of a customer's pasty and beans, washing it down with a long drink from the bowl of milk that had been put down for him.

"Don't feed him!" yelled Ray. "He doesn't belong here! He needs to find his way home, so let's just put him outside and say goodbye."

"I think he's a stray," commented Shirley, who had appeared at his side. "He's not wearing a collar, and he's definitely hungry. He's a lovely little fella. It might be that he's lost, and somebody's missing him."

"Well, they can come and collect him, and make a promise to keep him secure in his own garden in future," snapped Ray. "He's wandering around the neighbourhood making a real nuisance of himself."

"Oh!" Shirley looked at Ray in surprise. "You're not normally so grumpy. What's up?"

"It's this dog. He's been waiting in my garden every morning, and now he's following me to work. I've had enough. I need to find out where he lives and make sure he stays at home."

"Is he chipped?"

"Oh, don't you start! I've got no idea if he's chipped, and I don't think it should be my job to find out."

"Look, he's obviously attached himself to you. Let's do the right thing. You and I could nip out now, during our lunch hour. I'll ring Smith's and see if they can fit us in to check for a chip. That way we might find out where he lives."

Ray knew better than to argue with Shirley. With a shrug of resignation, he walked back towards the cleaning cupboard,

12

giving the dog a glare as he left. By the time he returned to the foyer, Shirley was waiting with her coat on. The dog was sitting obediently beside her, wearing an impromptu collar made from a bit of rope she had found.

"Come on, then," sighed Ray. "Let's get this over with."

As the trio left the building, Hope Hall Administrator Kath Sutton walked through the foyer on her way to the kitchen, where Catering Supervisor Maggie Stapleton was just pulling three freshly baked quiches out of the oven.

"Wow, they smell delicious!" Kath said. "Can I reserve a couple of pieces of that quiche Lorraine to pick up later? I've got a meeting at the town hall until about four o'clock. Will that be okay?"

Maggie grinned. "I'll put your slices in the fridge right next to mine! They may give it a posh French name nowadays, but my mum just called this egg and bacon pie. I love it!"

Kath laughed. "Me too! I just wanted to check with you about the harvest supper arrangements. The Women's Institute has volunteered to pull it all together, liaising with James Barnard, the vicar across the road at St Mark's, and all the other groups who would like to take part."

"Remind me of the date for that?" called Maggie as she leaned forward to ease a tray of hot pasties out of the oven.

"It's a six o'clock start on the 26th of September. That's the Saturday before St Mark's has its Harvest Festival service on the Sunday morning."

Maggie's head shot up as she reached over to place the tray on the work surface. "I was worried you might say that. I'm away that weekend, I'm afraid."

Kath smiled. "Going anywhere near Chichester?"

Maggie grinned. "It'll be my first visit down to see where Phil actually lives. He's been really good at popping up here once a week, but it's only fair that I take my turn at making the journey.

13

I did book the days off in the office diary. Did you see?"

"Yes, that's why I thought I'd come and see you. Is Liz likely to be available that night?"

"I've already asked her. She's got her sister-in-law's fiftieth birthday party that weekend, and she's doing the catering for that. But Jan here is perfectly capable of organizing the catering for the harvest supper. That would be all right with you, Jan, wouldn't it?"

Jan Hayward was concentrating on the coffee machine, where she was preparing a latte for a customer at the hatch. "The 26th? Yes, that should be all right. Who did you say was organizing the event?"

"The Women's Institute."

Jan looked around sharply.

"Brenda Longstone is the one we need to liaise with," continued Kath.

Jan quickly turned away to focus her attention on filling the coffee cup. "Er, on second thoughts, I'd better just check that date when I get home. Can I let you know?"

"Of course," agreed Kath. "See you later, Mags – and don't let anyone pinch my two portions of that egg and bacon pie before I get back!"

"*Two* portions? Not dining alone tonight, then?"

"Richard's coming over for supper."

"Enjoy!" grinned Maggie.

"We will."

Maggie waited until Kath had left and Jan had finished serving her customer before walking over to join her. "What's going on?" she asked.

Jan shrugged, as if she had no idea what Maggie was talking about.

"You've wanted to take on responsibility for events like this harvest supper for ages. You're more than capable of it, and you said that date was fine until you heard who was organizing it. What

14

have you got against the Women's Institute?"

Jan stiffened. "Nothing at all. I don't know what you mean."

"Jan, we've known each other a long time. Something's wrong here, I know it is. Can I help?"

Jan's expression darkened. "Not unless you can keep that Brenda Longstone well away from me."

"The formidable Brenda, queen bee of the WI for as long as anyone can remember? Have the two of you crossed paths before?"

"More like crossed *swords*! She's a terrible woman."

Maggie's expression was one of puzzlement as she stared at the usually calm, good-natured Jan. "She's certainly difficult."

"She's impossible!"

"She likes to get her own way—"

"She's a *bully*, Maggie. She's always been that way."

"How long have you known her?"

Jan sighed. "Since junior school. She was in the same class as me, and she lived just two doors away, so I was an easy target, whether we were at school or at home."

"That's all a long time ago now, though, isn't it?"

"Not for me. She belittled me, always putting me down in front of the other kids. I still have nightmares about the things she said to get everyone laughing at me. I can't work with her, Maggie. I'm sorry."

Walking across the kitchen to put her arm around Jan, Maggie was alarmed to find that her friend's shoulders were stiff with tension as she recalled these distressing memories.

"I understand. But I also know you are smart, hard-working and incredibly efficient. Perhaps it's time to let your old nemesis know just how capable you are. You have the ability to create a truly wonderful harvest supper menu – and I'd like to help, if you'll let me."

"But if the WI is involved, it'll be Brenda calling the shots, won't it?"

"Not necessarily. This is a joint venture between St Mark's and several other voluntary agencies in the town, as well as the WI. As Catering Manager for the supper, you would naturally take all their tastes and opinions into account, but you would have the final say on what's actually served."

Jan huffed in disbelief. "Brenda will never allow that – especially not from me."

"This event is being held at Hope Hall. You are a trusted senior member of the Hope Hall catering team. You will be preparing the meal. *You* have the final say!"

"Really?" Jan looked doubtful.

"Really."

"And you'll work with me on it?"

"There's a meeting on Wednesday morning to sort out the final details. You and I will go to that together, and we'll make sure we keep bossy Brenda firmly in her place."

"Oh, Maggie, I'm not sure. Can I think about it?"

"Of course. But I've seen you face all sorts of challenges over the years. Somehow it feels important that you don't back away from this one."

Jan nodded, still looking uncertain.

A couple of customers appeared at the hatch as they worked their way along the serving shelves trying to decide which treats to choose.

"Duty calls," smiled Maggie. "And you're going to need more coleslaw. I'll make some up now."

Half an hour later, Ray and Shirley returned to Hope Hall with the little dog trotting happily between them on his makeshift lead.

"Well, that was a waste of time!" grumbled Ray. "No chip, so no details of the mutt's owner."

"He probably is a stray," said Shirley, "although his coat's in good condition."

"So if the vet can't do anything, what happens now?"

"I'm going to take a few nice shots of him, and we'll make up some posters to stick on lamp posts around your area. Someone might know where he's come from."

"And where does he stay in the meantime?"

"With you."

"No!"

"Yes. That's the only reasonable answer. This dog seems to have taken a liking to you. He trusts you. You'll have to take responsibility for him until we've found his owner."

"I most certainly do *not*! I've never had a dog. I haven't the faintest idea how to look after one."

"They need one big meal a day, a good walk morning and evening, fresh water and a warm bed. That's it."

"I don't want that dog in my house."

"Where else will he be safe?"

"Someone else's house. Yours! Why don't *you* take him?"

"Because we've got a cat."

"Don't dogs and cats get on?"

"Only in Hollywood cartoons. Our cat would scratch this little fella's eyes out."

Ray sighed with exasperation. "Aren't there rescue homes for stray dogs? What about the RSPCA or the council? Can't we ring them?"

"Yes, but that vet said he knew for certain that they've got more stray dogs to care for right now than pens to keep them in. So what I suggest, Ray Brown, is that you stow our little friend safely in your storeroom while I run off those posters and you nip down to the supermarket to buy dog food and biscuits."

"What do dogs even eat? I've got no idea!"

"Ask the supermarket staff – they'll sort you out. Let's meet up again in an hour, then we'll head out to knock on a few doors and put some posters up."

"We are employees of Hope Hall!" retorted Ray. "We can't

go gallivanting around the town when we have jobs to do this afternoon."

"I started much earlier than I needed to this morning, and you've worked so much overtime that taking a couple of hours off will be absolutely fine. I'll pop back before five to make sure everything's ready for Brownies and Cubs this evening, and I'll nip back to lock up after nine when they've left."

"But that's *my* job."

"Not today. You'll need to be at home taking care of your new lodger."

Ray grunted with indignation.

"We need a name for him," said Shirley.

"No we don't. He's probably already got a name."

"Agreed, but what do we call him in the meantime?"

"Dog!" snapped Ray.

Shirley smiled sweetly at him. "Fine. Off you go, Dog. Take the nice man to his storeroom and make yourself at home!"

"Hello, you."

Kath could hear the smile in Richard Carlisle's voice as she answered the mobile call on her car's sound system.

"Hello yourself! How's your day going? Did you get through that finance meeting without too much trouble?"

"I think it was a challenge for all of us to keep our eyes open while the accountant was going through his huge list of nitty-gritty transactions line by line. But the devil's in the detail, as they say, and I know that to be true."

"You sound tired."

"A little. I burned the midnight oil into the wee small hours last night to make sure I had all the facts and figures ready for the meeting."

"You probably need a shoulder rub."

"I most certainly do. How soon can you get here?"

"I'm driving in the wrong direction at the moment. I had a meeting at the town hall this afternoon, and I need to get back to Hope Hall to catch up on a few things before I head home. Are you still planning to pop over for supper?"

"Definitely."

"Good, because I managed to bag a couple of pieces of Maggie's famous quiche Lorraine, made fresh this morning, so it'll be well worth your while."

"It's you I'm longing to see. Although Maggie's quiche Lorraine is a very welcome bonus."

"Right answer! I'll add some strawberries and ice cream just for that."

"You temptress! I'll be there about seven. That okay?"

"I can't wait," she said with a happy sigh.

As she said goodbye, she realized she really couldn't wait to see that lovely man again. It had all been such a whirlwind. Their paths had first crossed quite dramatically back in May, when she tripped over and dropped her files at his feet as he arrived at Hope Hall for a trustees' meeting for the Money Advice Service. Every Friday, experienced and caring volunteer financial advisors provided discreet help and support for those struggling with overwhelming debt, as many local people were.

Over the weeks that followed, the couple had bumped into each other on one occasion after another, although Kath had initially picked up the wrong impression that Richard, a widower, was romantically involved with Celia Ainsworth, who had actually turned out to be his cousin rather than his partner. That misunderstanding had finally been sorted out a month ago, and the pair had enjoyed spending time together ever since, growing closer as they got to know more about each other. Richard was such easy company – caring, funny, compassionate, clever and romantic. Kath felt as though her feet barely touched the ground these days.

Glancing at the clock to see it was already half past four, Kath parked her car outside Hope Hall and quickly grabbed her bag from the back seat before hurrying in through the main door. She had a lot to get through before she could leave that afternoon. She needed a coffee, an undisturbed couple of hours or so to concentrate – and a post-it reminder somewhere obvious to make sure she picked up that quiche before she headed home!

Dog burst into a frenzy of barking the moment he heard the front gate squeak open.

"Keep the noise down!" ordered Ray as he hurried to open the front door. "You'll wake the whole street!"

Dog was too busy jumping up and down with excitement to pay any attention. He loved it when Shirley's son Tyler came to the door, knowing it meant a half-hour walk around the park, with several stops along the way to catch or find sticks that Tyler would throw for him.

"I can't spend as long with him today," laughed Tyler as Dog stood on his hind legs to flatten his new friend against the wall in greeting. "I'll take him out for a nice walk, but I'll have to drop him off to you at the hall early enough to get down to the uni in Portsmouth by one o'clock. They're doing a special lecture before the new term starts. It sounds great. It's on machine learning and artificial intelligence."

"What's that all about? Robots?" queried Ray, trying unsuccessfully to pull Dog away so that Tyler could move. "Get down, Dog! Sit! I said *sit*!"

"It means that when you give a command, computerized technology and programming make sure your order is obeyed."

"Do they do a course for stupid dogs?" grumbled Ray.

"There's always the Waggy Tail Club at Hope Hall," grinned Tyler. "But I think they train the owners there as much as the dogs."

"I'm not this dog's owner!"

"Ah, but does *he* know that? No response to Mum's posters yet?"

"Not so far. Perhaps he doesn't live around here at all. Maybe he hopped into the back of a van and found himself miles away from home. If he's a genuine stray in need of a new owner, we'll have to contact one of the proper animal rescue organizations to arrange all that."

Dog was gazing up at the two men with great interest, finally sitting obediently at Ray's feet and looking up at him adoringly.

"Oh Ray, you can grumble all you like," grinned Tyler, "but I've watched you with this little fella. He might drive you mad, but he also makes you laugh, and I've heard you chatting away to him as you potter around the place. Go on, admit it – he's actually quite good company!"

"I don't want a dog."

"You *didn't* want a dog. But I think you've got one now."

"I need to get to work," mumbled Ray, barely noticing that his fingers were scratching the soft fur between the dog's ears as he spoke. "You two get off on your walk, and I'll see you up at the hall later."

Shutting the front door once Tyler had disappeared down the garden path with Dog trotting along beside him, Ray wandered into the kitchen to wash up his breakfast things. He bent down to pick up the ball Dog had carried into the kitchen earlier, hoping Ray might like to throw it for him to catch. He nearly tripped over the metal bowl left in the middle of the floor after Dog had used his nose to push it around the kitchen in his enthusiasm to make sure his long pink tongue had licked up every possible scrap of breakfast biscuit.

That animal is a nuisance, thought Ray. *He makes a mess everywhere he goes.*

But with Dog out for a walk, the uncomfortable blanket of absolute silence had fallen around the house once again, overwhelming him with a deep longing for the gentle, familiar sounds he remembered from a lifetime of sharing a home with Sara. He shuddered, then reached out to switch on the radio before turning on the hot tap and squirting washing-up liquid into the bowl.

Celia Ainsworth looked up from her desk when she heard her office door open.

"Hi, sweetheart. You look busy."

In walked Joe Munro, Financial Director of Apex Finance UK, the corporate institution with its parent company in the States that had employed her for the last two decades. She had been promoted to the role of Pension Fund Director eight years ago, which had not only given her responsibility for the pensions of hundreds of Apex employees across the UK, but also for the many thousands of employees in other businesses, large and small, who were members of staff pension schemes arranged by Apex through their employers. "Ah, you know me, Uncle Joe," Celia smiled. "Never happier than when I've got a balance sheet to pore over."

"I'm just checking you're still coming over for dinner tonight. Your Aunt Trish insisted I come and make sure you've remembered. She's cooking duck in some posh sauce. She's just bought herself another new cookbook, apparently, and she's very excited about it."

"I wouldn't miss one of Aunt Trish's special dinners for the world," grinned Celia.

"Are you coming straight from work? Do you want a lift?"

"I'll need my car, because I want to call in for a word with Douglas on my way over to you. There are a couple of points on the agenda for the Ainsworth Mill board meeting I'd like more information on before we all meet up next week."

"And you think Douglas is likely to give you sensible answers to any of your questions? Darling girl, Douglas might be the hereditary CEO of your family's highly successful breakfast cereal business, but you've got more business acumen in your little finger than that air-brained brother of yours."

Celia sighed. "I know. Douglas has neither the interest nor the capacity for financial detail, but there are two or three items in those notes that really do need more context before we discuss them. Have you looked at the paperwork yet? You're on the board too. What do you think?"

"I think you should forget your visit to Ainsworth Hall this evening and come straight over to dinner with me and Trish. We can talk things through together after we've eaten, and then perhaps I can bring up your queries with Douglas myself so he doesn't realize it's you who's asking. You know how he always reacts to any real involvement you try to take in the Mill's affairs. He knows you have to be on the board as a family member, but he definitely resents it. He feels threatened by you, of course – and so he should. You understand business; he doesn't. He enjoys the salary and prestige of being Chief Executive of Ainsworth Mill, but it should have been you who took on that role after we lost your father."

Celia picked up a handful of papers from her desk and tapped them into a neat pile. "That's the family tradition, Uncle Joe. The eldest boy takes the title. Dad never wavered in his wish to uphold that process, because that's the way his father and grandfather agreed it should be."

"I knew your father all his life. He was my dear friend, but I never understood his commitment to that old tradition when he was always so proud of your natural understanding of how things worked best at the Mill."

"Water under the bridge, Uncle Joe – and look what's happened instead. Here I am at Apex with a senior position that no other woman in the company has managed to reach. I love my work here. Yes, I will always take an interest in Ainsworth's, and I'll never stop worrying about how it's run, but I'm happy here. It's fine."

Joe smiled affectionately at her. "Seven o'clock for dinner then, and don't be late. Trish is longing to see you, and so am I."

He blew her a kiss before closing the door behind him, leaving Celia to turn her attention back to the complex set of figures spread out across her desk.

"Liver and bacon!" enthused Percy, rubbing his hands together gleefully as a plate of food was placed in front of him by a rather nervous-looking girl from the local senior school who was doing work experience in the Call-In Cafe that day. "With mashed potato, onions and carrots. Just the ticket! But I need more gravy. Liver and bacon needs lashings of gravy!"

Kitchen Assistant Kevin – who had first been introduced to Maggie and the catering team at Hope Hall back in the spring term as a work experience student during his final year at school – hurried across with a jug of extra gravy, which he placed on the table in front of Percy with a flourish.

"That's my boy!" Percy Wilson made a show of pushing his napkin into his shirt collar before picking up his knife and fork and tucking into his dinner.

His old friend Robert eyed Percy's plate with envy from the seat beside him. "I'd love to eat that," he sighed, "but Joyce has put me on a strict diet. She rang Maggie and told her the doctor says I've got to lose weight because of my diabetes, and now I'm only allowed salad at lunchtime."

"Your daughter has no right to do that. A man should be in charge of his own destiny," pronounced Percy as a drip of gravy trickled down his chin. "Especially when it comes to his dinner."

The Grown-ups' Lunch Club was in full swing around them, with the foyer of Hope Hall set up for more than forty pensioners all seated around tables covered in crisply ironed cloths adorned with shining cutlery and neatly folded serviettes. Sharing the table with Percy and Robert were their two regular companions, Connie and John. They all enjoyed the reflected glory of being on Percy's table, because he was a constant source of entertainment with his funny quips, insightful comments and his ability to come back with a one-liner capable of putting prim and prissy Ida Miller, their neighbour on the next-door table, firmly in her place whenever her acid comments drifted Percy's way.

At that moment, Ida was far too busy examining the plate that had just been placed before her to be concerned with Percy Wilson. "These carrots are overcooked," she announced, prodding her fork into the vegetables with disgust. "All the taste and goodness goes out of them when they're cooked beyond al dente."

"You what?" asked Betty from the opposite side of the table. "Did you say something about dentures? I've got some of those. Shouldn't I be eating this with them?"

"These carrots are so soft you could eat them with your naked gums," stated Ida, pushing the carrots to one side of her plate. "This is like baby food, it's been cooked so long."

"I like it soft," said Flora, shovelling a piece of liver laden with carrot into her mouth, "and this mash is delicious. I can never be bothered to make mash at home these days, but it's always good here."

"There's too much butter in it," retorted Ida. "It's not good for us at our age."

"Speak for yourself," mumbled Doris. "I like more butter than potato in my mash! And I love liver. It reminds me of my mum. She cooked it for lunch every Saturday, regular as clockwork. She didn't bother with bacon back then. We never had much bacon in those days."

"Kidney!" enthused Flora. "I haven't had kidney for years. They don't even put it in steak pie these days, do they?"

"Offal is awful!" grinned Betty. "That's what my granddaughter said before she turned vegetarian. Honestly, her generation don't know what they're missing."

"Liver is full of nutrients, especially iron," stated Ida. "And kidney is good for your heart. Anyway, let's stop talking and eat our meals while they're hot."

At that moment, Ray walked past their table on his way to speak to Shirley, who was always on hand during the Grown-ups' Lunch Club.

"Tyler's just rung me," Ray said. "He's bringing Dog in here because he's off to a special lecture down at the uni this afternoon."

Shirley smiled. "Yes, it's some sort of introductory event before the real term gets going in two weeks' time. Do you know, when you suggested a Computer Science degree might be just the right thing for Tyler, I have to say I was very doubtful – and I still am at times. That son of mine has been such a lazy so-and-so in the past. I know he likes computers and has a bit of a flair for them, but I worry that once he gets started on this degree course he won't stick at it."

"Well," replied Ray, "you've got to give him the chance to prove that he really wants to do it. Personally, I think his natural skill with computers is much more than just 'a bit of a flair'. He's got a real talent for it, so hopefully he'll prove you wrong, make a great success of this degree and have the prospect of a productive career in technology ahead of him."

"I certainly hope so, but then I am his mum," grinned Shirley. "I'm still going to nag him to put the seat down and wash behind his ears!"

"You need to let him grow up and take responsibility for his own future – and his personal hygiene!" smiled Ray. "Oh look, here he comes now."

Tyler hadn't quite made it through the main door of the hall before Dog, still attached to the old extending lead Shirley had dug out for him from her garage, flew into the foyer, weaving his way around one table, then another. As he approached Percy's group, Connie did a double take, staring intently at him.

26

"Banjo?! What are you doing here?"

Shirley was immediately at her side. "Do you know this dog, Connie?"

"Of course! It's Maud's dog. Well, not hers, exactly. I think he just turned up at her door one day and she let him in whenever he arrived. But yes, he's definitely hers."

Standing beside Shirley, Ray looked pale with shock. "We've put posters up everywhere with his picture on full display. Why didn't your friend come forward and claim him?"

"She's dead."

"What?!"

"She had a heart attack about two weeks ago. So tragic. They didn't find her for three days. No one noticed she was gone."

A flurry of comment rippled around the foyer as the others reacted to this sad news.

"I remember seeing all the police cars outside once they found her. I mean, I live just across the road from Maud. I've known her for years, although we were never very close. She always liked to keep herself to herself. I hadn't seen her for ages – I don't think she'd left the house for a couple of years or more. She never married, so there was no family. I saw a nurse going in to give her a check-up about once a week. Someone told me it was the nurse who found her."

"And what about the dog?" asked Shirley. "Didn't the police make arrangements for someone to look after him with Maud gone?"

"I don't think they even knew she fed him. I suppose he's just been wandering around on his own ever since."

Shirley turned to look at Ray, who was just staring down at the dog. "Did I hear you call him by a name?" he asked.

"Banjo. That's what Maud called him."

Ray's eyes suddenly shone with tears. "When I first met my Sara, her mum and dad had a dog she loved. He was Banjo too."

27

Shirley reached out to squeeze his hand. "Looks like your Sara thinks you need a Banjo of your own."

Ray nodded, rubbing his hands across his eyes before kneeling down in front of Banjo, who was sitting at Ray's feet, anxiously looking up at him. Ray's big hand cupped the dog's head, gently stroking his sandy-coloured fur. "Okay, boy. It looks as though you'll be coming home with me."

Chapter 2

"Mums, before you all leave this morning, can I just mention something I hope you'll be interested to hear?" Jen had to raise her voice to be heard over the babble of under-fives all scrabbling to change back into their outdoor shoes and pick up coats and bags as they left at the end of their preschool playgroup session, which was held every weekday morning in the old school hall.

"Can you take a look at the poster over there on the noticeboard, please? The Red Cross is organizing a series of first-aid courses here at Hope Hall over the coming month. The first one, starting at ten on Wednesday morning next week, is aimed specifically at people who look after children, in whatever circumstances that might be. Obviously, you should be interested as parents, but if grandparents in your family sometimes look after your children, or friends and neighbours, then this two-hour course is a must. Quite simply, it could save your child's life. The organizers are keen to have some idea of numbers, so could you please put your name on the list as soon as possible to secure your place?"

"What's happening to this playgroup next Wednesday?" enquired one mum. "I have to work that morning, so I won't be able to get to the course, and it'll be really difficult for me if the playgroup isn't running that day."

"Carol and I are already qualified first-aiders, and it's a stipulation of our job that we keep our skills and qualifications up to date, so we don't need to go on this course, because it isn't meant for us. It's a basic practical tuition opportunity aimed at parents and carers. So we'll be here to run the playgroup as usual, looking after the children while as many of you as possible go along to take part."

There was a murmur of chatter around the hall as the mums digested this.

"I'm definitely going to that," announced Cherie as she pulled her son Dylan's socks up before struggling to put trainers on the wriggling three-year-old's feet. "I've often worried about what I'd do if Dylan stopped breathing or fell unconscious after banging his head or if he had a really violent fever. It's the stuff of nightmares, isn't it? The idea that your toddler might be in trouble and you don't know what to do to help him."

Sitting next to her, Lorraine didn't answer as she sat Molly on her knee, helping the two-year-old toddler slide her arms into her favourite fluffy pink cardigan.

"You'll come, won't you?" asked Cherie. "I don't want to go on my own."

"I'm not sure," replied Lorraine.

Cherie turned to give her friend a direct look. "You've got to come. It's important. We'll go together, then you can remember whatever I forget."

"I'll have to see," said Lorraine, avoiding Cherie's gaze. "I might be busy that morning."

"You're never busy on Wednesday mornings except for coming here. You know Molly will be fine with Jen and Carol. Come on, Lorraine, this is a no-brainer. Of course you should come. You don't want to miss an opportunity like this!"

"Can I let you know?"

Cherie huffed with impatience. "Well, I'm going to sign up now. Do you want me to add your name just in case places are limited?"

"I'll have a think about it tonight, and I'll put my name on the list tomorrow if I can make it."

Cherie's eyes narrowed with curiosity as she looked at her friend. "Are you okay?"

Lorraine tried to smile, but it didn't quite reach her eyes. "Yeah, course I am."

Cherie regarded her silently for several seconds before grabbing Dylan's hand and bag, and heading towards the noticeboard. "Right, please yourself. I'm going, anyway. See you tomorrow. Bye!"

Lorraine waited until most of the parents and children had cleared the room before gathering Molly into her arms. It was then that she finally crossed the hall to look at the noticeboard. She read the poster carefully. The course looked excellent, and she knew it would be if it was hosted by a professional organization like the Red Cross. It was such a sensible and practical idea, and a wonderful opportunity for parents with small children like Molly to go along. And naturally, the techniques and information they would learn there could save lives. Any parent who loved their child half as much as she loved Molly should definitely make a point of going along.

Except her. She didn't need to learn the medical techniques that might be urgently required in an emergency involving her child. She knew them all. They came as second nature to Lorraine. She'd known them for years. If any child needed emergency treatment, she was the capable, efficient professional any parent would want to have at their side.

Except when it was *her* child, that is.

Every sensible thought had drained out of her head when it was *her* child in trouble. She had gone to pieces, and another darling boy had died.

"Nanny!" yelled Bobbie, struggling to keep hold of his favourite fire engine toy as he climbed the stairs up to the apartment.

Maggie was waiting at the top to scoop her grandson into her arms. "I've got a present for you. A very funny gingerbread man!"

"Why's he funny?"

"Come and see!"

Maggie had propped a gingerbread man she had decorated as a fireman up on the kitchen work surface, complete with a yellow helmet and big yellow boots. He had a lop-sided grin and a mop of soft brown hair that made him look just like Bobbie. Having just celebrated his third birthday, the little boy had already announced that he was going to be a fireman when he grew up, and that whenever he visited his nan he would have to bring his big red fire engine with him.

"Wow!" Bobbie's eyes were as big as saucers.

"Would you like a glass of milk with it?" asked his mother, Steph, who had followed him inside.

"It's me! I can't eat me!"

"Fair point," smiled Maggie. "I made us all some chocolate chip cookies, just in case. Coffee for you, Steph?"

"Oh, yes please! It's been a busy morning. I nipped round to one of my old customer's homes while Bobbie was at playgroup, to cut and colour her hair."

"Well, you're a great hairdresser. I'm not surprised your customers have been missing you."

"It got me thinking. Bobbie will be at playgroup so much more now he's had his birthday, and he absolutely loves being there. That would give me the chance to fit in a few more customers on a regular basis."

"That should work well, then. Will you always go to their homes?"

"I'd be happy to do that, but Dale suggested the other night that we could put a lay-back sink in our downstairs utility room, along with a special seat and mirror, so I could have a proper hairdressing area there."

"What a great idea!"

"Yes, it is. I'm quite excited about it really. It makes it easier that Dale's a plumber. He's not a great carpenter, though."

"Phil is. I know he'd love to help out with a project like that."

"Oh, I couldn't ask him. It's not as if he even lives in the town."

"Chichester isn't that far away, and you know how much he enjoys being here. I'm sure he'd love to help."

A slow smile crept across Steph's face as she looked at her mother. "You really like him, don't you?"

"I do. But it's just as important to me that *you* like him. I'm not being an old fool, am I?"

Steph chuckled. "No, but I'm beginning to understand how you must have felt when I brought new boyfriends home to meet you. I just want for you now what you've always wanted for me – happiness. You've been through a lot this past year, with Dad leaving and taking on a completely new family – and now that new little daughter of his, Aurora. All of that rocked your foundations. You've had to leave the home you lived in for twenty-five years, and you've been forced into a divorce. You've had a tough time of it. No one deserves happiness more than you do."

"And Phil does make me happy."

"I can see that. He seems like a genuinely nice man."

Maggie nodded. "He's always been a lovely person, right back to our school days. A whole crowd of us used to meet up to walk to school together, and I had such a crush on him."

"You walked down this very road, didn't you!"

"Past this house, which I knew so well because my best friend lived here. I never imagined I would be living here myself at this stage in my life. It's all come full circle, really. A new home, and another chance to get to know that very special man who simply walked back into my life as if he'd always been there."

"Well, he's certainly put a sparkle in your eye. You look great, Mum. Everyone's noticed the difference in you."

"But we're taking things slowly," insisted Maggie. "He pops up for a visit once a week, and I'm going down to Chichester in a couple of weekends' time. I'm looking forward to it, and he's excited that I'll be able to see him in his own surroundings at last."

Steph gave a cheeky grin. "So he's good at carpentry, is he?"

"It's one of his favourite hobbies."

"And you don't think he'd mind me asking?"

"I think he'd be pleased if you did. Anyway, it may be a while since he lived in these parts, but he grew up in this town, and he thinks of it as home. He always enjoys being here, and I know he'd help if you let him."

"Well, let's see how your weekend in Chichester goes first. Take a look at his cupboards and then report back!" Steph stepped forward to hug her mum as the two women laughed together.

Among the many things Kath and Richard were gradually realizing they had in common, they soon discovered a mutual love for creating tasty meals. From the first occasion when Kath had offered to make a curry with all the trimmings at her apartment, Richard had joined her in the kitchen; not simply as her "beautiful assistant", as he laughingly described himself, but as her companion at the cookbook. They discussed, suggested, tasted, added a pinch here and an extra ingredient there, and eventually chatted their way through the leisurely meal that had brought them as much pleasure in the making as in the eating. It was no surprise that the two of them were happily busy in the kitchen as they prepared a special Sunday lunch for Richard's son, William, the day before he was due to take up his place at the University of Plymouth.

William's A-level results – three As and a B – had clinched the deal. Two days after the results were announced, he had received a letter from the Royal Navy to say that he had been accepted onto its graduate training programme. He would initially be funded to study for a foundation degree in Maritime Science at the university, then go on to receive full officer salary while continuing to study towards a BSc honours degree in Nautical Science. When William realized there would be plenty of opportunity for practical naval experience at sea throughout his time at university, he simply couldn't wait to leave!

Richard was thrilled for his son, and clearly very proud of his achievements and potential, but Kath could read between the lines to see that he was having mixed feelings as William prepared to leave home. As a widower who had shared some very challenging times with his much-loved son in the five years since his wife's death, the exciting prospect of William moving away was tinged with a sense of loss and dread. The house would seem so empty without him. Richard would miss the constant thumping of music emanating from his son's room, and the sound of teenage voices on the many occasions when his friends came over and stayed for hours. He would miss their shared interest in Sea Cadets, and the many evenings when they would take themselves out for a plate of pasta before seeing the latest blockbuster together.

Quite early on in their relationship, Kath had gently broached the subject of how Richard was really feeling.

"William wasn't even twelve years old when Elizabeth fell ill," he'd explained. "It was a tough time for both of us, but especially for him, I think. His mum was dreadfully ill for several months, with nurses coming and going, which meant the atmosphere at the house was strained and tense, with William constantly being told to keep quiet and stay out of the way, or being foisted on to other families when Elizabeth was particularly poorly. By the time she died, the two of us had established a closeness that was so much more than the typical relationship between a young boy and his dad. We felt more like two floundering people who just clung together as things went from bad to worse to downright desperate. Since then, it's often felt as if it's the two of us against the world, and that's created a very special bond between us."

Kath found herself thinking about that conversation while watching the concentration on Richard's face as he stuffed cloves of garlic and rosemary into the slits he had made in the large leg of lamb he was preparing for William's favourite Sunday lunch. Drawing level with him as she passed by on her way to the vegetable rack to pick up the potatoes and carrots she needed to peel, she quietly laid her head on his shoulder. Richard tilted his head to rest against hers, and they stood wordlessly like that for a few seconds before they both went on with their tasks.

They had guests joining them for William's special lunch that day. The young man had enjoyed a rather wild night out with his friends on the Friday evening, then spent most of Saturday in bed recovering, but today was the family goodbye, when they would be joined by Celia, his uncle Joe and aunt Trish. Kath had yet to meet Joe and Trish, who were obviously dearly loved by Richard and his cousin Celia. It was Joe who had introduced Celia to Apex Finance, watching with pride as she had moved up the ranks.

When Kath had enquired about the family tree, and how Joe and Trish fitted in, Richard had explained that his mother, Nancy, had been the only sister of James, Celia's father. Joe, Nancy and James had grown up together, remaining lifelong best friends. Even though Richard and Celia had both lost their parents, Joe was as devoted to their family as he was to his own. The opportunity to see young William head off to his new life as a naval officer was an occasion he just couldn't miss!

Joe and Trish were the first guests to arrive. Richard greeted them at the door before William came downstairs to hug them both enthusiastically. He invited them upstairs to see how he was getting on with his packing, and to help him work out what to take and what to leave behind. Kath decided to let the family members greet each other at leisure, choosing to stay on duty in the kitchen at first, and then in the dining room as she set the table with everything they would need for lunch. She was just running a tea towel around all the crystal glasses to make sure they were absolutely sparkling when Richard walked in with the visiting couple so Kath could be introduced to them. Without hesitation, Joe and Trish hugged Kath warmly.

"I can't tell you how delighted we are to hear that this crusty old chap has finally relaxed enough to allow someone to share his life," Joe enthused. "You, dear lady, have broken through the shell, and we couldn't be more delighted. Welcome to the family!"

Deeply touched, Kath caught Richard's eye and was relieved to see that he was smiling at her with good humour, love and even a little pride. That look ignited a warm glow deep inside her as she realized how long she had waited to feel such genuine happiness in her life.

"Can I get you both a drink?" she asked as her cheeks turned pink with all the attention. "A gin and tonic, perhaps? Or a glass of wine?"

"Gin and tonic would be lovely," smiled Trish.

"I'm guessing you'll want a whisky, Joe," smiled Richard as he walked over to the sideboard in the dining room to fetch the decanter.

"Let's leave the men to it," Trish suggested to Kath. "Do you need a hand with anything?"

"It's all just cooking now," replied Kath, "but I'd love your company while I make up the starters and put the finishing touches to dessert."

"Give me an apron and a job!" grinned Trish as the two women headed for the kitchen.

It didn't take Kath long to realize that Trish was very easy company. They chatted about everything from the price of shellfish to the frustration caused by roadworks on the local bypass, and even managed to cover national politics and favourite radio presenters along the way. Finally, when the scallop starter was ready except for the cooking needed at the last minute, and autumn fruits in cherry brandy sauce had been made to accompany the hazelnut cream meringue Kath had already prepared, their conversation became more personal.

"It really is good to see you so at home here," said Trish. "Richard has needed this for so long. We've known all too well how lonely he's been. He's thrown himself into work and been determined not to wear his heart on his sleeve. I suppose most people would have thought he was just fine. He hasn't been fine, though, and that's even more obvious now that we can see how happy he is with you."

Kath smiled. "He's making me very happy too. It's unbelievable how quickly things have changed for us both. I really never saw this coming."

"Had you been on your own for a while?"

"I used to work in London as a senior administrator at a large teaching hospital. It was one of those jobs that was constantly demanding, although I must admit I enjoyed every minute of it. Then, when my mother became very ill five years ago, I had no choice but to return here to look after her. That meant breaking up with the doctor I'd been having a very relaxed relationship with for some time. He was busy; so was I. I suppose we'd never really got round to analysing our true feelings. I realized at that point that I was hoping he might want to stop me leaving London by reassuring me that we had a long-term future together."

"But he didn't."

"No."

"So you came home. Are you still looking after your mother?"

"She died nearly three years ago. I took on the role of administrator at Hope Hall soon after that."

"And I hear many good things about the difference you've made there. Hope Hall's fulfilling a much-needed role in the community. No wonder people speak so highly of it."

Kath smiled. "Well, there's never a dull moment at the hall, that's for sure."

"Is that where you and Richard crossed paths?"

"Yes. The Sea Cadets came to use our facilities during the summer months after asbestos was found on the roof of their hut."

"Oh yes. Richard's on the board of the local Sea Cadet unit, isn't he? You can take the man away from the sea, but you can't take the sailor out of the man..."

Kath chuckled at the memory of how they had met. "He kept popping in during their evening meetings."

"Much to William's frustration, I imagine."

"Well, I did suggest that William might prefer not to be constantly watched by his father while he was there."

"So the two of you went off to do something else instead?"

"We went to the pub for a meal and ended up talking so much that Richard almost forgot to go back and collect him!"

"And you haven't run out of conversation since."

"No. And I don't think we ever will."

Trish laid her hand on top of Kath's. "I can see that. Richard's a very lucky man."

At that moment the doorbell rang, heralding the arrival of Celia. All the family members greeted and hugged each other, while Kath held back, still a little uncertain around Richard's formidable cousin. Their relationship hadn't begun well, as Celia had been superior to the point of rudeness towards Kath on the first few occasions they had come across each other. However, the air had been cleared, and some misunderstandings had been put right when Celia invited Kath, Richard and Hope Hall's accountant, Trevor, to a sumptuous restaurant dinner. The two women had seen little of each other since then, and Kath still felt the need to be slightly reserved in Celia's company. She needn't have worried, though. Richard immediately made a point of drawing Kath into the conversation, and was right beside her as the two of them invited everyone to take their places at the table so they could serve lunch.

The meal couldn't have gone better, with the guests gushing over their obvious enjoyment of each course. The focus was on William, with everyone wanting to know as much as he could tell them about his university course, where he would be living and what he was looking forward to most of all. Kath was struck by how much she had missed Sunday lunches like this. When her parents were alive and her sister was still living in England – before she married her Australian farmer and headed off to the wilds of the outback – the Sutton family had enjoyed many chatty meals together just like this. Being accepted into the heart of another family, especially as the partner of a kind and fascinating man like Richard, moved her deeply, as each of the people around the table, even Celia, made a point of making sure her thoughts and opinions were heard along with their own. They laughed, they bickered in a good-natured way, and they slipped their shoes off under the table and made themselves comfortable as they drank coffee and after-lunch brandy. When they all raised their glasses to William and drank his health, Kath felt an overwhelming sense of belonging, having been so willingly welcomed into this delightful gathering.

It was gone five o'clock before Joe and Trish announced that they needed to get going, and as the couple gathered up their coats and went to say their goodbyes to William, Celia made her way over to stand beside Kath.

"So you're a wonderful cook too! As if you needed culinary skills to win Richard's heart, when you've obviously done that already. William leaving for university could have been completely devastating for Richard, yet you've come along at just the right time to soften that blow. You've put a smile on my cousin's face, Kath. Make sure it stays there. He can't be hurt again."

Then, to Kath's surprise, Celia leaned forward to air-kiss her in the vicinity of both cheeks before giving a friendly wave to the others as she headed for the front door.

Sometime later, once the table was cleared and the dishwasher loaded, Kath went upstairs to William's room to see how the packing was coming along. He was sitting at his desk with his earphones on, obviously engrossed in something he was watching on his laptop.

He got to his feet to greet her when he saw her standing there.

"I'm about to leave you and your dad to enjoy your last evening together," she smiled. "Good luck, William! I hope you love every moment of your university experience."

Without hesitation, he wrapped his arms around her in a great big bear hug.

She was surprised by how emotional she felt at this sudden show of affection. Ever since she'd started getting to know Richard and his son better, she had been anxious not to appear as though she were trying to take the place of William's mother. Before long, though, it had become clear that William was missing having a mother figure in his life. He had been warm and accepting towards her from the start of her friendship with his father, which had been as much of a relief to Richard as it had to Kath herself. She was under no illusion about the fact that if Richard were ever forced to choose between his son and the new woman in his life, his loyalty and love for William would be paramount, exactly as it should be.

"Take care of yourself." Her voice was muffled against his shoulder.

"I will – if you'll promise to take care of Dad for me. He's more of a worry than I am!"

She stepped back a little to look directly at him. "I will. I promise."

Minutes later, when she was back downstairs, Richard helped Kath into her coat before taking her into his arms and kissing her with heart-stopping tenderness.

"Drive carefully tomorrow," she said. "It's a long way to Plymouth."

"I will. William can arrive at the uni any time after one o'clock, so I suppose I'll just help him carry all his bags and boxes to his room, then leave him to it."

"I think he'll be okay. He's a very sociable lad. He always seems to get on with everyone."

41

"I hope so. He'll have his mobile. He can always call if—"

"If he wants you to come and rescue him?"

Richard laughed. "I know that's not going to happen."

"But you wouldn't mind if it did!"

Richard's expression darkened a little. "I *am* going to miss him, Kath."

"Of course you are. You adore him. But you know how prepared he is for this. He's about to start the career he chose for himself a long time ago. He's going to love doing this degree."

Richard gazed down at her for a while before planting another soft kiss on her lips. "Thank you for being here. Thank you for caring. Thank you, darling Kath, for happening to me."

She slid her arms around his neck, drawing him into a passionate embrace that lasted some time before she reluctantly pulled herself away. "Do you fancy supper at my place when you get back from Plymouth tomorrow night? Then we could cuddle up and watch a movie or two."

He sighed. "That sounds just perfect."

After one final lingering kiss, Richard opened the front door and walked Kath to her car, then waved until she had disappeared down the drive and was out of sight.

Brenda Longstone rapped her knuckles on the table to call to order all those who had come along to discuss the arrangements for the harvest supper – due to take place at Hope Hall on the last Saturday evening of the month. It was no surprise that the vicar, James, and his wife, Ellie, both of whom were very involved in various local clubs and charities, were sitting alongside Brenda. There were also representatives from Rotary, the Lions Club and the University of the Third Age. And because the supper was to be made and served at Hope Hall, Shirley was present, as were Maggie and Jan, the latter looking as if she wanted to fade into a corner as the group gathered.

Brenda had assumed the role of chairperson for the meeting because, as in previous years, the event was being pulled together by the local Women's Institute – and Brenda Longstone *was* the Women's Institute. Members might come and go, but she had been in charge for as long as anyone could recall. Known, not necessarily with affection, by the nickname "She Who Must Be Obeyed", Brenda expected her instructions to be heard, understood and implemented without question or deviation.

"Right!" she announced without even a hello or a welcome. "I have placed on the table before you the seating plan for the event, details of ticket sales so far, the running order for the evening and a list of what I expect in terms of contribution from each of you and your organizations. Please study the sheet for a minute. There shouldn't be any questions – but if there are, I shall be happy to answer them."

"I see you're down as the only person to speak during the event," said James. "It'll be wonderful to hear from you, of course, but as this harvest supper is traditionally part of the church celebration of the Christian Harvest Festival, I would appreciate the opportunity to speak too. Perhaps I could say something at the start of the evening, just to put the whole reason for having a harvest supper into context."

"I'm perfectly capable of doing that, Vicar," was Brenda's frosty reply.

"We have no doubt about that," said Ellie, the local senior schoolteacher whose popularity stemmed, to a large degree, from the tactful and friendly way in which she was usually able to get her way nicely. "But some of my pupils and their parents are coming along, and they're not necessarily churchgoers. It would be really interesting for everyone to hear a bit about the history and the reason behind this delightful meal."

Brenda's eyes narrowed as she observed the general mutter of agreement around the table. "Is there anyone else here who insists that their voice must be heard? I'm sure you'll agree that we don't want too much talking when people will be anxious to get on with their supper."

"That's a good point, Brenda," agreed Roger from Rotary. "The vicar gets my vote because he's completely across the local groups and organizations represented here, so I'm happy for him to welcome everyone and speak on behalf of us all."

Pursing her lips with fury, Brenda spent a good minute writing slowly and deliberately in her notes before looking up again. "You will see that I have suggested a menu for the evening. This is, after all, a traditional occasion, so people know what to expect. It has to represent the fruits of the garden and farmyard, so we will be serving home-made bread, locally reared organic chicken, the usual mixed salad, freshly made coleslaw, apple and blackberry pie with cream, and a cup of coffee. Maggie, as head of catering here at the hall, I hope this menu meets with your approval."

"Actually, Brenda, I'm afraid I can't be involved that evening, as I'm on annual leave. It'll be Jan here organizing the meal on the day." Maggie turned to smile encouragingly at Jan, whose face seemed to be growing paler by the second.

Brenda's hard glare homed in on Jan, just as it had back in their long-ago schooldays, and it was having much the same chilling effect on Jan now. Brenda turned abruptly back to Maggie. "This is a very important community occasion. We assumed that was completely understood. One has to ask, then, why the Hope Hall management would even consider fobbing us off with inferior staff."

Maggie's laugh was relaxed and friendly. "I can't imagine what you mean by that, Brenda. Jan here is perfectly qualified and experienced when it comes to leading the catering team for an event like this. In fact, she's put a lot of work and thought into an alternative menu for this year. Perhaps everyone would like to hear about that before we make any final decisions."

"How interesting!" responded James. "Come forward a bit, Jan. What ideas have you come up with?"

Tightly clasping her collection of papers, Jan moved towards the centre of the group and opened her folder to display a range of colourful photographs.

"Well," she began, rather too quietly at first, "harvest isn't just a British celebration. Since life on earth began, countries and communities around the world have given thanks for the produce of the land and prayed for a bountiful crop, which they recognized could only grow at the whim of the elements. So, bearing in mind that we have families from all sorts of traditions and backgrounds here in the town, why don't we reflect how harvest is celebrated not just here, but around the world? I've been looking up foods that are often prepared at harvest time in other countries, and I thought we could invite along some of our neighbours who have grown up with these traditional foods and share the pleasure of tasting and enjoying a multicultural banquet together."

"What a brilliant idea!" enthused Frances, representing the University of the Third Age. "I'm all in favour of being inclusive in everything we do. We can learn so much from each other that way."

Brenda's knuckles rapped sharply on the table, silencing the chatter that had broken out around the room.

"Excuse me, but I think we're missing the point here. We are *English*. We are celebrating the blessings of *our* harvest. That's what people expect. It's traditional. It would be a great mistake to move away from what people had in mind when they bought their tickets."

"You know, Brenda," replied Ellie, "when I look around our school assemblies, there's a very broad ethnic mix among our pupils. It's something we celebrate because we know how positive it can be for young people to learn from the life experiences of their friends and neighbours. Sowing the seeds of tolerance and understanding through shared gatherings and genuine friendship must surely be the key to good community relations in years to come."

"And there are occasions when that mix can rightly be marked," snapped Brenda, "but the traditional harvest supper is not one of them!"

"But just look at these pictures," commented Frances. "This food looks delicious. Can you talk us through these, Jan?"

"Well," began Jan, her confidence growing as she spoke, "every culture in the world seems to honour the bounty of their harvest by focusing on the benefits brought to communities, family life, good fortune and health. In southern India they mark the Pongal Festival with a feast of rice, milk, palm sugar and lentils. In Ghana and Nigeria they serve up a traditional diet of yams in a variety of ways, accompanied by parades, dancing and drumming in the streets. The Homowo Festival is also celebrated in West Africa, to remember famine in past years and to scorn hunger in the hope that famine will never strike again. And across the Far East, the autumn festivals of different communities often share the tradition of eating moon cakes, with the aim of bringing friends and families together, even though they might be living far apart."

"I recognize these moon cakes from when I lived in South Korea," mused Frances. "I even remember how to make them."

Encouraged by the positive response, Jan continued. "And some produce is so vital in different parts of the world, it is always part of the harvest celebration. Like corn, for example. There's mealie bread from Swaziland, street corn with lime and chilli from Kenya, potato and corn casserole from Argentina... the list is endless!"

"And there are the fruits from different areas too," added Maggie. "We may not be able to imagine a harvest supper without the home-made apple and blackberry pie Brenda suggested, but wouldn't it be nice to try pawpaw pudding or sweet pumpkin doughnuts from Chile as well?"

Conversations started up among the group, with fingers pointing at the illustrations and heads nodding in enthusiastic agreement. The sound of knuckles being rapped sharply on the table brought a hasty silence. Brenda was staring coldly in Jan's direction.

"And you'll be cooking all these delicacies, will you, Jan? You'll be purchasing all these exotic ingredients within the budget allocated for the event? And you'll be able to create this so-called banquet within the time frame of one day?"

"Oh no, I'm not thinking of doing it all myself," explained Jan. "I'm certainly not an expert when it comes to all these recipes. But there are many people within our town who've grown up with traditional food like this. Looking around this group here today, we collectively have a wide range of contacts from within our community. I was hoping we could all work together to see who might be willing to help us."

"Many of the tickets have already been sold," retorted Brenda. "Where are all these other people going to sit? It's too late to change everything now."

"Is it?" asked James. "There's a lot of space here at the hall. If we use the foyer and this balcony lounge, as well as the main hall, we could get a lot more people in than we initially planned."

"And it will obviously be a buffet," interjected Maggie, "so we might find people are happy to eat with plates on their knees instead of sitting at one long table. That way, we can encourage everyone to mix and eat a range of foods with different groups of neighbours."

"Well, I have to say this idea definitely gets my vote!" announced James, as others in the group also showed their support for the suggestion. "How do we pull this together?"

"The Women's Institute will be in charge, as arranged." Brenda's voice was stony. "And as head of the Women's Institute, I will let everyone know what their roles should be."

"Do you know, Brenda?" interrupted Ellie. "That's a really kind offer, but as you said, it's going to be quite a challenge to change direction from what we've traditionally offered, and draw in enthusiastic support from across the whole community. We can't expect any one person or organization to take on all that work, so let's decide now what we can individually contribute. All of us here are used to working together. As Catering Manager on this occasion, Jan must be the one making the final decisions on the food we can provide, how much it will cost and who will be doing the preparation and cooking, so we should all report to her. I'm happy to draw up a notice about what we're planning, in which we can ask for volunteers from different backgrounds in the town who are willing to prepare their own traditional dishes for us to share. I'll make sure you all have copies of that poster later today, so we can start spreading news of the event as quickly as possible. Shirley, can you be in charge of sorting out the seating arrangements and all other logistics here at the hall? And Roger, I know that your colleagues in Rotary will help with any staging and audiovisual requirements we might have."

"I'd like to investigate whether we could get some musicians from different cultures to take part too," suggested John from the Lions.

"And perhaps even some dancing," added Ellie. "I'll ask some of the girls at school about that. I know quite a few of them belong to traditional dance groups in the area. And, of course," she added with a warm smile towards Brenda, "you're right that if we're going to aim for higher numbers to come along, ticket sales will be paramount. You've always been brilliant at that, Brenda. Perhaps once you've had a chance to talk through this exciting new approach with your ladies, you can let us know if you feel there is any other way the WI might be able to help."

Brenda said nothing, but her expression spoke volumes.

"Right," said James, gathering his papers together as he stood up. "I'm due at a diocesan meeting. Must go. Thanks, everyone."

It was some minutes before the group finally drew their conversations to an end and moved away from the table, leaving Jan to collect up all the photo illustrations she had brought along. As she carefully fitted them back into her folder, she became aware of a shadow falling across the table in front of her.

"Once useless, always useless." Brenda was standing close enough to hiss venom into Jan's ear. "You're about to ruin an annual event with centuries of tradition. You'll make a mess of the beloved harvest supper that has always brought pleasure to so many. And when you fail, I will have great delight in reminding this ill-informed group of PC do-gooders that I told them so!"

Chapter 3

*L*orraine had never intended to go along to the Red Cross class offering first-aid advice specifically relevant to children in the home. She had come up with a lame excuse when Cherie quizzed her about it, knowing her friend was well aware that there was much more to this situation than she was letting on. Even though it might have helped Cherie to understand, Lorraine couldn't begin to explain why she wasn't able to go.

She decided to steer clear of Hope Hall completely that Wednesday morning until the evening beforehand, when she was putting Molly to bed. Her daughter's beloved Baa Lamb was missing, and in an instant Lorraine remembered seeing her hug the toy as she walked into playgroup earlier that day. Molly was inconsolable, finally dropping off to sleep through exhaustion after two full hours of wailing for her favourite cuddly companion. Lorraine had no choice but to collect it from the school hall the next morning. She would have to make sure she arrived after ten o'clock, when Cherie and all the other mums were safely in the main hall taking part in the Red Cross class. Then she could slip away before anyone realized she had been there at all.

It was a relief when she glanced at her watch at quarter past ten the following morning as she left the old school hall with Baa Lamb safely back in Molly's arms. The pair were about to make their escape, with mission accomplished, when Molly squealed and looked down in alarm at the tell-tale wet patch making its way down her pretty pink leggings. Lorraine sighed in exasperation.

She couldn't put Molly in the car like that, and she certainly didn't want to go back into the school hall. She had managed to avoid catching Jen's eye when she slipped in earlier, but she almost certainly wouldn't be so lucky next time, and she couldn't face the thought of being given a lecture by the playgroup leader about how irresponsible she was not to be at the first-aid class with all the other mums. Looking up, she realized the loos in the foyer were much closer, so she checked she had spare clothes for Molly in her bag, scooped the little girl into her arms and rushed through the main entrance of Hope Hall.

Five minutes later, Molly and Lorraine emerged from the ladies' to find a woman standing a few yards away near the glass panels that divided the foyer from the main hall. Lorraine had a feeling her name was Shirley, and they had even said hello to each other once or twice in the past. Lorraine groaned to herself, anxious to get out of Hope Hall as quickly as possible, so she grabbed Molly and buried her face in her daughter's soft brown hair as she turned towards the exit.

"Oh, hello!" called Shirley. "I thought you might be in the hall at the first-aid class with all the other parents and relatives."

"Not today. I couldn't," mumbled Lorraine.

"Pity," replied Shirley, turning back to peer through the glass panels into the main hall once again. "I've been watching from here, and it's really good. You never know when all this might come in handy, do you?"

Molly was wiggling so much in Lorraine's arms that she put the toddler back on the floor, watching for a few seconds while the little girl settled down with her legs crossed as she had a one-way conversation with Baa Lamb.

"Hey, look what they're doing now!" called Shirley.

In spite of herself, Lorraine found herself drawn to the window beside Shirley, staring at the manoeuvres going on inside the hall. Some groups were practising resuscitation techniques on child-

51

sized dummies. Others were learning to clean and seal wounds, apply dressings, and wrap wrists, ankles and limbs with bandages. There seemed to be a demonstration going on at the far end of the hall about what should be kept as standard in a domestic first-aid kit. It didn't take Lorraine any time at all to acknowledge that this was an excellent introduction to what was needed for keeping children safe in the home environment.

Suddenly, there was an ear-piercing scream behind her. She spun around just in time to see that Molly had climbed up on to a chair, which was tipping over on just two legs. Lorraine watched in horror as the little girl's body was flung through the air, as if in slow motion. Lorraine threw herself in the direction of her daughter just too late to stop her descent towards the hard wooden floor. Molly landed head first, with a resounding crack.

Shirley turned around just as the little girl's terrified mother threw herself to the floor, wailing like a wild animal in pain as she pulled her apparently lifeless daughter into her arms, calling out her name and shaking her frantically in an attempt to bring her round. Even before Shirley had found the presence of mind to open the door to the main hall and yell for the Red Cross first-aiders, she saw they were on their way.

By the time they reached Lorraine, her face was ashen and shiny with perspiration, her body shuddering uncontrollably, her eyes glassy with fear. Two first-aiders immediately fell to their knees to concentrate on the little girl's condition, while Rosemary, the senior Red Cross team member, gently approached Lorraine. She put a steadying arm around her shoulder, speaking quietly but firmly as she instructed her to breathe slowly… and again, slowly… and slower still until the shudders subsided a little. Eventually, her wailing became just a long low whimper as she watched with staring eyes while Molly was examined.

"Should I call an ambulance?" asked Shirley.

"I don't think that will be necessary," replied one of the first-aiders dealing with Molly, "but a pack of frozen peas would be useful to put on that bump. She didn't actually lose consciousness – she was just winded from the fall initially. She's coming round properly now. Hello, Molly. Look, Mummy's over there – but don't try to sit up just yet."

Bemused and intrigued by all the new faces around her, Molly didn't even cry. Someone handed her Baa Lamb, who immediately claimed her attention.

Lorraine, on the other hand, was still trembling and moaning quietly, apparently unaware of what was going on around her.

"Don't worry, dear." Rosemary's voice was soothing and gentle, although Lorraine felt as if all the sounds around her were reaching her from the other end of a long tunnel. "You've had a terrible shock, seeing Molly take a tumble like that."

"Molly!" Lorraine was mouthing the word, but couldn't hear herself speak. "Molly?"

"Molly seems just fine. We're keeping her quiet and still while we check that she's completely okay after her fall. She took a big bump to the side of her head, so we need to make sure she doesn't have any symptoms we need to keep an eye on."

Her mind suddenly clearing, Lorraine struggled over to her daughter. "Is she responding? Has she said anything? Is she being sick?"

"So far, she's doing well. We're taking good care of her. But we need to look after you too. Here – would you like a sip of water? I'm Rosemary. What's your name?"

"Lorraine."

"Can you tell me your surname, Lorraine?"

Lorraine didn't answer. Her eyes were fixed firmly on Molly.

"Molly's okay. See? She's having a drink. What's your surname, Lorraine?"

Lorraine suddenly stared directly at Rosemary. "I know what you're doing. I've had a panic attack and you're trying to decide if

I'm still suffering from the effects of it."

Rosemary looked at her with curious interest. "That's right."

"I felt a bit shaky, but I'm okay now. I just want to be with Molly."

"You're more than a bit shaky, Lorraine. Your pulse is racing, you're hot and clammy, and look at your hands. They're still trembling now."

"Please just help me up so I can get across to my daughter."

Nodding towards one of her colleagues, the two first-aiders gently supported Lorraine as she got to her feet and on to a chair near where Molly was playing. Seeing her mother, the little girl scrambled up on to her lap, still clutching Baa Lamb tightly.

A quarter of an hour later, Lorraine felt calmer as she watched Molly chatting away to Shirley as if nothing had happened. Two of the first-aiders had gone back into the hall to carry on with the course, while Rosemary remained at her side.

"Here," she said, passing a cup of hot sweet tea to Lorraine. "You look as if you could do with a cuppa."

For a minute or so, the two women drank in silence.

"So, I gather you work in the medical profession yourself?" asked Rosemary at last.

Lorraine's shoulders slumped as she considered the question. "I did, but not now."

"Were you a nurse?"

"Yes."

"With any particular specialty?"

"I was in paediatrics."

Rosemary's eyebrows shot up in surprise.

"I was a senior paediatric nurse at St Thomas' in London."

"Goodness! There's not likely to be anything I could teach you about first aid for children, then!"

Lorraine turned towards her, eyes brimming with tears. "I knew everything and nothing. I was very good at telling everyone else what to do; how they should react if their child had a sudden medical emergency."

Rosemary stayed silent, sure there was more to come.

"When you take all those nursing exams and end up in charge of desperately ill children, you feel a bit God-like, putting people back together, saving lives. I knew it all. At least, I thought I did."

"What happened?" asked Rosemary softly.

"I went to pieces. I was a complete wreck. And my boy died." Tears were coursing down her cheeks.

Rosemary placed a clean tissue in Lorraine's hand and waited. Minutes passed before the tearful mother spoke again.

"He was just about the same age as Molly is now. His name was Daniel, but he was Danny Boy to us from the moment we saw him. He was a mini version of my Geoff from the start. They were like peas in a pod. Danny Boy had a little digger suit he loved to wear that looked like the overalls Geoff put on whenever he was doing DIY around the house. I remember them being in the garden together when Geoff had taken down some fencing, and we had a skip there to put the debris in. Geoff gave Danny his own little wheelbarrow and told him his job was to pick up stones and twigs from the other side of the garden, then wheel them over so his dad could help him throw the contents into the skip. Danny loved it! He worshipped his daddy. They were very close."

There was another pause while she gathered her thoughts. "It was a Tuesday morning, just an ordinary day. Danny and I were walking down to the corner shop because I needed a few bits and pieces – milk, bread, the usual stuff. He'd made up his mind that he didn't want to be in the buggy any more. He was a big boy, he said, and I agreed with him. He was a normal, lively little monkey with bags of energy. He loved walking to the shop because he knew he'd get a treat while he was there and we'd call into the playground across the road on the way back."

Lorraine's voice faltered, her bottom lip trembling as she

struggled to continue. "He chose an ice lolly shaped like a rocket. They were his favourite. He was tucking into it as we walked back, hand in hand, chatting away like he always did."

There was another pause as her eyes glazed over, as if she were watching the scene unfold before her. "The park entrance was coming up on the other side of the road, and there were lots of children there because it was summertime. Then Danny spotted his friend Jacob coming up to the park gate and Danny yelled across the road to him. And then, without any warning at all, he just pulled his hand out of mine and started running towards Jacob. I tried reaching out to stop him, but he was off the pavement and charging into the road in seconds..." Lorraine stopped, her face frozen in an expression of realization and shock. "That driver didn't have a chance..."

Long seconds passed before she was able to speak again. "The noise was awful. The brakes screeching, someone screaming. Maybe that was me. I remember seeing the driver's face behind the windscreen. I still see that face now, whenever I close my eyes. His shock, his horror. And I knew I should get to Danny, but I couldn't. My feet wouldn't move. I just stood there. People started coming out of the park. I could tell from their faces it was bad – and there I was, rooted to the ground, doing nothing at all." Lorraine stiffened and started to shake uncontrollably as shuddering waves swept across her body.

Rosemary put a steadying arm around her shoulder, keeping a watchful eye, but remaining silent.

"I'm a nurse. A *good* nurse. A professional who knows all about how to care for injured children. And my feet wouldn't move. My mind went blank. I did nothing. Nothing at all. I could have helped him. Perhaps I could have saved his life. But I didn't – and I lost him. I lost our Danny Boy. It was my fault. All my fault."

Another pause followed. Rosemary was a solid support at her side, watching Lorraine carefully.

"Someone came over to me. I remember her talking, but I don't remember what she said. The driver got out of the car and was looking down at the front wheel. And then I saw him – Danny Boy. His shoes. His blue trainers. He was so proud of them. I could see his little legs and those blue trainers. And there was blood on the road. My baby's blood. And I knew he needed me, and that I should be down on the ground with him, making him better. And I couldn't – because I knew what I would see if I did. I couldn't… I just couldn't…"

At that moment, Rosemary became aware of a movement to one side of her. From the concern on his face, she knew this was Geoff, who had been contacted at work immediately after Molly had fallen and Lorraine had had her panic attack. Without a word, he came straight across to kneel in front of his wife, wrapping his big, comforting arms around her. Together, they gently rocked back and forth in a bubble of shared grief.

"Daddy!" called Molly, running across to join the hug. "Baa Lamb fell off the chair and I did too. Baa Lamb banged his head. He wants to go home now."

Geoff smiled at her, his eyes shining with tears. "And how are you, Molly Moppet? Did you bump your head as well?"

Molly frowned. "I don't think so. Baa Lamb did. Come on, Daddy, let's go! You can make Mummy one of her nice cups of tea and she'll feel better then."

"That's a great idea, love." Geoff glanced at Rosemary. "One minute, and we'll be on our way."

Lorraine's face brightened as Molly climbed up on to her lap. Taking that as their cue, Geoff and Rosemary stepped to one side so they could talk.

"Lorraine's had quite a severe panic attack, brought on by seeing Molly take a tumble. And she's just become very distressed talking about what happened to your son."

"I'm glad she told you. She rarely speaks about the accident,

57

holding all this pain inside for three years now,
lost him."

"...ime isn't always the healer we hope it will be," said Rosemary.

"You're right. She had counselling the first year, but I think her
grief was just too deep to respond to it. And she's overwhelmed
with a terrible sense of guilt, as if the blame for what happened is all
hers. But it isn't! It was just an awful, shocking accident, caused by
a little boy deciding in an instant that he wanted to run across and
join his friend. But however much I try to talk about it, she can't
get over the idea that she should have done something, anything,
to help him."

"Could she have saved him?"

"No chance. Danny Boy was killed the moment he went under
the wheels of that car."

"And these panic attacks – does she have them often?"

"No. Seeing her now with Molly, she looks like she's back to
her old self: a loving wife, a devoted mum, capable, organized,
happy—"

"But she's holding all of this inside."

"And it breaks my heart to know that. I mean, I adored Danny
Boy. His loss has been devastating for me. Lorraine and I have
mostly been able to share our dreadful loss. In many ways, it's
brought us closer. But people grieve in different ways, don't they?
I feel as if I want to talk about him all the time; to include him in
our conversations every day so he's still a real part of our family life.
But Lorraine's different. She can hardly bear to hear his name – and
that's really tough for me. It's like the elephant in the room. We're
both consumed with our thoughts of Danny, but his name is never
mentioned. It's as if Molly's just taken his place and we don't need
to refer to him any more. That breaks my heart, but I know it's the
only way Lorraine can deal with it."

"I wonder if, after what's happened today, Lorraine would
consider seeking help again."

Geoff nodded. "I think we've got to. Today makes that so clear. And Lorraine's a very experienced medical professional, who knows in her heart that's what we need. I'll talk to her."

"She told me she was a senior paediatric nurse. I was as a nurse too, but my specialty was mental health. I'm retired now, but I know that a wide range of therapies are available these days that might really help her – and you."

"Can we keep in touch?" asked Geoff. "I'd like to talk to you again about this. Here's my card. Would you call me when you can?"

"I'll ring tomorrow to see how Molly and Lorraine are feeling after what's happened today."

"Thank you." Geoff's smile was warm and grateful as he turned back towards Lorraine. Rosemary was pleased to see that the colour had returned to her cheeks, and that she was laughing at something Molly had said.

As Geoff checked that all their possessions were safely gathered together, Lorraine came across to speak to Rosemary. "Thank you. Thanks to all of you for taking care of Molly and me."

"I'm just glad we were here when you needed us."

Lorraine hesitated. "And about what I told you..."

"Whatever you shared with me will be held in the strictest confidence. But it's plain that you're still deeply wounded by what happened to Danny Boy. Perhaps this might be your cue to seek further help in coping with the memory of what happened."

Lorraine sighed. "That sounds very scary. It's so painful remembering."

"Then think about the future – not just for you, but for your whole family."

Lorraine nodded thoughtfully, then turned to walk across and join Geoff and Molly, who were ready to go home.

Just before Ray's alarm clock went off as usual at six thirty in the morning, he was in that twilight zone of being neither completely awake nor completely asleep when he found his nose was twitching. There was a strange smell, like a cross between dried meat and a dusty old carpet. Then he noticed the noise – a fluttering, wheezing sort of sound. His eyes shot open with alarm, and he found himself nose to nose with Banjo, who was snoring happily beside him with his mouth open and his pink tongue sitting in a damp patch on the pillow. *Sara's* pillow!

"This is *not* your bed!" he yelled. "*I* sleep here. *You* sleep downstairs in that posh new basket of yours!"

Banjo immediately leaped into action with an expression of pure delight that his master was awake. In one swift move he was off the pillow and standing over Ray on all fours, licking his face with slobber that smelled exactly like dried meat with a coating of dust.

"Don't *do* that!" roared Ray, throwing back the covers and pushing the dog on to the floor. "I hate having my face, or anything else, licked by dogs. This has got to stop, Banjo! You *have* to learn the rules."

Bounding enthusiastically alongside him, Banjo followed Ray to the bathroom, slumping back on his haunches with disappointment when the door was slammed firmly in his face.

By six forty-five, Banjo was trotting ahead of Ray at the end of his smart new extending lead. They were on their way to the park for their early morning walk, which had fallen into the pattern of Ray walking twice around the perimeter, throwing sticks while Banjo bounded backwards and forwards searching for them. He would drop the stick somewhere random on the way back, and return to Ray, who would instruct him to go back and pick it up. Banjo would then meander off to find the stick, sniffing every delicious-smelling item of interest on the way before dropping the stick at Ray's feet so the process could be repeated all over again.

Perhaps it was mostly because Ray was already mad with Banjo about the pillow incident, but he was aware that he felt generally out of sorts that morning. He was wondering whether he had bitten off more than he could chew by adopting this high-energy, ever-enthusiastic, smothering, totally devoted dog. He felt as though his life was no longer his own. He might have been through times of great loneliness since Sara was not there to fill his life and home with her comfortable, loving presence, but these days he almost longed for a chance to be alone – time to think, to remember, to simply be himself doing nothing at all if that's what he felt like.

His thoughts were interrupted when he realized Banjo was nowhere in sight. Looking around in all directions, Ray shouted the dog's name several times, but there was no sign of the little dog's familiar leaping figure bounding across to rejoin him. Ray felt a moment of alarm. Banjo had been a stray before the two of them had found each other. Perhaps his outburst of bad temper that morning had made Banjo decide to head off and find a kinder owner. Or perhaps he'd injured himself in some corner of the park. That wouldn't be such a surprise, considering how the little dog always ran at full pelt, taking no notice whatsoever of possible dangers and pitfalls.

Ray broke out into a run, yelling Banjo's name. He started to run in the direction he had been heading in, then thought better of it and turned around to search the area where he had already walked. *I'll go back to where I last saw him*, he thought, as panic gripped his stomach, twisting it into a painful knot. For more than ten minutes, Ray charged around like a headless chicken until he finally spotted another dog walker standing beside an area of woodland at the far end of the park. Thinking the stranger may have seen Banjo, Ray hurried towards him.

The man was short, round and practically bald. He was standing with his hands in the pockets of his well-worn jacket, which was probably kept just for dog walking, like the one Ray was wearing.

"Lost your dog?" the man asked.

61

Ray gave a sigh of relief. "Yes! A little sandy-coloured terrier-type. Answers to the name of Banjo."

"I've lost mine too," replied the man. "I bet they've gone off together. Bertie's like that. He meets a new friend, then just forgets I'm here. I wouldn't mind, but I'd rather be in bed at this time in the morning. I wish he wouldn't keep doing this."

"Where do you think they've gone?"

"Into those woods, I should think. That's Bertie's favourite place."

Ray started striding towards the trees.

"I wouldn't go in, if I were you. They'll think you're up for a game of chase. Better just to wait here until the blighters decide to come out again."

"But I've got to go to work this morning. I can't just hang around here until a couple of dogs decide I'm allowed to leave."

"Please yourself," shrugged the man. "Go charging in there if you want to. I did that the first time too. The dogs thought it was great fun and just kept disappearing further into the undergrowth. We'd be better off taking a seat on that bench over there until they come back out. I've got a flask of coffee and two cups. You're welcome to join me if you want some."

There was still no sign of the dogs ten minutes later, as Ray drained the last mouthful of surprisingly good coffee from the plastic cup. He glanced at his watch anxiously.

"Where do you work?" asked his companion.

"Hope Hall. I'm the caretaker there. I've got a lot of setting up to do this morning. I need to be there by eight at the latest."

"Oh, they'll be back any minute now. You'll be fine."

"Do you work?" enquired Ray.

The man smiled. "I'm retired now. I worked for British Telecom for thirty-five years. I'm getting used to this retirement business, though. It took a while. I couldn't work out what to do with myself for the first year. It would have been easier if my missus were still with me, but she died four years ago. We'd always looked forward to the idea of retiring together and perhaps going on a cruise or two. There were so many places in the world we wanted to see. But then I lost her at the start of my last year at work. I'm getting better now, three years on. My daughter's very good – she pops in most days. And Bertie's good company too."

"Your dog?"

"Yes. He's as ugly as sin – well, *I* think so, but then that's probably why I love him so much, because I'm no oil painting myself. He's an old-fashioned bulldog. He looks miserable, dribbles all the time and has this habit of leaning on me wherever I am, whether I'm standing or sitting. He's a real character, and I can't imagine life without him now. So, if he wants to go off for a bit of adventure for a while every day, that's okay with me. I just wish he didn't always demand to be taken out for his constitutional so early in the morning. I'm John, by the way."

Ray grinned. "Ray. It's good to meet you. My dog, Banjo – I've only had him a couple of weeks. He's a stray who ended up needing a permanent home with me. My wife Sara died six months ago…"

John grunted with understanding. "That's tough. Early days yet. If my Bertie's anything to go by, you'll find you've taken on a good friend in Banjo. He'll help you through."

"He just does whatever he likes, though. He's running rings around me. I bought a beautiful wicker basket for him to sleep in, and he loves being in there during the day. But then I put him in there at night-time and tell him to stay – and the next thing I know he's snoring away on the pillow beside me. My *wife's* pillow!"

"Shut the door, then."

"Sara and I always left the doors open at night so we could hear if anyone broke in."

"But you've got a dog now who wants to be with you all the time. If someone breaks in, he'll soon let you know, wherever he is. So just shut the kitchen door or the bedroom door, or both. Job done!"

"Is Bertie well behaved?"

John spluttered with laughter. "Bulldogs are friendly, inquisitive and much more agile than I imagined when I first saw the size of him. He won't do anything unless he wants to."

"Is that what I'm in for, then?" asked Ray with a sigh. "A dog who rules the roost; an animal calling the shots in my own home?"

"You could always take him to the Waggy Tail Club."

"What, the one at Hope Hall, you mean?"

"I've started taking Bertie there on Wednesday nights."

"I know the one! Six to seven thirty. I open the hall and set things up for Ali and the team."

"She's very good. Well, actually, she's extremely scary, but she says it's the owners who need to be trained as much as the dogs. When she yells 'SIT!' I have to stop myself falling to my knees and putting my paws up to beg!"

"Does it work? Is Bertie better behaved?"

John considered this question for a moment. "I think we understand each other better. Dogs don't think the same way we do, so I've had to learn to see things from his perspective as well as my own. In the end, I have to be the boss, of course, and I think Ali's teaching us that. Yes, I would say it's working."

At that moment, a commotion to the right of them heralded the appearance of two very happy dogs, each with his teeth sunk into one end of a long, thick branch. Running in tandem, they belted up to their owners and dropped the branch triumphantly in front of the bench.

"So you're here every morning at this time?" asked Ray.

"Reluctantly, yes."

"I'll see you tomorrow, in that case. And you'll be going along to the Waggy Tail Club next Wednesday, will you?"

"We definitely will."

"Then I think it's about time Banjo and I joined you. See you tomorrow morning!"

It had been a frantically busy day. Jan had been in the Hope Hall kitchen from seven a.m., knowing she would need every available minute to make sure the harvest supper was ready on time before people started arriving at six that evening. Since the committee planning the event had opted to move away from offering only the traditional menu of home-grown vegetables, freshly baked loaves, honey-roasted ham and organic chicken, along with pies and puddings made from the fruits of orchard and hedgerow, it had been action stations to pull together a new menu that represented the multicultural mix of residents living in the town. Once word had got out that they were hoping to reflect the harvest celebrations of communities from around the world, offers had poured in from families whose roots were in Asia, the Far East, several corners of Africa, across the United States of America, Europe and even from the frozen north. One Sámi family from the northernmost part of Finland had offered to bring along a huge pot of venison stew, made according to the recipe used by families that had been herding reindeer across Lapland for centuries.

Jan had spent time with all the cooks, learning the recipes and working out what could be made outside Hope Hall and brought in time for the banquet, and what needed to be made in the hall's own kitchen. Although both Maggie and Liz were away for the day of the event, they had been enthusiastically involved in the preparations, and quite a few dishes had been stored in the freezer until that morning, when they had been defrosted so that the final touches could be applied before they were displayed on the long row of serving tables that stretched across one side of the hall. Under teacher Ellie's guidance, work experience pupils from the sixth form of the local school had prepared some beautifully coloured and crafted labels for the various dishes, and Jan was amazed to count more than forty options when the labels were delivered that afternoon.

Helping her in the kitchen that day were some very capable

volunteers from the Women's Institute, who had entered into the project with enthusiasm and expertise gleaned from years of home cooking. They were assisting several ladies from the various ethnic groups in the community, who had come along not just to cook, but to gather together all the dishes needed for their particular section of the buffet, making sure they were heated properly and served well. It had also been suggested that there would be people from each community on hand at the relevant sections to explain which dishes were on offer and how they reflected the harvest celebrations in their part of the world.

Conspicuous by her absence as a volunteer in the kitchen was Chair of the Women's Institute, Brenda Longstone. She was far too grand to roll her sleeves up to peel sacks of potatoes or wash up the rows of pots and pans in which various types and flavours of rice had been cooked. Jan had heard Brenda sharply rapping a spoon on the tables as they were being laid out in the hall, giving orders, snapping out instructions and patronizing good-natured volunteers by telling them exactly what they were doing wrong.

A couple of times when Jan had needed to go into the hall to examine exactly how the buffet would be laid out, she had been acutely aware of Brenda's icy stare from a distance. Ordinarily, one look from Brenda would have been enough to have Jan heading for the door, but she was too busy on this occasion. She had been entrusted with the responsibility of organizing this imaginative and wonderful event, and she was determined to make a success of it.

The day flew past in a whirr of activity. All too soon, Jan realized she hadn't been to the loo since early that morning, and there had been no time even to put a lick of lipstick on before the doors opened and more than a hundred hungry people poured straight in. She looked around at the fantastic group of women in the kitchen who had been working so happily together throughout the day, and grinned.

"Right, we're on!" she cried. "Here we go, girls. We've got the most wonderful meal to serve. Good luck, everyone!"

The seating had been laid out so that people could take their plates over to a seat around the edge of the hall, where they could chat easily and meet old and new friends. Alternatively, they could find a place at one of the many tables across the hall, foyer and balcony that had each been laid out for either four or eight diners.

It was Ida who had decreed that a group of four from the Grown-ups' Lunch Club should be formed to come along to the event. Betty had immediately turned her nose up at the idea of trying foods that weren't familiar to her and had opted to stay at home and watch TV instead. Flora was always game to try anything, although she did say she would probably go for ham salad and apple pie, whatever else was on offer. Surprisingly, Doris had been the most enthusiastic, immediately confirming that she and her husband, Bert, would love to come. Bert had been posted overseas during his RAF career, taking the family with him on a couple of occasions, so they were both keen to try dishes from other parts of the world.

A long queue had quickly formed beside the buffet, so Ida suggested that she stay at the table to keep their places while the others went off to choose their food. She was quite happy people-watching from her seat until her friends returned to the table nearly a quarter of an hour later.

"It's wonderful!" trilled Doris. "What a magnificent spread. Look, I've gone all African. I've got a spinach and tangerine soup – named after Butha-Buthe, a district of Lesotho – and chicken done in a peanut and rice sauce, which smells wonderful. I'm going up for Indian next."

"And I'm trying this soy-braised pork belly with kimchi fried rice," enthused Bert. "I haven't tasted this for years."

Flora sat down at the table without explaining her choice. She reached out for the tomato ketchup in the middle of the table and poured a large dollop beside her honey-roasted ham. She saw Ida looking at the huge piece of lattice-topped apple pie smothered in hot custard that she'd placed in front of her.

"The pie was going fast, so I thought I'd grab a bit now. You need to go up, Ida. You don't want to miss anything you'd really like to try."

Pushing back her chair, Ida walked across to join the queue, which was considerably shorter now. As she gazed at the colourful display of food spread out along the table, she became aware that someone was standing close behind her.

"I didn't think I'd see you here. I'd pictured you as a roast beef and two veg kind of girl."

Ida swung around to see that Percy was in the line behind her. "For a man who hates to eat anything green, I wouldn't have thought these unusual foods would be up your street either."

"Oh, I like a good curry, and it looks like they've got some great Indian food up at the end there. I love chilli peppers too, and there are lots of dishes here that I reckon could bring a tear to my eye. What are you going for?"

"I'm not sure yet. I thought I might ignore what it says on the labels, take a spoonful of everything and see what I end up with."

"That would be daring," observed Percy, eyebrows raised over his twinkling eyes. "I'm glad to see you're game for anything."

She turned to him with just a hint of a smile twitching her lips. "Not *anything* – but I do like to take opportunities when they're presented to me."

"When you kissed me all those years ago, was *that* an opportunity you just couldn't resist?"

Ida picked an imaginary piece of fluff off the sleeve of her cardigan. "It was *you* who did the kissing, Percy Wilson, as you well know. And as our relationship didn't develop beyond that, you can draw your own conclusions about my opinion of your flirting technique."

"You were a bit of a beauty in those days."

She sighed. "Ah, well. Gravity's taken its toll since then. And you're no pin-up picture yourself these days!"

"Did you think I was back then?"

Ida turned to look him up and down thoughtfully, a slow smile creeping across her face. "I'm sure some people thought so. *You* certainly did."

"I tried to stay fashionable. The ladies seemed to think I was okay."

"I remember that paisley jacket of yours. You wore a black turtleneck jumper with it. In fact, you were always wearing that black turtleneck jumper. Was it the only one you had?"

"You seem to remember a great deal about me, young lady."

Ida laughed out loud. "Call me a young lady again and I'll remember a lot more!"

"So do you remember thinking I was a good-looking fella?"

Ida tutted. "I remember you were reasonably presentable to anyone who liked that particular sort of Mod style."

"And I remember that you were the prettiest girl in the street, and that I never thought I'd have a chance with you. The evening we took a walk together and ended up having that kiss – well, I couldn't believe my luck. But I wasn't really surprised that you didn't want to know me afterwards. You were way out of my league."

Ida didn't reply for a while. She just looked at him with an expression he really couldn't fathom. At last, she said, "You go first, Percy. I know you're hungry, and there's a gap up there by the curries."

He looked as if he wanted to say more, but instead he clicked his heels, gave a smart bow and moved ahead in the queue.

Chapter 4

"Will you just *stop*!" There was nothing, Ali thought, as piercing as a seven-year-old girl shrieking in frustration because she couldn't get her own way. Emily's squeals were hitting her mother's raw nerves with the precision of a guided missile.

"Tell him to stop being *wrong*, then!"

"Mum, tell her she's the one who's wrong!" her brother Zachary retorted. "She knows it's my turn to choose what we're watching. She chose yesterday."

"But it's my favourite programme *ever*," wailed Emily. "And Zach was on his computer game – he wasn't watching TV at all. He's just being mean. You're *mean*, Zach!"

Ali looked down at her twins in exasperation. "Well, it *is* Zachary's turn today, Emily, as you well know. Zach, what programme did you want to watch?"

"Er, well, I need to check what's on—"

"Well, if you're not sure what programme you're missing, you're just making a big fuss about nothing. You know that you can see whatever's on now on catch-up later. So you really *are* just being mean, aren't you?"

"But it's my turn!"

"No, it's *my* turn," stated Ali, taking the remote control from her son's hand. "The television is going off, and neither of you are going to watch it."

Emily wailed with indignation. "What? That's not fair!"

Ali looked down at her daughter sternly. "Emily, you aren't allowed to watch it, because screaming and demanding to get

70

your own way is never going to work. And Zach, you aren't really interested in watching television at all. You just want to stop Emily watching, and that's not fair."

Zachary screwed up his face with scorn. "She wants to watch that thing with all the fairies singing stupid songs."

"They're not stupid." Emily's face was red with fury. "Fairies like dancing, and they need songs to dance to."

"Fairies are for babies!" retorted Zachary, just as Emily burst into a spectacular bout of emotional sobs.

"Emily, stop that noise!" interrupted Ali. "You're not even crying real tears, and I won't listen while you're making that din. When you've finished, we'll talk about it properly."

The sobs abruptly stopped. Emily stood glaring at her brother for a moment of dramatic silence before announcing, "I'm too *tired* for this."

"Tired of what?" demanded Zachary.

"You!" Emily announced. "And *this*." She waved her arms in a circle, vaguely suggesting that she meant nothing less than the whole world. With one last smouldering look at her twin, she turned on her heel and stomped upstairs.

Ali sighed. "I need a coffee."

"Can I have one too?" asked Zachary.

"Kids don't drink coffee."

'Why not? Why can't I have one?"

Ali looked down at him, shaking her head in disbelief. "Because it would make you even more energetic than you already are."

"But you drink coffee all the time, and you're never energetic."

Astonished at the injustice of these words, two things happened. Ali heard the familiar sound of her husband, Clive, laughing as he stood in the doorway behind her. At the same moment, she saw Zachary's cheeky grin as he ran away, triumphant at the thought that he might actually have had the last word in an argument with his mum.

Clive walked in and wrapped his arms around Ali, who just sank into them, enjoying the lovely nestling feeling.

"Is he right? Do you think I'm lacking in energy?"

Clive held her at arm's length for a moment, his eyes dancing with amusement. "For heaven's sake, you're like a whirlwind. You never stop. And you're so organized, you just get everything done without making a big fuss about it all. You make it look too easy."

"Well, I don't know about running low on energy, but I'm definitely running at rock bottom in terms of patience with those twins of ours. They never stop. If they're not arguing with each other, they're arguing with me. They're exhausting."

"Don't you ever wish you could just blow a whistle and tell them to SIT?"

Ali laughed. "That only works on dogs. But then dogs are intelligent, logical and obedient when it comes to learning the rules."

"Well, some of them are…"

"True," agreed Ali, narrowing her eyes as she continued. "That Harley is definitely a hard nut to crack, and why Rufus's owners have let him rule the roost in their home for so long, I don't know."

"How many dogs has the Waggy Tail Club got at the moment?"

"I've got eleven booked in for the beginners' class this week, and one new dog starting, so that's just about the right number."

"You'll sort them all out."

She grinned. "The owners, you mean? Or their dogs?"

"Both! You were a senior dog handler in the army, for heaven's sake! You couldn't afford to let your dogs – or their handlers – be anything except absolutely obedient; lives depended on it. You'll have to train the dogs by training their owners!"

She nodded. "I have to agree with that. Whenever I said jump in the army, the dogs and their handlers hopped to it. We won wars that way." She sighed, sinking back into his arms. "So how is it that when it comes to two seven-year-olds, I never quite feel I win the battle, let alone the war?"

* * *

There she was!

Trying to look as casual as possible, Kevin stretched forward so he could peer a little further around the shutters at the side of the serving hatch. It was definitely her! Even with her back turned, he would know Chloe Evans anywhere. With her long blonde hair, slim frame and the naturally graceful movements she had learned from the dance classes he knew she loved, he simply couldn't take his eyes off her.

It was Saturday morning, and as usual the Call-in Café was packed with shoppers who had made a slight detour away from the High Street to take the weight off their feet over a cup of coffee and a cake, savoury snack or wholesome meal, for which the café was gaining a great reputation. Kevin Marley had started coming along to Hope Hall earlier in the year as a work experience student from the local school. Initially it was to help out at the Tuesday Grown-ups' Lunch Club, which was a highlight of the week for many elderly or isolated people in the area. Since then he had simply loved being in the hall's kitchen.

He came from a large, noisy family full of strong characters with wily ways, who made sure they got exactly what they felt was rightfully theirs. Kevin simply didn't fit the mould. How many teenage boys from that kind of background would name their favourite television programme as *The Great British Bake Off*? Or admit that they would rather spend an hour washing dishes and sweeping floors in the Hope Hall kitchen than be out with their friends? Maggie, Liz and Jan had soon recognized that this lanky, slightly awkward, creative young man was a real asset. He was anxious to learn, always taking instruction on board, and willing to do the most menial jobs if it meant he was simply allowed to be there.

73

Over the six months Kevin had been coming, Maggie had watched him grow in confidence. She had instigated a structured learning programme for him, allowing him the chance first to watch and learn, then to try for himself the skills and techniques needed to create cakes and pastries that tasted every bit as wonderful as they looked. His recent seventeenth birthday had practically been ignored at home, but it was celebrated in style in the Hope Hall kitchen with a cake in the shape of a chef's hat that Maggie had prepared specially for him.

"One day," she told him after he had blown out the candles, "you'll have a chef's hat of your own that you've worked for and really deserve. I'll be first in the queue to come to your café or restaurant."

Kevin had turned scarlet at the compliment, and had been mulling over Maggie's words in his head ever since, wondering if that future could really be his. She had assured him that he possessed all the qualities he needed to be an excellent chef, but suggested it would be best if he were able to go to college to study culinary skills, professional cookery, food and beverage preparation, and hospitality supervision.

His mind had boggled at the list she rattled off, but Maggie had just smiled and tapped his arm as she said, "You'll get there. And the best way to do that is to keep learning. Come on, I'm about to make a Thai green curry. Collect together all the ingredients you think I'll need, and we'll see how you do!"

And now, noticing Kevin leaning out to peer around the serving-hatch shutters, Liz sidled up to him to see what – or who – had caught his attention.

"Let me guess," she whispered just loud enough for him to hear. "The one with the blonde hair standing by the noticeboard. Am I right?"

He turned around with a start, obviously about to say that he had no idea what she meant. But on seeing the friendliness in her expression, his shoulders dropped as he pulled himself away from the serving hatch. "Is it that obvious?"

"You were exactly the same last Saturday morning when she came out of her dance class in the main hall. Your tongue was practically hanging out!"

He looked aghast. "You don't think she noticed, do you?"

"She didn't seem to mind, if she did. She was smiling at you a lot."

"Was she? Do you really think so?" Kevin stopped to think about that possibility for a few seconds. "No, that must have been a fluke. I don't think she'd even recognize me. I mean, I see her at school, but she's in the year below me, so our paths don't really cross."

"Could you make them cross? Is there anything at school she likes that you could try?"

He looked down at his trainers, deep in thought. "I know she goes to the drama club. I saw her in a play just before we broke up for the summer holidays. She was brilliant."

"And can new members join the drama club?"

He stared at her. "Do you mean *me*?"

"Why not? You'd have a chance to get to know her better if you joined."

"But I'd probably be terrible. I'd forget my lines and stand in all the wrong positions. She'd think I was an idiot."

"Would you really be so terrible? I've seen the lovely way you chat to our old ladies and gents on Tuesdays. You were singing with them the other morning, and you read out that poem you wrote that got everyone laughing. Perhaps you didn't think we noticed, but we did! Are you sure you wouldn't be interested in doing something like that? Maybe not just because of Miss Golden Hair over there, but because you'd actually quite like to give it a go?"

Kevin didn't answer, but it was clear that Liz's words had hit home.

75

"Is anyone serving here?" asked an impatient voice from the front of the hatch. "I'd like three coffees, a ham sandwich, a pasty and a plate of home-made ginger biscuits."

With a smile, Liz turned towards the lady standing in front of the hatch. "Certainly, madam! Coming up!"

"So, this is the new boy, eh?" Celia called out as she walked from her car towards the paddock where Uncle Joe was standing alongside a beautiful chestnut horse, chatting to Sam, the trainer he had known and used for years.

"He arrived yesterday," replied Joe, his face full of pride. "Four years old and just at the right stage to start proper training. He's come all the way from Ireland with a great pedigree to his name."

"What is his name?" she asked, reaching up to pat the horse's shoulder before moving up to scratch the usual favourite spot just behind the ear.

"You don't want to know his pedigree name, because that's all a bit technical. But what that pedigree tells me is that this horse has the potential to fly like an arrow. So that's what I've decided to call him, the Latin word for arrow: Sagitta."

She smiled. "You've got a knack for choosing good names for your horses. Optimus has been so successful for you over the years, but then when you give a horse a name that means 'the best', that's bound to bring out the fighting spirit in him. How's he doing, by the way?"

"He's getting on a bit now, feeling his age. His racing days are almost over. This young man will be taking over the reins before too long."

"My favourite was always Ventus. He really did run as fast as the wind he was named after. He just loved running as fast as he could, with the wind in his face!"

Joe smiled fondly at his god-daughter. "He was my favourite too... perhaps because he was my first. Losing him was devastating.

He'd become part of the family."

"And I learned to ride on him. Bearing in mind he stood at sixteen hands, I'll never forget looking down at the ground from that great height when I first sat on him. I'm trying to remember how old I was then. Five or six, perhaps?"

"You used to love being around the horses. I'm surprised you haven't kept it up. Did you ever think of getting your own horse?"

She looked thoughtful. "It's a nice idea, and at times I certainly have thought about it. But I'm just too busy, Uncle Joe. My work takes up a lot of time, as you know only too well."

"Apex certainly claims its pound of flesh from anyone who works there. I have to say, Celia, I'm ready to retire. I've done thirty years there. It's time for me to take things a bit easier. Smell the roses, as they say – on horseback, perhaps!"

"I can't imagine you not working." Celia looked at him fondly as she spoke.

"It's time for a new generation to take over – and that's where you come in, my dear girl. I probably shouldn't be telling you this, but the board is very keen on the idea of you taking over my role when I retire."

"Really? I thought they'd be looking at a wide range of candidates for the UK finance director's role, especially considering the bright stars who might be working at that level for the other major financial institutions."

"They've certainly done that, but they seem to think there's no substitute for experience in our particular business, and you've got that in abundance. You've worked your way up, absorbing so much of the structure, procedures, challenges and pitfalls of the different strands of our field of work along the way. You're smart, you're hard-working... and you're top of their list!"

Celia let out a sharp breath. "Well, that is exceedingly good news. When might I hear something?"

"The board will be meeting this coming Friday. They'll decide on a date the majority of them can convene, then invite you to come and discuss the possibility of you taking over."

She grinned. "I'd better make sure my diary's free."

"I think you should. Pop up to the house before you leave. Trish is just sorting out lunch. Tell her to put the kettle on. I'll be in after Sam and I have finished our chat."

"Come in soon, though. I can't stay long!" Celia waved over her shoulder as she headed for the house.

Drawing a quick breath for extra courage, Ray opened the foyer door leading into the main hall just an inch or two before peering inside. His first reaction was one of complete horror, and he hastily shut it firmly again. But as he stepped back, he found his getaway was stalled by Banjo sitting solidly behind him, flatly refusing to move.

"Don't you give me that look!" warned Ray, glaring at the dog gazing up at him, one ear pointing to the ceiling, the other to the window, and his tongue lolling to one side as if it were too long to fit inside his mouth. "It's chaos in there – and I know you! You'd think it was all a game and cause even more pandemonium."

Looking for all the world as if he understood every word, Banjo's head tilted to the opposite side.

"I mean, it's a daft idea to think that you could put all those untrained dogs in one room and expect it to be anything other than chaos. No, boy, this is not for us. You'll just have to learn to do what you're told when I tell you to do it, and no arguments. Do we understand each other?"

Banjo gave a sad little whimper, his enormous eyes filled with disappointment as he stared at the closed door, which, just at that moment, was pulled open by the Waggy Tail Club's organizer, Ali.

"Ray, you made it! And this must be your new housemate. Hi there, Banjo. Welcome!"

"Well, a-actually," stammered Ray, "I've just come to tell you I haven't got time for the class this evening. Pressure of work, you know, here at Hope Hall—"

"Nonsense!" grinned Ali. "I can tell you're terrified just by looking at you. But this is just the first few mad minutes as all the dogs show their excitement at being here and seeing all their friends again. We've not begun the training yet. Do you see anyone you know?"

Ray glanced around the gathering of owners and their motley collection of dogs, large and small – some bouncing with enthusiasm, their tails swinging like metronomes, others yapping as if in conversation (or was it competition?) with each other. A few stood disdainfully beside their owners, as if the whole affair was beneath them in both dignity and interest.

Then suddenly, a deep bark from the other side of the hall caught Banjo's attention, and he was off like a shot to greet his friend Bertie the bulldog, practically yanking Ray's arm out of its socket as the lead was tugged out of his hand. Before Ray could recover from the shock, he looked up to see Ali striding smartly across to where Bertie and Banjo were enthusiastically greeting each other, their tails swishing back and forth like frantic windscreen wipers.

"Bertie!" The authority in Ali's voice cut through the noise in the hall like a hot knife through butter. "You know better than that! SIT!"

Ray watched in amazement as Bertie's beaming expression turned to one of total submission as the dog sat back on his haunches and looked up at Ali adoringly. Everything he had been meaning to say about not having time to stay, needing to be somewhere *extremely* urgently – all those fictional excuses drained from his mind. *That's* what he needed. In future, when Ray said "SIT!", sit was exactly what Banjo would do.

So when Ali turned back to him and said, "We're about to start, Ray. Take your place at the end of the line over there,"

Ray obediently followed her instructions, with Banjo trotting alongside him as if that was how he always behaved.

"Right," announced Ali, "welcome to you all. Most of you have already met Jim and Gail, both experienced dog owners who work with me during these classes so we can ensure that you all get the individual help you and your dogs need. And let's start by saying hello to our new members this week: Banjo and his owner, Ray."

Ray grunted with embarrassment as all eyes turned in his direction, while Banjo seemed to be loving the attention.

"Those of you who have been before will know that this class is about so much more than just teaching your dog how to sit and stay. This class is about manners – helping owner and pet to understand the importance of good social behaviour, whether at home or out and about. There is nothing more irritating than a dog who doesn't behave reliably and appropriately in the company of other dogs and people. Your pet must learn to pay attention and listen to your commands while surrounded by distractions, and be able to socialize in all situations without causing disruption or annoyance to others.

"So, let's start with the basics: how your dog should behave on a lead. Form a large circle, please, with the end of the lead held loosely in your left hand, your right hand guiding the lead, and your dog on the outside of the circle to your right."

Glancing around in panic as he watched everyone else getting into position, Ray was relieved when Ali made her way across to him.

"That's far too short," she said, handing him a much longer lead. "A loose lead is best for training your dog to walk by your side. Think of the lead as an aerial between you and Banjo. Through the lead, combined with your voice commands, you can communicate what you expect from him. The first thing is to make sure that you have his complete attention – and the best results come from encouragement when he performs correctly rather than confused messages about what he might be doing wrong. Initially, you could reward him with a small biscuit treat from your pocket, to let him know when you're pleased that he's behaved correctly. But from the dog's point of view, you, his owner, are the most important person in his world. He relies on you for his home, his food and his security – so he is naturally anxious to please you. Although little treats are useful at the start to help him learn what you want from him, he's just as keen to earn the reward of your approval, which you can convey to him through your words and body language. Watch me."

Ali started to walk Banjo around their own small circle in one corner of the hall. Then she looked down at Banjo and gave him the instruction "SIT!", which he did immediately. Ali fed Banjo a treat from her right hand, which she allowed to linger near enough to the dog's nose for him to know that more treats were there to be earned.

Then, raising her right hand to her shoulder and calling out the instruction "With me!", Ali took one step before stopping and rewarding Banjo with another treat because he had stayed close and moved with her.

Not realizing that his jaw was dropping with amazement, Ray watched as Ali repeated the command, movement and reward until Banjo was following her instruction perfectly.

Then, as Banjo sat obediently when told to, Ali's gaze met Ray's. "You have a very bright little dog here, eager to learn. Now, let's see if you're a quick learner too."

From then on, Ray and Banjo practised walking on the lead, while the others around them got on with different manoeuvres that involved trust and partnership, polite greetings in specific situations, and walking to heel without a lead. The sound of dogs' names being called rippled around the room as each owner concentrated on one exercise and then the next. The pair were so absorbed in their various tasks that Ray couldn't believe how quickly the hour had flown by when Ali finally called time.

"What do you reckon?" asked John, coming over to greet Ray with Bertie at his side.

Ray puffed out a long breath of air. "Well, I wasn't sure what to expect. That Ali's very…" He searched for the right word.

"Definite?" suggested John. "Scary? Sergeant major-ish?"

Ray grinned. "All of the above."

"So are you coming again next week?"

Ray glanced down at Banjo, who was standing alongside Bertie, both dogs looking up at their owners as if waiting to hear the answer.

"I think we probably will," smiled Ray.

"See you both tomorrow morning, then. Usual time, usual place?"

Kath and Maggie decided that the discussion they needed to have about events leading up to Christmas could just as well take place outside of Hope Hall as inside it. So much had recently happened in the lives of the two friends that they felt a proper catch-up was long overdue, so they headed off to the lounge of a hotel on the High Street, where they could settle into comfy chairs in a corner by the fireplace over a big pot of tea that was refilled without them even asking.

"Shall I be Mum?" asked Maggie, reaching for the teapot. "Sugar?"

"Not for me, thanks," replied Kath, expressing her surprise as Maggie popped two sweeteners into her cup.

"Not for me either, as you see. I decided it was time to do something about my embarrassingly high sugar intake."

"Because of Phil?"

"Well, sort of. Not because he's asked me to, though, because he's been quite clear from the start that he likes everything about me, not just the way I look. I could blame my sweet tooth on the fact that I bake cakes for a living, but that would just be an excuse really. I'm beginning to realize I eat sweet things to make me feel better, because I actually have a very low opinion of myself. I know I'm not very tall, and I can't help that, but do I have to be so broad from side to side as well? Phil's helped me remember some of the other things I used to enjoy, like walking. I used to do a lot of that when I was younger, especially with such nice countryside around us and the coast nearby."

"All the things you'd find in Chichester as well. How did your weekend away go?"

"It was really good. We blew the cobwebs away with long walks on the South Downs. I can never get enough of that sea air."

Kath smiled. "Do you know, you're positively glowing?"

"I feel as if I'm glowing inside too. Who'd have thought something as wonderful as this could happen to me? I mean, look at me – not far off my fifties, definitely no oil painting, dumped by my husband and losing my home all in one year? I couldn't have been in a worse place. And then Phil just walked in and changed everything."

"It's been a bit of a whirlwind…"

"I know." Maggie eyed her friend thoughtfully. "You're wondering if everything's happened so fast that I haven't had time to grieve or think. I'm probably on the rebound. This will all end in tears."

"Well, what do *you* think?"

"All of that! I'm more aware than anyone of how my settled old life has been turned upside down over the past few months. The last thing I need is another man complicating things with his own agenda. I should be concentrating on forging my own path to find what I really want and need. But actually it took no working out at all, because Phil just found me, and through that friendship I've discovered what being happy really feels like – and it's wonderful!"

"Friendship? Is that what you have with Phil?"

...nitely. I've never had a nicer friend – present company excluded, of course! But yes, I think we're simply the best of friends. Getting on with each other is just so easy. We never run out of things to talk about, or laugh over, or want to do together. We both like being busy. He loves my baking, and I love the way he can't wait to get his tool kit and electric drill out to repair, make or create anything that anyone wants. He's coming up on Saturday to turn Steph's utility room into a hairdressing area, so she can invite clients over to her place. She's missed working, but doesn't feel she can commit to being in a salon with Bobbie still so young. To have her own set-up at home is a great idea – and Phil immediately offered to restructure the room for her. He's just good that way; always ready to lend a helping hand."

"He sounds like a very special man – and a great *friend*."

"Oh, I know what you're asking. How do I *feel* about him? Am I being swept away on a cloud of romance?"

"Are you?"

Maggie took a few moments to consider her answer. "Yes, it does feel romantic, but that's because Phil is such a thoughtful man. Every time he rings to say good morning and wish me a great day, or calls last thing at night when we're both tucked up in our beds to talk about the day and say goodnight – yes, it *does* seem very romantic. Especially after twenty-five years with a man who thought romance was buying me a new ironing board so he had nicely pressed shirts lined up for work. But this isn't love's young dream. Phil and I have both been a bit battered by life. Our hearts might be fluttering, but our feet are still firmly on the ground."

"You're not planning to run off into the South Downs sunset, then?"

"As nice as that sounds, I've just got myself settled with that lovely new flat – and my job, of course, which you know I love. I'm not ready to give any of that up for someone else right now, however wonderful that person may seem."

"And what does Phil think about that?"

"He feels exactly the same way. He completely understands, to the point that when it all came up in the first heady days after we'd just met up again, we realized we were both a bit worried the other person might get the wrong idea and want to move too fast. It was such a relief to hear him say exactly what I was thinking – so we agreed then and there to enjoy this for what it is, taking things nice and slowly. And I'm so happy just to savour this lovely feeling for as long as possible, because I can't believe it'll last. I mean, Phil's great – and I'm, well, I'm just ordinary old me."

"Are you worried that you're falling in love with him?"

"Neither of us has mentioned the word, and that suits me fine. For me, it would be a commitment to say it. Even though it's a word that could easily slip off my tongue whenever I think about how much Phil means to me, I'm not going to use it until I'm ready to commit long term. And I'm nowhere near that. I wonder if I ever will be."

Kath nodded. "Yes, it's hard to trust your feelings after you've been hurt by someone you love."

Maggie looked at her friend with understanding. "Jack hurt *you*, didn't he? You loved him for so many years, and then he hurt you, not just once but twice after that Family Fun Day at his new hospital."

"Yes, but I've come to realize that there are many kinds of love. Looking back, there was never a blinding flash of emotion at the start with Jack. We were work colleagues who always got along like a house on fire, and on that basis we drifted into a relationship that was certainly very caring – but was it true love?"

"And now you love Richard."

Kath's eyes shone as she answered. "I think I probably do, but I'm not sure I can put into words something I've simply never felt before. It's exciting because it's new, but the roots feel deep and solid between two people whose lives are slotting together in the most comfortable and compatible way. We've both been alone for a long time, but we're used to that, so I suppose our independence could be a problem if we're each too set in our own ways. But actually, nothing's been a problem because we find it so easy to talk about anything and everything. We're interested in each other's work. And we're enjoying meeting each other's friends and family."

"What about Richard's son? He's had his dad to himself all these years since his mum died. How does he feel about you being the new woman in his father's life?"

"He's okay about it. He told me so before he went off to university. He said he was really pleased to see his dad enjoying life again. He even asked me to take care of Richard, because he was worried that the house would seem empty if his dad spent too much time there on his own."

"And Celia? She was the woman you once described as Richard's 'other half'!"

Kath chuckled. "I can't believe how badly I got my wires crossed. I really thought they were a couple. They always seemed to be together. The truth is, they grew up more like siblings than cousins. His father and her mother were brother and sister, and the children lived close enough to spend a lot of time in each other's company. Richard adores Celia."

"But she was very off with you when you first met. Can you trust her now? What happens if she takes a sudden dislike to you? Where would Richard's loyalty lie then?"

"I'm really not worried about that. I understand that Celia has always seemed very confident and headstrong, but she's actually quite vulnerable, especially where her brother Douglas is concerned. Richard told me that she had always adored her father, because it seems they were very alike in interest and ability. She inherited her good business brain from her dad, but then the key job at Ainsworth Mill went to Douglas, because he was next in line for the inheritance, even though he had no interest whatsoever in finance.

Richard has kept an eye on Celia over the years. He's been there to listen and work things through when she's gone through tough patches, especially with Douglas. There was never any romance between them. In fact, they both laugh hysterically at the idea."

"And there's been no wedding bells for her?"

"Richard says she's never shown much interest in a relationship like that, or even in having a family of her own. She's married to her job, I think. She's happiest of all when she's got a nice complicated spreadsheet in front of her."

"And she's okay about you and Richard?"

"She really is. I worried about that at first, but there was no need. She loves Richard enough to want him to be happy, especially after all the turmoil he went through when his wife was ill. She stepped in to be the woman in his life when it was needed, and I have to say she has a terrific relationship with William, which seems to bring a lot of pleasure to them both."

"Can you see yourself with Richard, slippers on and cuddled up together, in your dotage?"

"Oh, I don't know. That would be very nice, but I can't think that far ahead. We're both a little overwhelmed by what we feel as we spend more and more time together. Who knows where it'll all lead? But I have a feeling the best is yet to come."

Maggie reached across to lay a hand on Kath's as the two women looked at each other with matching expressions of sheer contentment. Then Kath's grin turned into a chuckle, and Maggie joined her in a moment of delighted laughter.

Chapter 5

"Hi. It's Kevin, isn't it?"

Kevin had just finished a final clean of the tables used by members of the Grown-ups' Lunch Club that afternoon and was in the process of stacking the chairs away when he heard her voice behind him. Even without turning around, he knew it was Chloe – and he couldn't possibly have looked any worse than he did right then, after all the cleaning and floor mopping he had just done. He slowly swivelled around to face her.

"Yeah, that's me."

"You probably don't remember me. I'm Chloe Evans. We go to the same school, but I think you're in the year above me."

"Oh, really?" he asked, hoping he sounded cool and interesting in spite of the fact that he was covered in dust, and his hair was sticking up in spikes all over his head.

"I have a feeling I saw you last night at the after-school drama club. I thought you'd come into the hall during our rehearsal, but when I looked again you weren't there. Was that you?"

"Er, yeah. I was just walking by, you know, and I saw something was going on, so I took a quick look."

"I wondered if you were thinking of joining."

"Oh, a drama club, was it?" Kev stuttered, hoping she wouldn't be able to tell that he was lying through his teeth. He knew full well it was the drama club, of course – and yes, he had been thinking of joining until he saw the other people there. It seemed as though every student known throughout the school for being popular, good-looking or a great sportsman was in the hall that evening. You need confidence to act on stage and that crowd had it in bucketloads! It was when he recognized two of the best-known characters at Broad Street Upper School – Jason Harding, the head boy, laughing loudly with Callum James, captain of the senior football team – that he'd turned on his heel and sped away. Whatever had made him think he could fit into a group like that? They'd be laughing before he even opened his mouth to say a line.

"We rehearse in there on Monday evenings," Chloe explained. "It's just that we're always looking for new members, so I was hoping you were thinking of giving it a try."

Wow! She was looking straight at him with those enormous blue eyes of hers, as if she were really interested in him. Kev felt his knees buckle and had to pretend to shift his weight a little so he could nonchalantly grab one of the chairs behind him.

"Drama? Well, I've never been on the stage. I'm not sure I'd be any good at it."

"Oh, it's such good fun – and we all work together. It's a really nice group. You might enjoy it."

"Wouldn't I need to be able to act?"

"Perhaps you already can. You never know until you try."

Kevin could hardly breathe, owing to the heady sensation of sinking into that gorgeous gaze of hers. "What are you rehearsing for at the moment?"

"We're doing an end-of-term revue. You know, lots of different sketches and songs. It should be really good."

"What are you doing in it?"

"Oh, I'm acting in a couple of the cameo pieces. I've got a solo song at one point, and I'll be dancing, of course."

"I bet you'd be good at all of that."

"You've never seen me do anything on stage, have you?"

"I've seen you arrive for dance classes here once in a while, so I'm guessing you'd be okay."

Okay? Did that sound insulting? He could hardly tell her he

89

knew how brilliant she was. He'd watched her through the foyer doors that led into the main hall on several occasions – not that he was prepared to own up to that. *Be cool*, he told himself. *Girls like it if you play it cool.*

"You served me a coffee on Saturday the other week," she said.

"Yeah, you're usually here for the Saturday morning dance class, aren't you? But it's Tuesday today. What are you doing here now?"

"I've got a ballet exam coming up, so I've come in for an extra class."

"You must really love it to be putting in so much practice time."

"I've been taking lessons since I was four years old. I'm hoping to study dance in London when I finish school."

"We'll be seeing you on the telly, then, performing in all those big shows!"

"Well, it's ballet I like best, although I do enjoy the modern stuff too – you know: jazz, hip-hop and contemporary – as well as tap, jive and Latin American."

Kevin was beginning to feel a little out of his depth when it came to different types of dancing, so he just nodded, hoping she would think he understood exactly what she was talking about.

"Anyway," she said, filling the awkward silence. "I'm holding you up. I can see that you're busy. You're here a lot, aren't you? Have they given you an after-school job?"

"It's the kitchen I like. I'm keen to learn about baking, and they do some really interesting patisserie stuff here at Hope Hall. I came through school for work experience first of all, but I liked it so much I pestered them to let me keep coming."

"So I'll be on the dancing shows, and you'll be on *The Great British Bake Off*, eh?" She laughed, and he couldn't help but join in. When the laughter stopped, there was another bout of silence while Kevin struggled to think of something else to say.

"Well, I'll see you around, then," he finally said.

He wondered if he'd struck a suitably casual pose as he leaned back against the stack of chairs behind him, hoping she'd think he wasn't fussed one way or the other whether he saw her any time soon.

"Okay. See you, Kevin!" With a quick wave, she turned away towards the main door, leaving him in a pool of sweaty embarrassment as he thought about the way he looked and all the things he had and hadn't said.

As usual, Celia used her own key to let herself into Richard's house, calling out his name as she made her way through to the kitchen. She found him with the morning paper stretched out across the old oak table that stood in the middle of the room.

"I need a tea," she announced. "Have you got any of those decaf bags I like?"

"In the brown jar on the work surface. Do you need breakfast too?"

"I'm on the 5:2 diet, and today's a fast day."

"That doesn't sound very healthy, especially when you're working such long hours."

"I refuse to get podgy."

"Just eat healthily. Cut back on that gorgeous ice cream I know you tuck into every night."

Celia huffed with indignation as she popped a teabag into a mug and poured hot water over it. "It helps me sleep."

"You only sleep about five hours a night at most. That can't be healthy either."

"The trouble with you," she retorted, "is that you know me far too well and never pull any punches. A girl could get a complex with all this criticism, you know."

"A complex? You? Never! You're always forthright and completely sure of yourself."

Celia sighed, kicking off her high heels before sinking down on to a wooden stool opposite him. "I have news!"

He gave up trying to read and looked directly at her. "Well, spit it out!"

"I've got an interview."

"For the UK finance director's role?"

"Apparently they're planning to call a special board meeting, and I will be the only item on the agenda."

"That sounds promising. Does that mean you've got the job?"

"According to Uncle Joe, I have. He says this meeting is just to iron out the details. As long as I don't say anything terrible and promise to make them lots and *lots* of money, the post is mine."

"Congratulations! You'll be brilliant at it."

"Well, I'll save my celebrations until I know what kind of package they're offering."

"Of course. You'll strike a hard bargain – and an international financial institution like Apex wouldn't want you as their UK finance director if you aimed for anything less."

"Uncle Joe's already planning his retirement party, but I guess I'll be easing out of my present role for several weeks before that. I'll need a decent amount of handover time with him just to make sure I'm properly across everything, but I may well be making myself at home in that great big office of his before Christmas."

"How do you feel about that? Are you excited?"

Taking a sip of her tea, Celia considered her answer before speaking. "What words would I use to describe my feelings right now? Flattered? Honoured, even? Amazed I've got so far that they're even considering me? Daunted? Terrified?"

Richard's smile was affectionate as he reached out to touch her hand. "My darling Celia, you are fearless. This job was made for you. You have all the right experience, and you know Apex's UK business through and through. You're well respected in the financial sector. You've got this!"

She puffed out a long breath. "I've got this," she said, looking anything but certain.

"But are you sure this is actually what you want? It's a lovely feeling to be flattered and honoured and all the other things you said, but is this the job you would really choose for yourself?"

"It's what I've been working towards for years, so I guess it is."

"You'd be taking on a lot, and you'd have to be right up to speed from the start. But then you're so familiar with all of this, and you're great with figures. You have a nose for good investment and have already proved yourself to be a safe pair of hands."

"Do you think so?" Her usual confidence had slipped from her expression.

"Of course I do. So does Joe – and the board of directors. And if you're honest, so do you. You're just fishing for compliments, but they're coming your way from every direction!"

Celia fell silent as she settled down to sip her tea for a while. "I have other news!" she eventually announced, pushing Richard's newspaper to one side to make sure she had his full attention.

"I can see you're itching to tell me, so go ahead."

"Douglas is leaving to drive Diana to Berkshire first thing in the morning. Her mother rang last night, and apparently Lord Harry is quite poorly."

"What do you mean by *quite poorly*? You're talking about a man who's always been such a powerhouse and taken great pride in the fact he's never had a day's illness in his life. Do you know what the problem is?"

"Douglas isn't one for detail, is he? I don't think he bothered to ask – he just sees it as a chance to take some time off. We've got that big contract starting at Ainsworth Mill this month, as you know, and everyone's working overtime to keep it all on track. Douglas doesn't do overtime, because he doesn't do work. He's marching around telling everyone that Lord Harry and Lady Eleanor desperately need him in Berkshire, and that he has to be there to support his beloved wife in her distress and worry."

"And is she distressed and worried?"

"Diana's far too well schooled to show any emotion in public. But I have to say, she answered the door last night when I popped into Ainsworth Hall to pick up some papers for Uncle Joe, and she looked quite wretched – not her normally coiffed and elegant self at all. She's always been very close to her mother, as you know, and they speak every day. So if Lady Eleanor's concerned about Harry, Diana will be worried too."

"What about Matthew and Barnaby?"

"The boys are away at school, so Douglas and Diana can take however long they need to make sure things continue to run smoothly while Lord Harry's under the weather."

"You don't mean to say that Douglas is going to be in charge of her father's estate while he's there, do you?" guffawed Richard. "Douglas can't organize any aspect of his own life – or even his day – without people waiting on him hand and foot!"

"I imagine he's planning to lord it over everyone working there, telling them what's what and how things should be done."

"That's not going to help Lord Harry's health! Surely he knows how hopeless Douglas is at business."

"I suspect Douglas puts on a very plausible performance for his in-laws. He wants their approval, and he likes moving in their social circles. He'll play the role of the concerned son-in-law very diligently while he's there."

Richard hesitated for a moment. "This probably isn't a tactful thing for me to ask, but there's no possibility the estate will come to Douglas if anything happens to Lord Harry, is there?"

"None at all. Diana is their only child, but the estate has to go to a male heir, and the only one who qualifies for that is David, the son of Lord Harry's younger brother, Charles. That's all been organized."

"Well, that's a relief," replied Richard. "How about things back at Ainsworth Hall while Douglas and Diana are away? I guess the housekeeper and estate manager will be there to hold the fort. They don't need us to keep an eye on anything, do they?"

"Nothing has been said."

"We'll keep out of it, then. I'm sure they'll ring us immediately if they need something."

"Ring *you*, you mean," retorted Celia. "Douglas would never dream of asking me for help."

Richard nodded. "That's very sad. Your parents would be upset to know that the two of you don't get on."

Celia shrugged. "Not for any lack of trying on my part."

"I know," agreed Richard. "Douglas is a very difficult character."

"My little brother is an arrogant, lazy, ignorant show-off. I wouldn't choose him as a friend."

"But you still love him as your brother."

She sat back from the table a little. "Of course. He was a great kid, but unfortunately he grew up to be a very self-centred man. I really don't know where he gets that trait from, because Mum and Dad were both such dedicated, hard-working people. They constantly went to great lengths to show their care for everyone they knew or had responsibility for."

"I think your father would turn in his grave if he saw how Douglas is behaving now."

"Well, in that respect I'm glad Dad is no longer here to see how things are. It would break his heart."

Richard nodded his agreement without further comment.

"Speaking of affairs of the heart, how's your romance going? I know you've been seeing a lot of Kath lately."

Richard's face lit up with warm affection. "I will simply say that I'm a very happy man. Kath's good for me, as I hope I am for her. We feel very comfortable in each other's company."

"Comfortable? It sounds as if you're talking about your favourite armchair!"

"Celia, I'm fifty-one years old, and I've been widowed for going on six years now. I've not looked at another woman since Liz, because she's a hard act to follow. But very gently, with no pressure at all, Kath and I have just been drawn to each other. We get along well."

Celia tilted her head so she could peer closely at him. "You're going all soppy. I've never seen that look on your face before."

"I don't do soppy," he said with a laugh.

"It looks as if you do now."

He thought about that for a few seconds before answering. "Kath is lovely, and our time together is becoming very precious to us both. It's so long since I've had the company of a warm and loving partner. I'd forgotten how good it feels."

"Well, that's true. You've been acting like a crusty old hermit since we lost Elizabeth."

"Liz was my life. I could never replace her, so I've had no interest whatsoever in filling the gaping void I've felt since losing her. But Kath certainly isn't a replacement, because I'm beginning to realize that getting close to her doesn't make me love Liz any less. It's as if my heart is expanding to include a new kind of love that's right for me now – and it feels good."

Celia expression softened as she gazed at Richard. "I'm glad. It's good to see you smiling so much these days. You've become a proper Cheshire cat!"

"Well, put it this way: I know how it feels to be the cat who got the cream!"

"Have you got a minute, Jan?" Barbara Lucas popped her head around the kitchen door.

"Hi, Barbara. Nice to see you," smiled Jan. "What brings you to Hope Hall today?"

"Della's got dance exams coming up for a lot of her pupils, so she's fitting in extra lessons that the kids can come to straight after school. I've been helping her out with the extra ballet and tap tuition some of the girls need, but I've got to hang around for a while this evening because a few of us are having an initial chat about this year's pantomime at six."

"Goodness. Are we planning the Christmas panto already? Where did the year go?"

Barbara laughed. "Jan, are you tied up at the moment? Is there any chance we could have a quick chat?"

Jan grinned. "I'm all organized and my feet are killing me. Two coffees up in the balcony lounge in five minutes?"

"Perfect!"

Before long, the two of them were comfortably settled on a soft sofa in the upstairs seating area, alongside the large window that looked out across the park on the opposite side of the road from Hope Hall.

"Della seems to be doing really well with her dance classes," commented Jan. "Those street-dance moves she teaches look absolutely terrifying! I like the tap steps, though, and the senior citizens are just queuing up to join the armchair exercise class. She must be very pleased."

"She is. As you know, she'd been dancing on the cruise ships for several years, which was all very glamorous and took her around the world, but after a while she got homesick. And, of course, she and Steve have been an item since she was fifteen, and she really missed him while she was at sea. It's amazing that their romance survived all that time apart, but they seem stronger than ever now. I caught her looking at a wedding dress magazine the other day!"

"Oh, that would be nice. A wedding in the family!"

"It certainly would. But more than that, I spent all those years building up a very substantial dance school here in the town, and although my style of teaching is traditional, Della brings a freshness to it because she can teach all those modern styles young people want now."

"Mother and daughter, each bringing her own experience and skills to the school. I can see that it works really well."

Barbara nodded. "It does, but I've chosen to take a big step back

97

from it all, as you know. I don't want the responsibility of running a school any more. It's not the dancing, because I'll always love that, but the paperwork and admin that goes into running a business of that size just became too much. Della loves it all, but then she doesn't have a computer that hates her, as I suspect mine does!"

"Mine too!" laughed Jan. "Young people seem to have been born with a chip in their brains that means they just *get* all this high-tech digital stuff. I can't tell you how often I end up shouting at my computer – as if it can hear me or cares a fig about how frustrated it makes me feel."

"I'm happy to leave the technical challenges to other people these days, and I've enjoyed having more time to spend with Stu. You know, I was teaching night after night, and he was very good about it for all those years, but it's our time now, so I'm happy to leave Della to get on with developing the school in her own way. I just enjoy popping in every now and then to help with the traditional dance styles I enjoy."

"I remember doing ballet classes as a kid," mused Jan. "I was terrible at it, and I still have two left feet when it comes to dancing."

"Ah," said Barbara, leaning in a little closer, "but you have other talents, my dear Jan – and it's those I want to talk to you about."

Jan looked surprised.

"A significant group of WI ladies have asked me to have a word with you," Barbara continued. "We were all so impressed with that magnificent harvest supper evening you organized, and we think we need you in our ranks."

Jan sat back suddenly. "Join the Women's Institute, you mean? I can't do that – not with that awful Brenda at the helm. She hates me. She made a point of telling me so in no uncertain terms at the end of that evening."

"But you handled her brilliantly. She might have blustered and threatened, but it didn't stop you coming up with an event that was different and imaginative, and really well planned and prepared.

Our ladies are full of praise for what you achieved – and it's started a very loud undercurrent of distaste for Brenda's attitude; not just towards you, but towards all the other members who aren't in her inner circle of cronies."

"No one's going to change that attitude of hers. She belittled and bullied me at school, and she's still doing the same thing now. And honestly, Barbara, whatever we might have achieved for that harvest supper, Brenda always has a way of making me feel like an idiot, sucking every bit of self-confidence out of me. I'm glad it all went well that night, but I really don't want to be in her company again anytime soon."

"We want you to join our institute, and we want you on our committee."

"I can't, Barbara."

"Please think about it. Brenda has ruled our group with a rod of iron for more than a decade. We're supposed to change our Chair every year, but no one's ever dared to stand against her, for all the reasons you've mentioned. But there's change afoot. A group of us is planning to stand for election to the committee at the next meeting, which takes place early next month, and we have enough support from our members to replace Brenda and her gang of officers with a new generation of practical ladies who'll work together as friends to make our branch all that it should be. So many of them have asked me about you, and not just because they know they would enjoy your company at our monthly meetings. They saw how you ignored Brenda's jibes and simply got on with the job. Whatever you might feel about her, you've become an inspiration to us all. So, I've been sent with this plea from everyone in the branch – except Brenda, of course!"

Jan let out a long breath as she reconsidered the request. Finally, she said, "I promise I'll think about it. I have to say that the WI ladies who came to help with the prep for that supper were just great. I certainly enjoyed their company. But I really don't fancy being at loggerheads with Brenda ever again."

"Let me and the rest of the ladies do the loggerheads bit. You simply fill in a form to join the branch and turn up at the next meeting. I promise you'll be enthusiastically welcomed."

Jan's worried expression changed almost imperceptibly until there was a slight cheekiness about her smile. "I'd never have the courage to stand up to her on my own. But if I was in a group with all of you—"

"You might get your own back at last," finished Barbara.

As Jan nodded in thoughtful agreement, that smile broadened to a grin. "Okay!"

Plainly delighted, Barbara moved a little closer to Jan. "In that case, I wonder if I might put another proposition to you. It's about the panto…"

A week later, pianist Ronnie Andrews was singing loudly as he climbed the stairs to the balcony lounge.

"Here we go, here we go, here we go again," he chanted as he glided and twirled his way over to the far corner of the balcony lounge where the pantomime team had gathered, as if he were a famous diva greeting adoring fans. "Sorry we're late, sweeties!" he announced to the group. "The little darlings in that last dance group just didn't want to go home."

Following closely behind him was Della Lucas, who had just finished her last dance class for the evening. As usual, she looked immaculate in chic dancewear that clung to every inch of her elegant slim frame.

"Exams are coming up," she explained as she dropped gracefully into a soft armchair next to her mother, before pulling out a large notepad and pen from the bulging leather holdall she used to carried her shoes, paperwork, props and all the other items she needed during her classes. "They're all getting a bit twitchy and emotional."

"And that's just the pianist," quipped Ronnie. "I'm exhausted with all this pressure."

Barbara looked across at him fondly. "Pressure, my foot! You love being busy and in demand. You're in your element at the moment."

Ronnie grinned as he took a flamboyant pose. "It's showtime! Oh YES, it is! Remind me what we're doing this year. Is it Aladdin, Snow White or Jack in the Beanstalk?"

"It's Cinderella this Christmas," announced Maurice Guilford, who was seated on the table next to Della. Brenda from the WI had taken her place directly opposite Maurice on a high-backed dining chair that allowed her to look down on the others, who were all settled into low settees and armchairs.

Maurice laid out his papers on the table in front of him. He had been producing the show ever since the tradition of having a town panto began at Hope Hall. As Deputy Headteacher of Broad Street Upper School, English teacher Maurice had taken on the role for every school show there for as long as anyone could remember.

"No matter," chuckled Ronnie. "We'll only need to change the names and the costumes. All the sketches and jokes will be exactly the same whichever story we choose!"

"Quieten down, please, everyone," called Maurice, looking pointedly at Ronnie. "I think we're all here now. Let me just run down the list of who's involved this year. For anyone who's new to the panto, I'm Maurice Guilford, the producer."

"The Admiral of our Fleet!" heckled Ronnie.

Maurice drew a slow breath before starting again. "I'm also the scriptwriter."

"Will it be the same script we used for Cinderella three years ago?" asked Barbara.

"No, there's a lot of new material in this one – as well as plenty of familiar old favourite bits, of course."

"Have we got a ghost sketch?" asked Hope Hall's accountant, Trevor, who was sitting with his wife Mary.

"Of course," nodded Maurice. "Only this time it's not ghosts but

101

giant spiders that the two Ugly Sisters and Buttons encounter in the deep, dark wood."

"That sounds good," said Trevor amid the general chatter of enthusiasm for the idea.

"Spider costumes?" snapped Brenda. "My ladies can't organize intricate costumes like that at such short notice. You'll have to change it. It needs to be a ghost sketch. We've got all the white sheets for that."

"It's going to be a spider sketch this year," stated Maurice in his best deputy headteacher voice – it had stopped many teenagers in their tracks over the years. "They will be giant spiders wearing ultraviolet costumes, which will look great at the start of the second half, when they do their night dance in the deep, dark wood. If your ladies can't cope with making costumes like that – and of course we understand – we will make other arrangements to have them put together elsewhere. Actually, our school art department is very keen to come up with something for us."

"Their help will not be necessary," huffed Brenda. "They certainly wouldn't have the needlework skills my ladies have – *high-standard* skills, I hasten to add, that are much in demand in the lead-up to Christmas. I'm simply saying that a little more notice would have been polite and helpful."

"My dear Brenda," replied Maurice in a tone that was as conciliatory as he could manage, "I only finished writing the script last night. The vision for this year's scene in the dark wood only occurred to me then, and this is the first official planning meeting of the pantomime committee. The script for the year is always revealed at this meeting."

"And the pantomime is to be staged during the second weekend in December, I believe," came Brenda's pointed reply. "Eight weeks away, to be precise. Leaving things a little late, aren't we?"

"Certainly not," retorted Barbara, fixing her eyes directly on Brenda. "Most of us are old hands at pulling the panto together, and this is our usual time for getting started. We already know who some of the main parts will go to, and our adverts are being widely displayed, giving details about auditions for all the other parts to be held early next week."

"Oh, I love the auditions," enthused Ronnie. "Sometimes they make me laugh more than the panto ever does. Who's going to be on the panel – apart from me, of course, as the musical director?"

"Well, I will be," replied Maurice, "as the producer and director. Then there will be Della and Barbara, the choreographers, and Jan Hayward, who unfortunately isn't able to be here this evening, but has just agreed to take on the role of stage manager."

Brenda spluttered with indignation. "I will *not* work with that woman! What experience has she had in stage management? That is a totally unacceptable appointment. We have several ladies in our group who would be first-class at the job. Jan Hayward would be a disaster!"

"Oh, I don't think so," said Barbara, her face the picture of friendly innocence. "Jan has already proved herself to be an excellent organizer. Just think what a wonderful job she did with the harvest supper the other week. We all enjoyed that, didn't we?"

Enthusiastic approval rippled around the group.

"And what's more," continued Barbara, "Jan did a lot of am-dram backstage work over the years before she and her family moved to this town. And she comes as a double act with her husband Keith, who is well known as a terrific handyman. He's really good at carpentry, painting and decorating. Keith is in Rotary, of course – a great friend of Roger Beck, who'll be in charge of the sound and lighting for the panto. Don't you remember that wonderful staging they erected for the Easter Centenary Fayre? It was Keith who designed that, and it was just perfect for the occasion. So I think it's great that he's offered to be our set designer and builder, with Jan as the overall stage manager. They'll make a really strong team."

"I repeat, I will *not* work with that woman! If you insist on going ahead with this unwise decision, I will resign. And I'll be taking my WI ladies and all their skills with me."

"I'm sorry you feel that way, Brenda," replied Barbara, her voice deceptively calm. "Let's hope it doesn't come to that. After all, the WI is all about working together for the benefit of our community, so I guess each of us will have to make our own decision on whether we want to be involved with the panto or not. As the branch chairperson, I'm sure that's something you'll wholeheartedly endorse."

Brenda gathered up her belongings, got to her feet and, with one last furious stare aimed at Barbara, turned on her heel and headed for the exit.

"Brilliant!" enthused Steph, running her fingers over the lay-back sink, the sleek shelf made from pale varnished oak and the large mirror, in front of which stood a shiny new hairdressing chair. In just a couple of days, the utility room in Steph and Dale's house had been transformed into a neat, flexible area where Steph could offer hairdressing appointments that fitted in with their family life.

"Thanks so much, Phil. This is better than I ever thought it could be."

Phil was obviously pleased with the compliment. "I couldn't have done it anywhere near as quickly without Dale's help."

"Oh, I'm just the plumber, putting in the finishing touches like the sink and taps," laughed Dale. "I'm no carpenter, but I can certainly appreciate talent when I see it. You've done a great job, mate. Thanks."

"So, this room has got to earn its keep now," sighed Steph, slipping down into the new chair and staring at her reflection in the mirror. "I already have quite a few customers I've known for years. I've been visiting them at home until now, but with Bobbie being such a handful it'll be much easier for them to come here, especially in the evenings when he's safely tucked up in bed."

Her face beaming with pride, Maggie stepped forward and put her arm around Phil's waist. "See, I told you he's a good 'un, didn't I!"

Phil chuckled. "Well, that's nice – but isn't it usually the hopeful partner who has to go, cap in hand, to his beloved's parents to get their permission to woo their daughter? And here's me, old fella that I am, hoping that I now have her daughter and son-in-law's approval to spend time with their mum."

"Who cares if your intentions are honourable," laughed Steph, "when you're not just willing but *able* to do wonderful work like this? I'm really grateful, Phil. Thank you. Consider yourself part of the family!"

Phil smiled down at Maggie, clearly relieved and delighted by Steph and Dale's reaction.

"I'll put the kettle on, shall I?" beamed Maggie. "Cake, anyone?"

"Cake?" repeated Bobbie, pushing his way through the grown-ups so he could look pointedly at Maggie. "I want cake!"

"And what word do you have to say if you want cake?" said Steph, her voice stern.

The little boy gazed hopefully at his grandmother. "Nanny?"

Chapter 6

"Have you seen the new notice on the board?" Flora almost broke into a run as she headed back to the table where Ida, Doris and Betty were sipping welcome cups of tea while they waited for lunch to be served. "They're holding auditions for the panto. It's Cinderella this year."

"You're not thinking of trying for the part of Cinders, are you?" drawled Percy, who was sitting at the next table. "The idea is that Cinderella's coach is made from a pumpkin, not that the leading lady should be the shape of a pumpkin!"

Flora burst into peels of good-natured laughter, while Ida pursed her lips in silent disapproval.

"No, I just thought it might be fun to be in the chorus. You know, as a court lady or a villager."

"The village idiot, you mean?" Percy's eyes sparkled with mischief as he teased Flora.

"No, that's always a man. You'd be good for that role, Percy. You wouldn't even need a script. You play the part so well already."

"But Percy can't sing," retorted Robert. "Doesn't the village idiot in a pantomime have to sing? Never sit next to Percy during a singalong. He's got a voice like a foghorn."

"Hang on," said Betty, joining in the conversation. "Isn't Buttons supposed to be the village idiot, even though he's actually very canny and clever? Everybody loves Buttons. He's the one who gets all the kids yelling, 'It's behind you!'"

"It's been ages since I went to a panto," sighed Doris. "I used to take the grandchildren when they were little, and I reckon I loved it even more than they did. They're all teenagers now and wouldn't dream of going to anything like that."

"Well, why don't we try for the auditions?" suggested Flora. "It would be fun – and after all, we proved at the Easter Fayre that we're star tap dancers now! We could be very valuable members of the chorus line. Plus we stole the show at that Centenary Fayre for our performance with the Can't Sing Singers."

"Do the men have to wear tights?" Percy directed this question at Ida, whose mouth twitched with just the smallest flicker of amusement that only he noticed before she answered.

"They do. And powdered wigs that itch like mad for the elegant minuet they have to dance during the ballroom scene. You'd never keep up, Percy, but I'd love to be in the audience to see you try."

The sound of someone noisily clearing his throat suddenly caught everyone's attention. They looked up to see Kevin manoeuvring his serving trolley, loaded with steaming plates of food, into position. And then, with a last-minute adjustment to the false moustache that was stuck at a jaunty angle to his top lip, he burst into song:

> *"Mind your elbows, ladies, please,*
> *If you want your steak and peas.*
> *And Percy, move your bloomin' cap*
> *Or this will end up in your lap!*
> *Robert, if I'm not mistaken,*
> *This is your poached egg and bacon.*
> *It's for sure... a Hope Hall dinner*
> *Is never gonna make you thinner!"*

Kevin hung on to his moustache as he took several comical bows in acknowledgment of the delighted applause and laughter he received from all the nearby tables.

"Kevin, you can sing!" squealed Flora.

"No, I can't. You've just heard me."

"You should audition for the panto."

"You could put me in a soundproof box, but I still can't sing."

"And you're a good-looking chap. You could be Prince Charming."

"He's the one who gets the girl," quipped Percy. "It might be worth your while."

"Look, you lot, do you want these dinners or not? I can always take them to the other tables over there."

There was no more discussion after that as all the plates were delivered to the right people and everyone tucked in. No one had noticed that over by the serving hatch someone had been watching the proceedings with great interest.

"Oh, I don't know how Bertie's going to get on with all this lot."

Standing just inside the door next to Ray and Banjo, with Bertie on a lead at his side, John was staring with dread at the array of agility equipment that had been set up in the hall. There were cones, ramps, single and double jumps, cross poles and tunnels – and several dogs and their owners were already queuing up to take their turn.

"Well, the dogs look as if they're enjoying themselves," said Ray, thinking that they also looked incredibly well behaved. He glanced down at Banjo, who was panting with excitement and tugging on his lead, as if he couldn't wait to join in. He had a sudden image of the wayward dog flying around, knocking over one piece of apparatus after another. Perhaps this hadn't been such a good idea after all.

The two men's eyes were drawn to a collie who had disappeared into a long tunnel. He shot out of the other end in triumph a few seconds later, to be met with a great welcome from his owner.

John looked down at Bertie's rotund body and sighed. "You'd never make it out the other end, would you, Bertie? You'd end up wearing that tunnel!"

"Shall we leave it for tonight, then?" suggested Ray.

"Hello, Bertie!" Ali's voice cut across the hall and stopped the men in their tracks. "I can see you're raring to go, Banjo. And I can see that you two gentlemen are considering whether to scarper or not. Well, I don't think your dogs are going to let you. Keep them on their leads and head over this way."

Ray and John exchanged a resigned look before trailing across the hall like naughty schoolboys to join Ali in the far corner.

"All of this is great fun for a dog," she explained. "Agility training is good exercise, it takes concentration and coordination, and it brings out the competitive spirit in them. They love to succeed. They enjoy pleasing their owners by doing well."

Sitting impatiently beside Ray, Banjo's tongue was flapping with enthusiasm as he tried to take it all in. Next to him, standing forlornly at John's feet, Bertie bore the expression of a condemned man.

"We're going to start with the cones. It's nice and easy, with the owner initially leading the way around the row of cones. Your dogs will soon get the idea that they have to weave in and out, and that there's a little treat waiting for them at the other end if they do it well. Who's going to go first?"

Banjo was up on his feet and tugging to get to the first cone before Ali had finished asking the question.

"Banjo, heel!" she commanded, the authority in her voice stopping Banjo and Ray in their tracks. "Walk nicely!"

Hastily manoeuvring himself into the right position to get around the course, Ray listened to Ali's instructions as Banjo rushed along beside him, making his way between the cones and even going around one cone twice for good measure.

"Well done, Banjo!" said Ali, stroking his head to show her appreciation. Ray wondered if he was about to get a tickle under the chin for good behaviour too.

"Now you, Bertie. Take up your position, John – and off you go."

Bertie did go off, but not in the right direction. Without a backward glance, he pottered towards the main door with John trailing behind him.

"Control him, John. You have the lead. Show Bertie who's boss! Bring him to heel and make sure you have his full attention."

Under Ali's eagle eye, John pulled Bertie to heel, painfully aware of the look of appeal in Bertie's eyes. At that point, Ali strode across to take Bertie's lead. Speaking quietly to him as she stroked his head, she led him slowly between the cones while Bertie trotted at her side without ever taking his eyes off hers. He'd made it! As John went up to the other end of the cones to make a fuss of Bertie and tell him what a good boy he was, it was clear that the plump dog wasn't just getting the idea, he was beginning to like it.

What a difference an hour makes! By the end of the session, Bertie was quietly trotting from one challenge to the next. Banjo could hardly contain his excitement, turning his body in a complete circle to whizz around in delight at the thought of the next game he was about to play.

There were a lot of challenges to be worked through by dogs with various levels of expertise and experience. As beginners, Bertie and Banjo and their owners were only able to watch from the sidelines as the more practised dogs tackled the intricacies of wobbly boards, ramps and double bar jumps. Bertie's face was expressionless. Banjo, on the other hand, dribbled with anticipation, and Ray felt a sudden jolt of affection for his new canine friend, who had such a zest for life. He was certainly a handful, and his complete disregard for house rules had turned Ray's life upside down, but the disruption had pierced the terrible silence that had shrouded the house from the moment Sara lost her battle with cancer. Banjo still needed to know who was boss, but Ray couldn't shake the feeling that this little man was a gift from Sara herself, and that she would be laughing out loud at the battles of will he and Banjo had throughout each day.

"Right," said Ali, making her way over to where Ray and John were watching the star dog of the gathering put on a remarkable performance as he worked his way across an agility course that had been specially put in place for him. "Don't look so gobsmacked. There's no reason why your dogs won't be doing all of this in time. It's up to you. They're only here for an hour a week, though. You have every other hour to continue their training. Lead work, voice control, learning instinctively when certain actions or responses are required – that's your homework for this week and every week."

She bent down to make a fuss of Bertie, who looked up at her with adoring eyes. "Well done, Bertie. You were very good tonight. Make sure you keep training John!"

Then she turned to Banjo, who was on the point of jumping up to lick her face with total devotion, but then the look in her eye reminded him he was likely to get more praise if he just sat on his haunches, as he knew he should. "And you, Banjo, are a very bright young man with bags of potential, but you've got to listen. When Ray gives you a command, you listen and you obey. We both know you understand perfectly. Prove it! Make Ray – and me – proud. I'll see you both again next week, okay?"

With a knowing look, Banjo managed to appear quite serious as he gazed at her – before excitement took over and he yapped his goodbyes.

Maggie pulled her coat collar up around her ears as she dashed across to her car through the drizzle of rain. Now the clocks had gone back, any memory of summer had been left behind as people found themselves making their way home from work in pitch darkness at five o'clock. It was dark and wet, and there was a definite nip in the air, hinting at the winter chills to come. She thought about her new home and how cosy it felt when she put the central heating on in the evenings. She was so content to be there. In fact, "content" was a good word to describe how she felt about every aspect of her life at the moment. At the start of the year, she had thought she would never be happy again, but everything had changed.

Her phone buzzed just as she was climbing into her car. *I bet that's Phil*, she thought. But the moment she saw the number, she recognized who the caller was and knew exactly why he was ringing.

"Richard! I was going to phone you this evening. You've beaten me to it."

She could hear the smile in Richard Carlisle's voice as he returned her greeting. "Well, I think I'm getting things sorted," he said, "but I'd like to run it all past you. Can you talk now, or would you prefer me to ring you in an hour or so when you're home with a cuppa in hand?"

"No, this is fine," replied Maggie, making herself comfortable in the driving seat. "Fire away!"

"Well, as you know, Kath's fiftieth is on the 6th of November, which is a Friday. She's insisting that it's a working day, and that any birthday celebrations can wait for the weekend."

Maggie chuckled. "She's definitely not going to get away with that."

"Precisely. Are we still thinking of a surprise gathering for her on that Friday, from around the time she's likely to think of heading home?"

"Kath usually keeps Friday afternoons for catching up on the accounts and other paperwork, so we wouldn't expect her to be in the main body of the hall until she walks through at the end of the day to say goodbye and cast an eye over everything before she leaves."

"And she's not likely to be late leaving that day, because she thinks she and I are going to have a special dinner to celebrate. William's coming back from Plymouth to see her, although she won't know that until the great reveal at her surprise party."

"Well," said Maggie, "Shirley's brewing up some great ideas for decorating the balcony lounge, and the invitations have been quietly sent out to everyone we think might like to come."

"I've managed to glean a few bits of information to help me make contact with her closest friends around here and some from her time in London too. Anyone who can't come has said they'll send a recording for her birthday video," continued Richard. "I actually spoke to her sister Jane, in Australia, who sounded thrilled that we're doing this. It's just too much of an undertaking for their whole family to come over here now, unfortunately, especially as they are planning a trip over next spring, but Jane says she'll make sure they get their birthday greeting recorded in good time so we can include it in the video."

"That sounds great. Ray has volunteered Tyler, Shirley's boy, to put the birthday video together, and I hear he's very talented at that sort of thing. What's the plan for the surprise party?"

"Trevor will keep Kath occupied with questions about the accounts from mid-afternoon, and as she's right at the back of the building, we'll ask people to park along the road rather than in our car park so she doesn't see everyone arriving on their way to the main door. The invitation says we would like them to be safely settled in the balcony lounge by five o'clock sharp. Trevor will think of something to get Kath over to the main building at that point, and he or someone else will lead her up to the balcony lounge. 'Happy Birthday' will start just as she gets to the top of the steps and sees everyone."

"That sounds wonderful," grinned Maggie. "Everyone loves a surprise."

"Will Kath, do you think?" asked Richard with a note of doubt in his voice. "She's not one for making a fuss about anything. Are you sure she'll enjoy this?"

"I've come to know Kath very well over the last three years, and you're right. She's not one to fuss for herself, although she would be the first to organize something like this for any of the rest of us. She'll be flabbergasted, astonished and deeply touched by the fact that so many people are keen to tell her how special and loved she is. Take it from me, she'll be thrilled."

Richard let out a long breath. "I really do hope so."

"So, are there any plans for the rest of her birthday weekend?"

"Well, she says that the next day, Saturday, she'd like to go to London for a walk around the National Portrait Gallery. I've managed to get matinee tickets for *Swan Lake* at the Coliseum that afternoon, which she doesn't know about yet. Then we'll round it all off with a meal at the restaurant we went to for our first proper date when we went up to London for the evening. She's always saying she'd love to go there again."

"That sounds like a wonderful day, and we'll make sure the evening before is pretty wonderful too. Let's keep in touch, and let me know about numbers whenever you can, so we know how many to cater for."

As they said their goodbyes and brought the call to an end, both Richard and Maggie were smiling to themselves.

"Well," said Uncle Joe, slipping into Celia's office fifteen minutes after the Apex Finance board meeting to which she had been summoned. "You never do things by halves, do you? That was a magnificent performance. You had every board member eating out of your hand. They're going to offer you the job, of course."

Puffing out her cheeks with relief, Celia felt her shoulders drop a notch or two as she beamed back at him. "Do you think so? Are you sure they didn't have any reservations? I felt I was floundering a bit with the nitty-gritty detail of the comparative overseas

114

money markets, but then that's not my usual area of expertise."

"If that was you floundering, I can only imagine how spectacular you'll be when you've got your head around that particular area of finance. You'll learn – and fast."

"How fast? Did they say when they're going to let me know officially? I'll obviously need some handover time with you, as well as a chance to help choose a replacement for this role. I've worked so hard to build up Apex. I don't want to see it all fall apart because they've appointed the wrong person to take over the role."

"Tell me, who *should* take over the role? Brian Reynolds?"

'There you are, you see. That's just what I'm afraid of. Brian Reynolds isn't a team player. He's ambitious, but he wants the show all to himself. And what's needed in this role is someone who can recognize the different gifts and talents of the team, then bring out the best in them. That's the way to make money."

"Who is good enough to fill your shoes, then?"

"Jenny Williams is way ahead of the field, in my opinion. She's bright, creative, disciplined and hungry. She'd be the perfect candidate to take this department on to the next stage."

Joe smiled. "I'll bear that in mind when the board meets to consider that position. First of all, they have to consider *your* new position. You certainly played hardball when it came to the package you'd expect to have."

"Did I overdo it? If they give me anything like what I asked for they don't know me very well! I pitched high expecting to compromise. But the truth is, I want that job so much, my fingers are itching to get at it. Whatever they suggest, I won't put up much of a fight. I just want to get started."

"Well, I'd better get back. This is just a coffee break before we get stuck into discussing the annual report. If I hear any more, I'll let you know. Stay cool."

"As cucumber," she grinned. "As if I don't give a fig!"

She watched as the door closed behind him before getting to her feet and clenching her fists with excitement. It was all she could do to stop herself throwing her head back and screaming with sheer delight. She finally perched on the side of her desk with a smile that lit up her whole face.

She had to calm down. They hadn't asked her yet, and when it happened, that would be a moment she wanted to savour. She quickly moved around to her seat to open her top left-hand drawer. Pulling out a magnifying mirror on a foldaway stand, she unzipped her cosmetic bag and set to work repairing her make-up by dusting her face with a fine film of powder before adding a cloud of blusher and a touch of lipstick. She flicked the mascara wand over her eyelashes, then plumped up her hair before spraying her wrists and neck with a breath of expensive perfume.

If the best job in the world was just about to fall into her lap, she intended to look her best. And when the chairman finally got around to offering her the position, she would not only look the part, she would be prepared and ready to take on the board, the banks, the clients and the world.

Kevin was just putting the finishing touches to cleaning the coffee machine after the Saturday lunchtime rush when he did a double take. There was Chloe! He had noticed that she hadn't arrived that morning for her usual Saturday dance class – but here she was at three o'clock in the afternoon, making her way towards the main hall and chatting away with several of the students he recognized from the time when he had almost called in to the drama club at school.

Leading the group, laughing and talking loudest of all, were the ever-popular Jason Harding and Callum James. There was another lad from that year whose name Kevin thought was Sean something-or-other, but he wasn't quite sure. He recognized the two girls who were walking either side of Chloe even though he didn't know their names, as they often went to the same dance class. Their voices dropped as they reached the double door that led into the main hall, peering through the glass to see what was happening inside.

"How many are there on the audition panel?" one of the girls asked. "Is Mrs Lucas one of them? She's been my dance teacher since I was three. I'm sure she'll give me a good part when she sees my name on the list."

"I'm going for Cinderella," retorted the other girl in a very loud stage whisper. "If I don't get the lead I'm not really interested in anything else – especially if Jason gets Prince Charming."

"Of course I'll get Prince Charming!" Jason turned towards the girls to give them an elaborate, over-exaggerated pantomime bow. "I can act and sing – and I'll look great in a pair of tights!"

"Isn't Prince Charming traditionally played by a girl dressed up as a boy?" asked Chloe, joining the group.

"Well, that won't be you, Miss Evans," replied Jason, moving closer and treating Chloe to a slow, smouldering smile. "You're far too pretty to be a boy. You could be Cinders, and I could be the dashing handsome prince who rescues you from every danger."

But Chloe wasn't really listening because her attention had shifted beyond Jason and towards the kitchen. When she smiled and gave a wave in that direction, Jason snapped around to see who she was waving at.

"Who's that?" he demanded. "Do you know him?"

"It's Kev," smiled Chloe. "He's in your year, but I think he mainly does technical subjects, so he's in the other block from you."

"What – Kevin Marley? Is he working here?"

"Yes. He's training to be a pastry chef."

Jason spluttered with laughter. "Not a man's man, then!"

"Oh, I don't know. I rather fancy the idea of a man who can wow me with his cupcakes," laughed Chloe. "Actually, Kev's really nice. I'll just go over and say hello. He might know how the auditions have been going."

But before she could move, the door of the main hall swung

117

open and their deputy headteacher, Mr Guilford, appeared, taking stock of the newcomers. "Which parts are you three girls auditioning for?"

"Cinderella," smiled the tallest girl.

"I thought you might be," said Mr Guilford, making a note of her name, Gina Welbeck, on his form.

"Are you going for that part too, Chelsey?" he asked.

"Yes, or the Fairy Godmother. I'd like a part with lots of dancing."

"And you, Chloe?"

"Oh, I don't mind which part I get. I'll just fit in wherever."

"Okay then, girls. Why don't the three of you come in together? I'll be calling you next, gentlemen, so spend this time practising your best lines."

Looking back towards Kev and giving him another quick wave, Chloe followed the other girls into the hall, where the door was shut firmly behind them.

"So Old Man Guilford's producing the panto again, is he?" said Jason. "He's been doing it for years. Too many, some might say."

"Oh, I don't know," replied Callum. "Isn't the whole point of panto that it's pretty much the same every year?"

"But why should someone who's basically just an English teacher be any good at directing stage productions? Do you think he missed his true vocation, and he really wanted to be a great actor – but his mum wouldn't let him?"

The boys sniggered at the thought.

"Yeah, he saw himself playing the villain in *EastEnders* but ended up as the back end of a horse instead," scoffed Jason.

At that moment, the main door to Hope Hall opened with a bang, letting in a blast of chill air. In walked three elderly ladies, who looked around with curiosity until their gaze settled on the boys.

"Are you here for the auditions?" the first lady asked. "Have they got as far as the villagers and court ladies yet? I know we're early, but we didn't want to risk being late."

"They're auditioning for Cinderella at the moment," replied Jason, struggling to keep a straight face. "Were any of you thinking of trying for that part?"

"Well, if you were Prince Charming I might give it a go," the same lady cackled. "Is that what you're trying for?"

"Can you sing?" her friend asked him, taking off her glasses so she could study him more closely. "Yes, you look just the part. I can see you as the prince. Very dashing."

"I certainly can sing. Can *you*?" asked Jason, pinching himself to keep from bursting into laughter.

"Oh, we have several talents. We can dance. In fact, we were the star turn at the Easter Centenary Fayre when we did our soft shoe shuffle. Perhaps you were in that very large audience when we brought the house down. And as for singing—"

"We *love* singing," interrupted the third lady in the group, who was almost as round as she was tall. "May we introduce ourselves? I'm Flora, and these ladies are Doris and Betty. We belong to a very esteemed group here at Hope Hall."

"Really? Does the group have a name?"

"Yes, we're called the Can't Sing Singers."

Jason erupted with a belly laugh, and Callum and Sean joined in.

"Well, I'm glad you're laughing," retorted Doris, raising her voice to make herself heard, "because that is the general idea with the Can't Sing Singers. We're perfect for panto, as you'll see."

"Oh hello, Kev!" squealed Betty, as she caught sight of him at the serving hatch. "Please tell me you've got the kettle on. We're all parched, and singers like us need to take care of our voices."

Kev gave them a thumbs-up, then disappeared out of sight as he went to prepare their drinks.

"He should be auditioning," Flora muttered to her friends as she made her way across to the serving hatch, rearranging her handbag as she went. "Kev would be brilliant."

"Yes, but I reckon he's too nervous to give it a try," retorted

Betty. "Let's go and see if we can persuade him to put his name on the list."

Kevin reappeared at the hatch with a tray bearing three bone china cups of tea, each with its own matching saucer.

"Here you are, ladies. This should get your tonsils in tip-top shape. Pinkies up!"

"Kevin," said Betty in an urgent tone. "Those lads over there are going in for the Prince Charming audition. That's *your* role! Get that apron off and get yourself over there."

Kevin gave a wry smile. "That's Jason Harding, Head Boy and most fancied student in the school. And the other one is Callum James, who all the girls dribble over because he's the captain of the rugby team. I wash dishes. I can't compete with them, and I wouldn't want to try."

"Go for one of the other parts, then," said Flora, who had arrived just in time to join the conversation. "You've got such a great sense of humour, and those little songs of yours are really good."

"And we don't think you get out enough," added Doris, popping two spoonfuls of sugar into her teacup. "You're always here, a bit of a Cinderella yourself, with your nose at the window while others get all the good chances. Come on, Kev. Show 'em what you're made of. This could be your moment."

Kevin smiled at the trio of ladies with affection. "I'll think about it, but I'm on shift here for the next halfhour. And look, those lads are going in now, so I've left it too late."

"They'll be on to the villagers and court ladies next," cried Betty. "Look, there are more people coming in to audition for all those roles now. We'd better take our cuppas over there with us so we don't lose our place in the queue."

With squeals of excitement, the three ladies bustled away to prepare to do battle for their starring roles.

An hour and a half later, Barbara Lucas sat back in her chair and rubbed her neck, just as her daughter Della walked back from the door, having checked whether there was anyone else in the foyer waiting to be seen. The committee had staggered the times to audition for each character throughout the afternoon, and now they were faced with the challenge of working out who would play which part, who might need a bit of TLC because they would not be getting the part they hoped for, and whom they still needed to find for roles that hadn't been filled.

"This should perk us up," called Jan as she walked back in from the kitchen pushing a trolley loaded with coffee, tea and a selection of Maggie's home-made biscuits. "Tea or coffee, everyone?"

As orders were taken and drinks handed out, Maurice ran his pen down the side of his pad, making notes here and there beside the names and parts that were listed.

"So there are some parts I think we all agree on. Jason Harding did a great job as the prince. He looks the part and he sings well. Is everyone okay with that?"

There were nods all round.

"Both Callum and Sean tried for that part, but also for Dandini and Buttons," he continued. "What do we think about those two?"

"Sean was quite good, and he moves well," said Della, "but his singing isn't great. I think he was really nervous, so I don't feel he's confident enough to play Buttons. I suppose he could be Dandini."

"Could Callum be Buttons?" suggested Maurice.

"His voice isn't bad," commented Ronnie, "and he's quite good at delivering lines."

"Callum is definitely *not* a Buttons for me," said Barbara. "As a dancer, I can only say that he's an excellent rugby player. I guess he has to be solid and lumbering on the field, but Buttons has to be light on his feet; able to move and dance with confidence."

"Point taken," replied Maurice. "So are we agreed that Callum should be Dandini? He'll be a good foil for Jason as Prince

Charming. Callum's a good-looking chap, his voice is okay, and that part doesn't require much dancing, except in a crowd with lots of others. We can put him at the back. He'll be fine."

"And Sean?"

Silence fell.

"He could be Major Domo," suggested Maurice at last.

As no one in the group could think of an alternative, he made a note of this decision on his pad before putting a large question-mark alongside the role of Buttons. "We'll come back to that, but let's think about the leading ladies now. Cinderella. We saw Chelsey, Gina and Chloe. One stood out for me, but I'd be interested to hear what the rest of you think."

"It *has* to be Chloe," stated Barbara.

It was immediately clear that everyone agreed with her.

"That'll go down like a lead balloon with Gina," smiled Della. "She's been mad about Jason for ages. She was hoping that if she was chosen as Cinderella and he was the prince, he would suddenly see her in a whole new light the moment he kissed her."

"Well, we've got a lot of dancing numbers in the show," said Barbara. "The villagers are always bursting into song and dancing around the stage. Then there's that scene in the woods when we do the ultraviolet spider dance, and during the court scenes and at the ball. Gina and Chelsey are both excellent dancers, and we have a wide range of ages, ability levels and personalities in the chorus. I suggest we could make them both head girls for the chorus, so they've got time to help anyone who's struggling with the dance moves get up to speed."

"Chelsey also auditioned to be the Fairy Godmother. She'd look very pretty and do a capable job in that part," said Della.

"Our Fairy Godmother is quite a character, though," replied Maurice. "She's a bit absent-minded and gets things wrong, but is really endearing all the same. I picture her as an older person."

"And that's Mary Barrett," said Barbara. "She's like that in real life. She drives Trevor to distraction, but you can't help loving her. I thought she did a great audition. Didn't you?"

"Absolutely!" Maurice put Mary's name down on the list for the Fairy Godmother, and underlined it. "And that's a good idea about Gina and Chelsey. That'll make them feel important – and I guess you can feature them quite a bit in the dancing."

"I'll give them starring roles," noted Della. "They'll be quite happy with that."

"Talking of starring roles," continued Maurice, "the characters we've really got to get right are the Ugly Sisters. I don't think there's any doubt about which duo walked away with those parts, is there? Trevor Barrett and Derek Jessop make a great double act. It must be all that barbershop singing they do – dressing up in stripes and moustaches to look the part. It's odd, really, because Trevor's quite a reserved sort of fella when he's in accountant mode, but put him in some stage make-up and a wig, and he's a hoot."

"I thought William Fenton did a great audition as Baron Hardup," said Jan. "And it's a good joke that he's the man in charge of the Money Advice Service here. This could ruin his sensible reputation for ever!"

"So that just leaves the other major role we've got to fill: Lady Devilia Hardup. I know we had a few people going for that part, but no one really knocked my socks off. What did the rest of you think?"

"I think," said Barbara, "that the perfect candidate for Lady Devilia didn't actually come along to the audition."

Every eye turned towards her.

"We have someone at Hope Hall who plays that part every day. She's bossy, she's scary, and she makes sure her opinions are heard loud and clear—"

"Shirley!" breathed Jan, her face lighting up at the thought. "You're right. She *is* Lady Devilia. But would she be interested in doing a panto?"

"She will if I tell her she has to. I'm her big sister. She'll do as she's told!"

"Then you must tell her at once," grinned Maurice. "That's a fantastic suggestion. I have no doubt she'll be brilliant if we can persuade her to take on the role. So that just leaves Buttons. Bernard Whitehead auditioned, of course, and he's brilliant at panto comedy, having done it for years. And he's certainly played the part of Buttons before, several times."

"Didn't you go along to his seventieth birthday party a couple of weeks ago, Mum?" Della asked.

"Don't exaggerate. It was his sixtieth," retorted Barbara.

"He's ancient," declared Della. "And bald. He's absolutely wrong for Buttons."

There was silence as the committee considered their dilemma.

It was Jan who eventually spoke. "May I invite you all for coffee in the foyer here at Hope Hall next Tuesday lunchtime? I think we might be able to solve this little conundrum then."

Chapter 1

"Come on, you two. You're going to be late again. The school bell will be going in fifteen minutes, and it takes us ten minutes to walk there."

The note of frustration in Ali's voice was obviously lost on her seven-year-old twins, who seemed to feel no sense of urgency whatsoever. A sulky Zachary appeared at the top of the stairs. "You should have started yelling at us earlier," he said.

Ali heard a chuckle from the lounge door and turned around to see Clive grinning at her. She glared at him.

"I can't find my book bag," wailed Emily from the depths of the twins' bedroom.

"That's because I've got it!" Ali held the bag up for all to see, just as Emily peered over the banister.

"How did you find it?"

"I *looked*."

Clive walked across to put his arm around Ali's waist. "Do you want me to take them?"

"No, I'm going to walk the dog round the park anyway, and it's right next to the school."

"I'll probably have left before you get back. Remember I've got that squash match with Chris this evening straight after work."

"Oh Clive, it's Wednesday. I've got Waggy Tail tonight."

"I know that, but I did tell you two weeks ago. You said you'd ask your mum to babysit."

"It's a bit late now. I hate springing things on her at the last minute. She's so good at helping us out. The least we can do is give her a decent amount of notice."

"You do remember me telling you two weeks ago, right?"

She sighed. "Oh, I don't know. Perhaps I do, but I have a lot on my mind, and the twins would try the patience of a saint. That class is my only chance for a bit of *me* time, just for a few hours. Couldn't you have arranged your squash match for another day of the week?"

"Chris and I are in a tournament. It's the final tonight. You could wish me luck, you know."

She laid her head back against his shoulder. "I do wish you luck. I just wish you weren't doing it on a Wednesday."

"Come on, Mum," said Zachary. "We're going to be late. Can I take my scooter? It'll be quicker."

"No, because I'm taking the dog for a walk straight afterwards, and I don't want to be dragging your scooter all the way round the park."

"You never let me take my scooter," he moaned.

"Dad, don't you think we should go in the car?" demanded Emily. "We'd get there on time if we did. All the kids come by car except us."

"We're not getting the car out for a three-minute journey!" snapped Ali. "You kids just need to get your act together in the mornings. I've got your packed lunches, your book bags and your PE kits. You just grab your coats and backpacks, and let's get walking!"

"Love you," smiled Clive, holding the front door open as they bundled outside.

She pecked him on the cheek on her way out. "Love you too, you rotter."

It wasn't until she was saying goodbye to the twins at the school gate that Ali realized she had left the dog in the kitchen with his lead on, obediently waiting to be called for his morning walk. She

126

had forgotten him. Suddenly, she felt her eyes well up with tears. How could she have done that? How could she – a woman who had commanded respect for leading the whole dog handler section in her army regiment – feel so out of control on days like this? How could she be in command of twelve dogs and their owners at her dog training class, yet feel that she lost the battle every day with two children who should just do as they were told because she was their mother and she said so?

And Clive was infuriating too. It wasn't that he didn't help, or that he didn't care. They were far too strong a couple to feel anything except total love for each other. But she hated it when he laughed while the kids ran rings around her. She hated it even more, though, if he took over and the twins did whatever he wanted them to do without arguing at all. Was she really such a terrible mother? She had always succeeded at everything until she became a parent.

Ali allowed herself a minute to wallow in self-pity, then pulled herself together before turning back in the direction of home. She took her phone out of her pocket as she walked.

"Mum?" she said as the call was answered. "I'm sorry to ask, but are you doing anything tonight?"

"So the Can't Sing Singers are going to have a star spot of their very own." Doris was practically bouncing up and down like an excited child as she made the announcement to anyone close enough to hear. "Ronnie's the musical director of the pantomime, you see, and he says he wants us to have a number to perform all by ourselves."

"What sort of characters will you be?" asked Ida. As she spoke, her eyes scanned the crisply ironed linen cloth on the table in front of her, which had been neatly laid out ready for the Grown-ups' Lunch Club guests. She flicked away a couple of minuscule and probably imaginary flecks of dust before looking up at Doris.

"Well, Ronnie says we'll need to be very versatile. He hasn't quite decided yet, but I guess we'll be villagers in the opening scene, courtiers at the ball and maids of honour at the wedding. Just imagine how lovely the costumes will be."

"Do they have costumes in unusual shapes and sizes?" enquired Percy with a look of total innocence.

"I hope they have ones that are large in the middle but short in the leg," frowned Flora, "because I'm heavier at the top than I am at the bottom, and that's always a challenge when you're only five foot two."

"The wibbly-wobbly woman. How do you manage to stay upright?" asked Percy, then grinned to himself as he noticed Ida's head had suddenly dropped, as if she were also suppressing an uncharacteristic giggle.

"I wonder what the colour theme for the wedding will be," mused Betty. "Red and gold, perhaps, or blue and silver? I always like that scene best of all."

"Are you going to come and join us, Ida?" asked Doris. "After all, you'll be in demand now you're a tap dancer."

"Oh, please do," coaxed Percy. "I hear they're planning a spider scene. I would certainly pay money to see you in your black tights and leotard, my dear Ida."

The conversation was brought to an abrupt halt by the spectacle of Kevin wheeling his trolley, loaded with lunch orders, across from the kitchen door. Belting out the conga, and swinging his hips like an overenthusiastic ballroom dancer, he boogied and sidekicked his way around the tables, beckoning to several of the ladies to join the chain.

"We love to do the conga
To make our lunchtime longer!
Just join the line,
It will be fine!
You swing your hips like this, this,

And give someone a kiss, kiss.
Grub's on its way,
Hip, hip, hooray!"

The crowd loved it. By the second verse, they were lalah-ing along with the song, giggling and swaying in their seats. A couple of ladies over on the far side even got up to do their rather chaotic impression of the rumba.

As he wove his way in and out of the tables, Kevin managed to deliver the right meals to each diner with remarkable accuracy – although they all seemed to be having so much fun that it was likely none of them would have minded too much if they had ended up with toad-in-the-hole instead of spaghetti Bolognaise.

"See what I mean?" said Jan with a note of triumph in her voice. "Our Kevin is a hit with our ladies and gents. He makes up these silly little ditties week after week and has them all eating out of his hand. If he's not a real-life Buttons, I don't know who is."

Maurice, Ronnie, Maggie and Barbara were all watching with fascination from inside the serving hatch.

"Well," said Maurice, "he's certainly got personality. I'm guessing he's done quite a bit of stage work."

"I don't think he's done any. In fact, he can be quite shy with people of his own age, and is generally not as confident as you'd think he might be. He's become very fond of the pensioners who come along to this lunch club, and he's good fun with the little kids who come into the Call-in Café for lunch with their mums and dads at the weekends too. Kevin is just a really nice lad."

"Well, that's one of the most impressive auditions I've ever seen. The part of Buttons is his, if he'd like it."

Liz and Jan glanced at each other, both obviously delighted at the producer's reaction to their young kitchen assistant.

"Wait until after lunch to have a word with him. Don't hold him up," warned Maggie. "It'll cause a riot if our grown-ups don't get their lunches pronto. As far as they're concerned, Kevin's our head waiter."

"He can obviously dance," commented Barbara, "judging by the way he was swinging his hips to the conga."

"Ladies," announced Ronnie. "A star is born!"

"All we need now is our Lady Devilia," added Maurice.

A round of cheering and applause broke out when Kevin reached the end of his song and took a theatrical bow.

"Come along now, you lot!" announced a booming voice. "Eat up, because we've got a speaker this afternoon who'll be giving a talk on how to live with arthritis. So, look lively and tuck in!" Shirley's voice echoed around the foyer for a few seconds after she had finished speaking.

"And there she is," said Barbara. "Lady Devilia. She doesn't know it yet, but our Shirley's got the part. It's not just made for her; it *is* her!"

Once lunch was over the committee had put their invitation to the two would-be stars, who reacted in completely opposite ways to the idea of taking up leading roles in the panto.

Shirley didn't hesitate for a second. "I've always wanted to play the baddie," she exclaimed. "I would have preferred it to be Hollywood calling, asking me to become the next evil world ruler that only James Bond can stop – but Lady Devilia in the Hope Hall panto is definitely a step in the right direction."

"Can you manage the rehearsals alongside your schedule here at the hall?" asked Barbara in her sternest big sister tone. "I know you often have to work evening shifts."

"Oh, I'll just tell Ray which ones I can't manage. He'll be fine about it. We always help each other out if we need time off for anything."

"The panto is the last weekend before Christmas, and it's the first week in November now. That means we've only got seven weeks to get this panto into shape – and you'll be playing one of the main characters. There'll be at least two rehearsals each week, okay?"

"Have you got a script for me to look at?"

Barbara pulled a large envelope out of her voluminous bag with a flourish. "Read it as soon as you can, and just yell if you want me to come and run through the lines with you at home."

Shirley thumbed through the pages, then asked, "Do I have to stick to these lines or is there room for interpretation?"

"Basically, you stick to the script unless you've got ideas that are better than ours. Run anything you fancy changing past Maurice. He's always open to suggestions to make things funnier."

Shirley's eyes were shining when she looked up from the script. "Oh, I'm going to love this. Do you know what I'll be wearing?"

"The WI ladies are keen to help with costumes..." started Barbara.

Shirley grunted. "And they've got their own Lady Devilia. Is Brenda going to be in charge? Because I'm not sure I'll feel safe having a costume fitting with her if she's got a pair of scissors in her hand. We've clashed on a couple of occasions recently when she's marched into the hall demanding this, that and the other."

"You gave her a bit of the other, didn't you?" chuckled Barbara, picturing the scene as those two strong personalities faced up to each other.

"I simply gave her my professional opinion as a senior member of the Hope Hall management team," retorted Shirley with a grin.

"Right. Well, in that case it might be better for us to ask Ellie and the art department at the upper school to work on your outfit. Their A-level students have great talent and imagination, and Ellie reckons they could come up with some really creative costume ideas, especially for your character, who's supposed to make the Wicked Witch of the East look like a goody-goody!"

"Right. I'm going home to have a good read," announced Shirley, reaching out to give Barbara a big sisterly hug before grabbing her bag and coat, and heading for the door.

Kevin's reaction, on the other hand, had been decidedly cooler, to the point of icy fear.

Maurice and Ronnie had blocked his path as he was heading out of the kitchen after the Grown-ups' Lunch Club members had made their way into the main hall for their talk on arthritis care. At first, Kevin had been anxious to keep working, worried that Maggie would be annoyed that he was taking too long to clear the tables. Confusion had set in when he saw his boss waving to him through the hatch, making it clear that he should take ten minutes to go and have a talk with the visitors. He had suspiciously lowered himself into the chair Maurice had held out for him, and the three men had taken their places around the table.

As Maurice explained that they had seen him performing the conga earlier on, and just knew that he would be perfect for the role of Buttons in the panto, Kevin's jaw dropped and the colour visibly faded from his cheeks. "I'd be a jabbering wreck. I'd forget my words."

"You didn't forget your words today, and Jan and Maggie tell me you come up with words for different songs each week."

"Yeah, but I make those words up. If I forget what I meant to say, I just think of something else on the hoof. I've never really tried to learn words that someone else has written."

"This is panto," declared Maurice, striking a theatrical pose. "Half the fun is people forgetting their words or just making it up as they go along. It sounds to me as if you would be perfect at that."

"But what else does Buttons have to do? Would I only have to learn a few lines?"

"There are quite a lot of lines, actually, but most of them are played to the audience, because Buttons is the lovable joker who gets everyone laughing and singing along."

"Singing?" Kev's eyes widened with alarm. "What sort of singing? I mean, you've heard my voice. I'm no singer."

"But you're great at putting songs across, and the sillier the song, the better you are. That's Buttons. The audience laughs along with him – just as all the lunch club crowd did today."

"Who else is in this panto? Would I know anyone?"

"Do you know Jason Harding?"

Kevin sighed. "Yes, I know who he is."

"Well, he's Prince Charming."

"And Shirley's going to play the wicked stepmother, Lady Devilia."

Kevin managed a wry smile. "Oh, I can imagine she'll be good at that. When it comes to laying down the law, she's definitely had a lot of practice."

"And the part of Cinderella has gone to Chloe Evans."

Kev's head shot up at that name.

"Do you know her?" asked Ronnie. "She comes to dance classes here every week."

"Er, yeah. I think I know which one she is."

"Well, I know that Chloe would really help you with the part, because she's done a lot of stage work," continued Ronnie. "And of course, most of your scenes involve Cinderella, so perhaps you could rehearse together until you feel really comfortable with what you have to do."

Kevin's Adam's apple shot up and down against the neckline of his sweatshirt as he swallowed, his expression unreadable.

"You'd need to put in plenty of rehearsal time," warned Maurice. "Two nights a week: one for the main characters and the other for the group scenes. And because you have such a central role, I'd be willing to fit in extra practice sessions with you for the audience participation numbers you'd be leading."

"So?" demanded Ronnie, impatient to get an answer out of the young man.

Kevin gulped again, but his voice was firm as he looked directly at Maurice. "Okay. I'll give it a go."

As Ronnie clapped his hands together with glee and Maurice cheered, Kevin rubbed his sweaty palms across his jeans under the table and wondered what on earth he had let himself in for.

Throughout her married life, Maggie had never really liked walking. Over those years while she was bringing up her two children and running a busy household with Dave at work all day, she'd sometimes felt that she was never off her feet. But the thought of walking just for the sake of it simply didn't appeal to her. Neither had she ever felt the slightest interest in going to keep-fit classes, or getting a bike to make short journeys around the town rather than taking the car. All the same, she rarely sat down. She was constantly cleaning, tidying or baking something, and had always felt that was exercise enough, and she didn't need to walk around the perimeter of the park three times because other people said it would be good for her. Fair enough if the family had owned a dog, but with her son's allergy to any kind of animal fur, there was no need to lap the park or run around the block for the sake of exercise.

But once she and Phil started spending time with each other, she had discovered the joy of walking for quite a different reason. Phil had always loved the countryside, and it wasn't long before he was suggesting that they nip out for a spot of lunch at some out-of-the-way country pub, but he would always build in time for "a bit of a walk, so we can work up an appetite".

And to her great surprise, Maggie realized she didn't mind it at all. In fact, she found herself looking forward to their strolls down winding lanes in the dappled autumn sunshine, with golden brown leaves crunching beneath their sensible walking boots. From their very first outing, Phil had taken her hand in case she needed a steadying arm on uneven terrain, and she enjoyed the feeling of his fingers entwined with hers as they chatted with comfortable ease about what they saw around them, or reminisced about shared moments from the past, or discussed what they thought the other might be interested in hearing about from the long years during which they'd lost touch.

At the beginning of their friendship, Maggie had worried about mentioning Dave and their twenty-five years of family life together. But Phil seemed unfazed, commenting every now and then, or adding to the conversation with a memory of his own family growing up and the times he remembered with his wife Sandra. After all the months of pain and bitterness following Dave's decision to walk out on his family, these conversations with Phil, with his down-to-earth responses and his insights from a man's point of view, were surprisingly helpful. It wasn't as if Phil was agreeing with Dave or letting him off the hook for the hurt he had caused Maggie and their children, but Phil provided a broader point of view, based on his own experience of the way Sandra and he had gradually grown apart because they had different personalities, interests and opinions.

It took a while for Maggie to recognize that some of the painful knots of anger and resentment in the pit of her stomach were loosening their grip. One day it struck her that she barely thought of Dave at all, and she realized that she had changed. And it was Phil who was helping to bring about that transformation, with his gentle humour, his wide general knowledge gleaned from all those years of travelling the world in his work as an architect, his understanding of the ups and downs of family life, as well as his own sadness that his marriage had faded away until there was nothing left to keep him and Sandra together.

Maggie was beginning to understand that feeling, and to recognize that there was no marriage left for her to cling on to either. Dave had moved on. In recent weeks, he had let her know that he was struggling with his new life. The old Maggie would have found that knowledge impossible to bear. Now, though, she knew her feelings had become detached enough simply to wish him well. She had no desire to have Dave's presence in her life, and even less inclination to know any further details of his new situation with Mandy, her children or their new baby. Maggie had moved on too, and she knew that the new contentment and clarity in her life came from the confidence and pleasure she was discovering through her growing feelings for Phil.

Why this lovely man should choose to spend his time with her, Maggie still couldn't fathom. She certainly wasn't a looker, and she had a list as long as her arm of shortcomings that he would surely recognize for himself before they went much further. But whenever she plucked up the courage to question him about whether he really knew what he was doing by choosing to spend his time with her, he brushed her worries aside with tender good humour. He simply didn't want to know. He would change the subject, make her laugh and slide his arm around her to draw her close until every sensible thought seemed to slip from her mind.

However, the question that often kept her awake in the darkest hours of the night was: where is this all going? She had been divorced for only a few months. She was happy in her beautiful new home. She had a responsible job and a loving family. She was settled, and was discovering how capable and content she could be on her own, without a man at her side whose opinions might be expected to override hers. She wasn't looking for a long-term partner... was she? And even if she were, surely this had all happened too soon and too quickly. Whatever would people think? She would come across as a racy divorcee who had found herself another man to spend time with in no time at all.

Then she would feel the pleasure of her fingers interlocked with his, and a surge of pleasure flooding through her, as if she had never known such ease in the company of another person. She felt like a teenager. Her mornings began with his phone call, and his voice at the end of the phone wishing her goodnight brought her day to a close. She thought about him when she was working. She would revisit the most recent chat that had made them laugh, and realize she was giggling about it again as she drove, walked or cooked. When she did the rounds at the supermarket for the week ahead, she found herself searching for what she knew he would like, from his favourite brand of peanut butter to the tubs of salted caramel ice cream he knew he should resist but just couldn't. He made her feel interesting, entertaining, cherished and cared for – and she loved it.

But she couldn't fall in love with him. She wouldn't allow herself to do that. It was too soon, and most definitely unwise. She wasn't some giddy teenager. She was a rather plain-looking grandmother built for comfort rather than speed, and he was the most beautiful man she had ever known. He'd tire of her – of course he would – and she would understand and wish him well as she let him go. For the time being, though, she was determined to savour every glorious moment, storing up memories that would warm her wounded heart when he finally realized his mistake and left her alone again.

The cork exploded out of the champagne bottle with a satisfying pop. Richard and Douglas held out a number of glasses so they could be filled up in turn, with Richard handing the first glass to Celia.

"Congratulations, my dear Celia," announced Uncle Joe, once he'd finished pouring, his face beaming with pride. "Good luck in your new position as UK Finance Director at Apex Finance Incorporated. May you have as many happy and fulfilling years in the role as I've had!"

"Cheers!" was the call all around, as everyone got to their feet to drink a toast to Celia, who raised her glass before taking a sip.

"I think, Uncle Joe, that your shoes will be very hard for me to fill. But although I know I have a lot to learn, I can't wait for the challenge of this new role. It's hard to believe it's actually coming my way."

"Nepotism." There was a sour note in Douglas's voice that instantly jarred with Celia. "In Joe, you have a doting godfather in high places, and you're right that his act will be a hard one to follow. You'll have your work cut out for you trying to live up to his reputation after all his successful years in the job."

"Well," interrupted Richard as he felt Celia stiffen in the seat next to his, "we all know that Celia has shown a flare for business ever since she was a very young girl. That early promise has made her highly successful in every task she's undertaken."

"It's a *man's* job," retorted Douglas, "and frankly, I'm surprised Apex has appointed a woman to such a responsible role."

"Douglas!" Diana was clearly embarrassed by her husband's blunt comments.

Celia glared at her brother furiously. "I am the first woman within the worldwide Apex Finance network ever to be asked to take on the senior role of finance director in a country that ranks as highly in the world economic market as the UK does. Along with the States and Japan, the UK is right at the beating heart of world finance, particularly for fund management and investment. In that complex and constantly changing context, I will be leading the way for Apex Finance investments. That's the role they've entrusted to me."

"And it's a post Celia will be able to fill with great aplomb," added Joe, raising his voice in a bid to block out any further inappropriate comment. "Everyone around this table knows without a doubt that once our girl has her feet comfortably settled under that huge old desk of mine, she'll quickly get to grips with the complexities of the job."

Douglas sniffed, looking away as he spoke, as if he were

beginning to find the conversation boring. "I was simply saying that I'm surprised Apex made a decision like this; not because of any lack on my sister's part, but because you rarely see women in the top jobs there. I would have expected a major corporation like Apex to appoint a man."

"They've appointed the right person for the job, and that person happens to be a very accomplished woman." Kath's voice cut across the conversation like a sharp knife, calm and authoritative in a way that probably surprised her more than anyone else. "Many congratulations, Celia, for breaking through the glass ceiling that so often prevents the talent and potential of female managers and directors from being more widely recognized. You have proved your business acumen, and that alone has led to you being offered this very important position. Well done!"

Glasses were immediately raised around the table again, and there was a flurry of conversation as everyone sat back in their seats, as if they were all trying to change the subject and the mood. Kath felt Richard reach for her hand under the table and squeeze it. She squeezed back, giving a small smile without looking directly at him.

"When do you start?" asked Celia's Aunt Trish. "You're leaving just before Christmas, aren't you, Joe? How much handover time will that allow Celia before you go?"

"The board has already advertised my present role as the head of UK Pensions," replied Celia, who was still seething after the exchange with her brother. "But both my assistants in the department are excellent, and each would be very competent in taking over my position in their own way. I don't think it'll be long before a decision is made, which will allow one of them to be promoted so I can spend as much time as possible learning all I can from Uncle Joe before he retires."

"I have to say, Joe," mused Richard, "that I can't imagine you ever truly retiring."

Joe smiled. "Well, I do have plans to fill my time. I've enjoyed dabbling in racehorse training and breeding in the past, and I'd like to get more involved with that now. You know – turn the hobby into a business. I believe I have a potential winner in the stable at the moment and I have my eye on another, so I'm certainly planning to expand on that. I'd like to establish our position as a first-class training yard, and build up my reputation as an owner, with horses competing in races on a regular basis."

Richard smiled. "I've heard you speak of that plan of yours so often over the years. It's good to hear that you'll finally have the time and opportunity to make your dream a reality."

"I'm just glad to hear there'll be something to keep him out from under my feet," laughed Trish, reaching over to cover Joe's hand with her own.

Her husband's eyes sparkled with humour as he feigned offence. "Are you saying, beloved wife, that you aren't looking forward to having every minute of every day in my wonderful company?"

Trish grinned. "I'm saying, my darling, that this filly you married over forty years ago has much better things to do with her day than wait upon you hand and foot. It'll suit me fine if you want to spend all day at the stables. It'll make me very happy to know you're getting your own way there rather than getting in my way at home."

"Agreed." Joe looked at Trish with undisguised devotion, and Kath, sitting opposite them on the other side of the large round table around which they were all gathered for dinner, felt quite touched by the deep, comfortable love the older couple so clearly shared.

At that moment, two waiters arrived to serve the party their starters, and conversation halted for a while as everyone settled down to what they knew would be a delicious meal at the excellent restaurant Joe had chosen for Celia's celebration. Still feeling a little overwhelmed by this group of strong characters who wielded such

140

power over the lives of others, Kath was glad to feel the warmth of Richard's leg brushing against her own beneath the table. This was his family, and she hoped in time she would have a chance to get to know them better. But in these early days of their relationship, Kath still felt like something of an interloper in this hallowed circle of wealth and influence. She listened without comment as they chatted about subjects mostly unfamiliar to her: family members she hadn't met, business colleagues she didn't know and occasions from long before she'd had anything to do with this family.

Once the starters had been cleared away, Trish turned to the woman sitting beside her. "How's your father, Diana? I hear he's been ill."

"Oh, Lord Harry's okay," answered Douglas before his wife could open her mouth to reply. "Strong as an ox, that man."

"But haven't you two just come back from spending a couple of weeks up there because of his poor health?" asked Richard.

"Just a bit of a chill," replied Douglas.

"*Pneumonia*," corrected Diana. "The doctor was really worried about him."

"It's a good job I was there to take over for a while, wasn't it?" retorted Douglas. "He knew his interests were in good hands while I was around to keep an eye on things."

"But he has an estate manager and a full-time team on hand to keep things going, doesn't he?" Richard asked.

"My dear Richard, of course a man in Lord Harry's position has a team working for him on a day-to-day basis, but when it comes to major decisions relating to the future of the estate, it's family he trusts. That's why we were there, to ensure the smooth running of the family business."

"It was my mother who invited us," interjected Diana. "We went up there to support her because she was so worried about Daddy. And pneumonia is nothing to be flippant about, especially not at Daddy's age."

141

Douglas gave a dismissive wave of the hand. "He'll outlive the lot of us, that man. The estate is huge and very challenging for him as the lord of the manor. There are forty-six cottages and houses on the estate, you know. They're rented out, but it means he has the bother of looking after all those tenants with their complaints and problems."

"If the tenants have problems with their properties, the estate manager, Mike, takes care of everything. He's worked with us for years."

Totally ignoring Diana's comment, Douglas raised his voice as he continued. "And Lord Harry, poor chap, doesn't have many people of the right calibre with whom he can discuss the responsibilities that rest so heavily on his shoulders. He doesn't want to appear weak or indecisive to the staff. It's family he needs to speak to – which is why he was so glad I was there. As a landowner myself, I'm able to understand the complexities of running a large estate."

"The Ainsworth Estate here is two hundred acres, with just four tenanted houses." There was a firmness in Diana's voice that matched the cold frustration in her eyes. "Our family estate in Berkshire is five thousand acres. There is a considerable difference in the complexity and responsibility between Ainsworth and my family's estate."

"I know that, my dear Diana." As he spoke, Douglas leaned across to grip his wife's hand in a gesture that appeared more controlling than soothing. "But regardless of the size of the estate, we landowners speak the same language. Your father has spent years making the job look easy because he hasn't wanted you or your mother to be bothered with the detail. That's why he values my company so much. We understand each other, your father and I."

Silence descended on the table. No one knew quite how to respond to the obvious tension between Douglas and Diana. Fortunately, the waiters reappeared at that moment with the first of their main course orders, and the moment passed. Conversation was deliberately general after that, and as the wine flowed and tensions mellowed, Joe regaled the group with stories ranging from jokes they had shared at the office to the progress of his horses at the stables. They talked about neighbours and the approach of Christmas, and how the prices were rising in the shops. Richard talked about a new area of farming machinery his company was promoting. This became a popular topic for discussion, as farming was the lifeblood of everyone there apart from Kath. She joined in whenever she could, but was often out of her depth when the topics covered everything from high finance to the basics of the farmyard.

"And how are things at Hope Hall?" asked Trish with genuine warmth in her eyes as she looked at Kath. "This must be such a busy time for you."

Kath smiled. "You're right. There are Christmas parties and celebrations galore booked in for the coming weeks – but the big topic right now is Cinderella, our panto for this year. It looks as if they've finally managed to fill all the parts; some with rather surprising people who have never trodden the boards before now."

"Which part are you playing, Kath?" asked Joe. "Oh, but of course you'd be perfect as the Good Fairy!"

Kath chuckled. "I'm delighted to say the answer to that is I'm not – but you may be interested to hear who's got the part of Cinderella's father, Baron Hardup. It's William Fenton!"

There was an eruption of laughter around the table at that news.

"William? The former area bank manager and financial advisor," exclaimed Celia.

"And the manager of Hope Hall's Money Advice Service, of which you and I are trustees," finished Richard.

"Better still," smiled Kath as she continued, "another member of that group of trustees – our own accountant Trevor Barrett – has also bagged himself a major role in the panto."

"Not Prince Charming! Trevor definitely doesn't have the legs – or enough hair – for that," declared Joe.

"Dandini?" As she spoke, Trish seemed to be racking her brains to remember which characters traditionally appeared in a pantomime version of Cinderella.

"The back end of the horse?" suggested Douglas.

"Better than that," laughed Kath. "He's Cheryl, one of the Ugly Sisters, complete with bustle, false boobs and all."

"Oh, that's priceless," guffawed Joe. "We're going to need tickets to see that performance. Many people in the finance world around here would give a lot of money to see Trevor Barrett in make-up and a fancy frock."

"Apparently, he's been a member of a barbershop choir for ages, with the false moustache, stripey waistcoat, the lot! Another member of that choir, Derek Jessop, is playing the other sister, Beryl. You probably remember him, Celia, from the Hope Hall centenary event in August. His mother Joyce spoke so movingly about the letters we found in the time capsule that was put into the wall a hundred years ago, straight after the First World War."

"I certainly do," smiled Celia. "Well, we must book our tickets in good time. I don't want to miss that."

Before they knew it, coffee had been served and other guests at the restaurant were starting to leave.

"Thank you all so much for a lovely evening," said Celia. "This job is a dream come true for me, although I'm a bit nervous about taking on such a huge responsibility."

"You'll be fine," smiled Joe. "Congratulations again, my dear."

"Well, thank you, Uncle Joe, for this wonderful meal. It was very kind of you to organize it."

"It's the very least I can do for my favourite, and very talented, god-daughter. And on that note, I most definitely need my beauty sleep if I'm going to be fit for duty at the office tomorrow morning, so I bid you all adieu. Trish, my darling, say your goodbyes while I collect your coat."

Kath found herself being warmly hugged by Trish before she

followed Joe towards the exit. After that, Celia came across to air-peck Kath by each cheek, then threw her arms around Richard in the comfortable way that was usual for the cousins. Diana was already moving away from the table, looking back with a quick wave, as Douglas propelled her towards the door without a backward glance.

What a complex family this is, Kath thought, as she felt Richard's arm slip around her waist.

"They're completely mad, aren't they?" he whispered in her ear before planting a soft kiss on her willing lips. "Please don't judge me by my rather unusual family."

Kath smiled. "You're so unlike any of them. You're not a changeling, are you?"

"Do you think perhaps you're spending too much time thinking about pantomimes?" he laughed, drawing her closer to him.

"Oh no I'm not!" she declared in her best panto voice.

"Well, I'm *behind* you, so you'd better watch it!"

Chapter 8

"Did you see this?" Doris was sliding her outdoor coat off her shoulders so she could hang it on the hooks in the foyer while she had lunch. On her way, she had stopped to stare at the new poster on the Hope Hall noticeboard.

Flora, who had travelled to the hall on the bus with Doris that morning, walked over to join her friend to see what was being advertised.

"A quiz night," enthused Betty. "I really fancy going along to that."

"Oh, me too," agreed Flora. "I'm a sucker for quiz programmes on the TV. I like having a go at the answers, even though I always get them wrong."

"Remind me not to be on your team, then."

"My Eric is good at quizzes," mused Connie, who had come to stand alongside them. "His father was a schoolteacher, you know."

"Did someone mention a team? Whatever it is, I volunteer – as long as it's not for downhill skiing," interrupted Percy as he came across to read the notice for himself.

"How's your general knowledge, Percy?" asked Betty. "This quiz is being organized by Rotary, so it's a sensible affair. We don't want any of your nonsense."

"Or your smutty jokes," added Flora, who had just arrived to see what they were all looking at.

"Oh, I rather like Percy's jokes," quipped Betty.

"I never understand them," sighed Connie.

"Ladies and gentlemen!" They all stopped in their tracks as

146

Shirley's voice rang out across the foyer. "Lunch is served. Kindly take your seats if you want your grub."

Settling the Grown-ups' Lunch Club members into their allotted seats was always a long-winded affair, as some needed more help than others. Ida was already sitting bolt upright in her seat with an impatient expression on her face as Betty, Flora and Doris joined her.

"The four of us need to form a team," announced Betty as she pulled her chair out ready to sit down. "What shall we call ourselves?"

Ida looked across at Betty with disapproval, as if she were an overexcited child.

"It's a quiz night, Ida," explained Flora. "Rotary's running it here on Saturday week."

"There's a buffet included," added Doris. "I'd come just for that."

"Oh, do let's put our names down." Betty's face was full of excitement. "Ida, you will come, won't you? We'll need you as our team captain."

Ida didn't answer immediately, but after a pause she turned her attention towards Flora. "Did you say that Rotary is organizing the evening?"

"That's what it said on the advert."

"And their evenings are always good fun," interjected Betty.

"It's for charity, then," stated Ida. "We should always support charitable causes. Yes, I agree we should form a team, and I will be the captain."

"Did you say that you intend to take part in this venture, ladies?" Percy demanded to know from his seat on the next table. "Our team, the Conquerors, will be glad of a bit of healthy competition before we sweep the floor with you."

"The Conquerors?" giggled Flora. "The Tailenders would be a better name for you four."

"Well, you'll certainly have your tails between your legs when we win first prize," snapped Robert from Percy's table.

"What's your team called?" demanded John, who was sitting next to him.

Ida's eyes narrowed as she icily stared at Robert, John and Connie in turn, until her gaze finally settled on Percy. "We're the Know-It-Alls," she declared. "Let battle commence!"

The first rehearsal for the panto main characters was the following evening. Kevin had been a bag of nerves all day, arriving at the hall half an hour earlier than necessary so he could hang around inside the kitchen. From there, he could take cover behind the hatch shutter while he looked out at all the other panto performers as they arrived.

The main hall began to fill, and Kevin sighed with dread as he saw that most of them seemed to know each other. How long would it take for them to realize the key role of Buttons had been given to someone who would be an absolute disaster at the part? He had thought about joining the cast of various shows at school over the years, but nerves had always got the better of him before reaching the auditions. It was one thing larking about with his silly songs and dances for the Grown-ups crowd, but taking a lead role in the town pantomime was quite another matter.

Peering out from his vantage point behind the hatch, he didn't hear Jan approaching until she spoke right behind him. "They're probably every bit as nervous as you are."

He responded with disbelief. "That's not true. Just look at them. They're used to this. They know each other. They're old friends. I'm going to make a fool of myself, I just know it."

"Maurice has been producing shows like this for years," Jan calmly continued. "He knows talent when he sees it – and I can tell you that he wouldn't have been so enthusiastic about casting you as Buttons unless he was completely sure you'd be great in the role."

The young man's shoulders fell as he let out a long sigh. "Can't you just tell him I've changed my mind? Tell him I'm too busy. Tell him my grandma needs me. Tell him that, with Christmas coming up, I'm going to be working extra hours here."

"No," replied Jan. "I won't do any of that because it's not true. What is true is that the whole audition committee is thrilled at the prospect of you playing this role. Perhaps you can't see the natural talent we saw in you as you performed at the Grown-ups' lunch the other day. I know you can do this, Kev. We do understand that this is your first experience of being on the stage, and it must be really daunting. But you're going to enjoy it, I *know* you are. If I promise to keep a close eye on you all evening, will you give this first rehearsal a go? And after that, if you really haven't enjoyed yourself you can tell me, and I will inform Maurice then that you've changed your mind. Is that a deal?"

Kevin swallowed hard as he looked back at her. "Okay," he said at last. "Just tonight, though. I'm not promising any more than that."

As Kevin trailed into the hall behind Jan, he was surprised when Maurice abandoned the conversation he was having and marched straight over to greet him.

He was followed closely by Shirley, who gave him a big bear hug as she whispered in his ear: "We're both new to panto, but it's going to be great, Kev. I've got no idea what I'm doing as Lady Devilia, but I do know I'm going to have a lot of fun with this. You will too."

"Is that who I think it is?" drawled Jason Harding, watching the proceedings from the other side of the hall. Jason's good looks, strong singing voice and years of stage experience had earned him the part of Prince Charming. His best friend Callum, who was playing the prince's sidekick, Dandini, stared across at the group surrounding Kevin.

"Apparently, he's playing Buttons. Someone said he's in our year, but I don't remember seeing him around much."

"What's his name?"

"Kev, I think they call him."

"How come we've never come across him if he's good at drama?"

"Don't know," replied Callum. "Shall we go and find out?"

Just at that moment, someone else was making her way across the hall to welcome Kevin to the first rehearsal. Chloe smiled broadly as she arrived at his side. "You made it! Congratulations on getting the part. We're going to be working together a lot."

Kevin couldn't help the grin that spread across his face at the sight of her. "I'm really new to this, you know," he confided. "I hope I don't let you down."

"Of course you won't. They're a great crowd here. We'll all be helping you make the part your own."

"Chloe," said Jason, as he came up to place a possessive arm around her shoulders. "Aren't you going to introduce me to your new friend?"

"This is Kevin, who's going to be brilliant as Buttons. He's a bit nervous because he hasn't done much stage work before, but I've told him what a friendly lot we all are. We'll make him feel welcome, won't we?"

Jason watched with interest as Kevin gazed at Chloe with a look of pure adoration. Finally, Jason held out his hand towards the newcomer. "Pleased to meet you, Buttons. I'm Prince Charming. I'm the one who gets the girl."

As November mornings went, the day was just perfect. Cool sunshine cast dappled patches of light and shade through the brown and auburn leaves that still clung to branches or gathered in piles on the grass and paths. Kath's feet crunched through them as she took her usual jog around the park. She loved early mornings. As soon as she was aware of one coherent thought breaking into her slumber, she couldn't wait to open her eyes, throw back the covers and get on with her day. Whatever the weather she would reach for her trainers and head out of the door, spurred on by the thought of getting her limbs moving and filling her lungs with the freshness of a new day.

That morning, her thoughts weren't so focused on what the coming day was likely to bring her way, but instead drifted towards the past. She remembered how her father had always enjoyed running, and how, when she was a small girl, the two of them had often gone off together for a gentle jog, or at least a purposeful walk along the local country lanes. Sometimes her dad had suggested taking the car to the base of a comfortable sized hill or driving south to the coast, so they could run along the shingle shoreline together until the backs of her legs ached in the most satisfying way.

How Kath missed her dad. So much time had passed since they had lost him, but she still felt a comforting warmth sweep over her when she thought of how his eyes had creased with affection whenever he spoke to her, or the silly jokes he loved to tell that had made *him* laugh more than anyone who heard them. She remembered how he would take her cold hand and tuck it into his pocket as they walked back from their frosty outings. And how he would make a big show of pulling off her muddy boots on the doorstep before they went into the house to be greeted by the welcoming mug of hot chocolate her mum always had ready and waiting for them. Such happy memories, so long ago. Kath never really thought about how the days flew by, or how months came and went, but whenever she found herself savouring those old memories, it occurred to her that the years were slipping by without her really noticing.

Pulling herself together as she turned the final corner back to her small, elegant apartment block, she slowed down as she approached the main door of the building. A delivery man was peering at the name plates as he tried to work out which bell to press.

"Can I help?" she offered.

The man glanced down at his clipboard before answering. "Apartment 4. Miss Sutton?"

"That's me."

"Well, this is for you then."

He reached down into a large box at his feet and pulled out an enormous bunch of yellow blooms. "Happy birthday!" He grinned as he placed the huge bouquet into her arms. "Have a nice day."

Standing on the doorstep with her face buried in the fragrant flowers, Kath found herself smiling with surprise and pleasure as she fumbled to open the door, then navigated her way up to her first-floor apartment, carefully cradling the unexpected gift. Once inside, she laid the flowers on the table and opened the envelope perched in the middle of the bouquet.

> *Happy Big-O birthday, my darling.*
> *I can't wait to see you tonight.*
> *All my love,*
> *Richard*
> *Xxx*

Kath let out a sigh of pleasure in response to the flowers and the message. He really was the dearest man. She chuckled to see that he had been tactful enough to avoid mentioning that she was fifty, in case it upset her. But it really didn't. She was the age she was, having lived the life she had. She didn't regret a moment of it – from the lovely childhood she had enjoyed, to the career she had followed in London, to her decision to come back to her home town when her mother was ill and alone – and finally to the piece of luck that had come her way when the administrator's job at Hope Hall had landed in her lap. Life was good, and had probably never been better than it was right now with Richard Carlisle as her most loving companion.

She hadn't mentioned her special birthday to anyone at Hope Hall. She just didn't feel the need to make a big fuss and bother about this milestone occasion in her life. It was just another day among so many other good days for her right now.

With that thought, she dug out her favourite vase, which would display the bouquet beautifully, then glanced up at the kitchen clock to make sure she had time to ring Richard and thank him before leaving for Hope Hall punctually, as always.

Later that afternoon, Kath's heart sank as she sat with Trevor Barrett in her office for their customary Friday afternoon meeting.

"It would be really helpful," he had just said, "if we could look at the financial projections for the next six months this afternoon."

Kath hoped she had successfully hidden her disappointment at Trevor's suggestion. He was absolutely within his rights to ask, because Friday afternoons were always set aside for the two of them to discuss the accounts and any financial matters associated with the running of Hope Hall. The end of their financial year was looming, and the board of trustees would be looking for detailed plans about potential demands or shortfalls on their resources in the coming months. It was just that she had been hoping to get off smartly at five o'clock that day. Richard had intimated that he had a special birthday treat lined up for her that evening, and she was looking forward to a soak in the bath and a bit of getting ready time so she looked her best before he called to collect her.

She became aware that Trevor was gazing at her in his usual good-natured way, obviously hoping for an answer. "Erm, how long do you think this is going to take?" she queried, quickly checking the time on her laptop to see that it was already four o'clock.

"Oh, not long," he replied, pulling out a folder from his briefcase. "I've drawn up some notes, and I'm sure we'll be able to get through it all quite quickly. It would be a great help to me, if you don't mind us doing this now. I like to have everything prepared in good time, as you know."

Kath hoped he was unable to detect the sigh in her voice as she stretched over to take hold of the pile of papers he had pulled out of his briefcase.

"The first page, then," he announced with enthusiasm. "Item number one."

Kath had never been one for wanting to get away before the allotted time of departure, so she assumed it was just the special occasion that was making Trevor's detailed analysis of the projected accounts feel longer and more pedantic than usual.

Therefore, it came as a bit of a surprise when he suddenly stopped mid-sentence and stared at his watch. "Sorry, Kath, but it's five o'clock. I'm picking Mary up at quarter past five after she's had her hair done. Shall we stop there? We've made a good start, and we can finish the rest next Friday."

Feeling relieved and a little bemused, Kath started to pack up her things without hesitation.

Trevor eyed her with feigned curiosity. "Oh dear. Were you wanting to get away promptly this evening? I hope I haven't delayed you. Can I offer you a lift home? I'm parked on the road by the main entrance."

Kath readily accepted, and leaving her office, they made their way down the small corridor that joined the old school building to the main block of Hope Hall. Chatting together as they continued on through the main hall, they were soon approaching the glass double doors that led to the foyer and the front entrance.

"Oh, Kath, I'm so glad I've caught you!"

Kath looked up in surprise to see Maggie leaning over the balcony from the first-floor lounge area.

"I could do with a very quick word, if you've got a minute. Would you mind coming up here? I can't come down just at the moment."

Grimacing inside, Kath stuck on her brightest smile as she turned to Trevor. "You get going, or you'll be late picking up Mary. I'll walk home. Have a good weekend, and I'll see you on Monday, okay?" With that, she started up the stairs to the balcony lounge to get whatever it was over with as quickly as possible.

"SURPRISE!"

Kath stood at the top of the stairs in shock and amazement. The bar was full of familiar faces, all smiling and waving at her as they burst into "Happy Birthday".

Kath suddenly became aware of someone standing alongside her. She turned to see Trevor grinning like a Cheshire cat.

"You didn't think we were going to let a special birthday like this one go without celebrating in style, did you?"

Just then, Richard stepped out from the crowd to take her hand with a broad smile. "Come on, birthday girl. There are a lot of people here who've been waiting very patiently for you to arrive."

In a daze, Kath allowed herself to be led around the gathered group, gasping with delight as she spotted familiar faces from Hope Hall: the kitchen team, Shirley and Ray, and members of the board, as well as leaders from many of the clubs and activities that were held at the hall. Della and Barbara were there with several of the older dance students who were well known to Kath. Over in the corner, already tucking into the buffet – which was so glorious only Maggie could have organized it – were some of her favourite Grown-ups' Lunch Club members. Percy, Iris, Betty, Doris and Flora gave her a cheery wave as she spotted them.

Then she felt a touch on her arm and found Councillor Norman Radcliffe, the town mayor, standing beside her, clearing his throat as someone over the other side of the room called for silence.

"Kath, it gives us all great pleasure to mark your birthday here at Hope Hall. Since you took on the job of administrator, you have made such an impact; not just on this place, but on our town. Gathered here, we can plainly see the success of your work – the skilful, inspired, enthusiastic way you've built up the range of activities going on here each week to encourage local people of all ages, needs and interests to become part of the Hope Hall family.

"A hundred years ago, people in this town had a vision of Hope Hall as a place that could offer interest, vocation, education and entertainment for all. You've built on everything that has gone before to make that vision an impressive reality, achieving a potential that surpasses anything our forefathers could have envisaged. Whenever your name is mentioned people speak of your kindness, insight, sensitivity, hard work and immediate instinct to go the extra mile. So, this is our chance to thank you, and to wish you every possible happiness, today and always."

Touched beyond belief, Kath felt her eyes mist over as cheers echoed around her. At that moment, Maggie led the way and Kevin followed behind with a trolley on which there was a huge cake covered in yellow roses and swirls of icing. Taking the long knife Maggie handed her, Kath triumphantly made the first cut to the sound of spontaneous applause.

From then on, Kath felt as if she were floating on air as she worked her way around the crowd, delighted to greet old friends and colleagues who had come some distance, and current neighbours, colleagues and friends, as they took turns to congratulate her on her birthday. Time flew by, and she was surprised to see that it was going on for eight o'clock when Richard eventually took her hand to lead her out of the building and over to his car. She settled in, leaning back against the headrest with an expression of sheer joy on her face.

"Kath."

His voice was so quiet that she wasn't quite sure she had actually heard him. She sat up a bit to see that he was gazing across at her, his face shadowed by the dark interior of the car.

"I was really proud of you in there," he said softly. "So touched and moved to hear how appreciated and admired you are."

She smiled. "They were all extremely kind. I can't get over how nice it was of everyone to arrange all that. I honestly didn't suspect a thing."

"People simply wanted you to know how much they love you. And I understand just how they feel. You are such a remarkable,

156

warm-hearted, special person, Kath. I've never met anyone like you. You've turned my life upside down in the most wonderful way. I can't imagine life without you now. I only know that I long to spend every minute of every day with you."

Kath sucked in a deep breath, unable to reply.

"Darling Kath, I love you so much, and I hope and pray that you feel the same way. I want to devote myself to your happiness for ever. I'm asking you to marry me. Please say you'll be my wife, my love, my everything."

She stared at him in the darkness, seeing that the longing in his eyes was tinged with uncertainty at the thought of what her answer might be. Then she leaned forward until her lips met his in a soft, lingering kiss.

"Yes, Richard. With all my heart, my answer is yes."

He almost didn't notice her at first. He was walking across the old square in the centre of the town, where on Saturday mornings there was always a small market with stalls selling vegetables, flowers and plants, greetings cards, and several different kinds of clothing, when he caught sight of the distinctive lilac-coloured scarf she often wore. She was sitting alone on a bench to one side of the square, with a shopping bag at her feet that was brimming with fresh vegetables and a bunch of bright yellow chrysanthemums. He took his time wandering over in her direction, but she seemed to be so deep in thought that it wasn't until he was standing right in front of her that she came to, and realized who was there.

"Good morning, young lady," he said, raising his hand to salute her. "Is there room for another on this bench?"

A look of amusement quickly crossed Ida's face before she changed her expression into one of stern disapproval. "Percy Wilson, are you stalking me? I can't seem to make myself comfortable on a bench anywhere without you coming along to disturb my peace."

"Oh, then it *is* free," continued Percy as if she hadn't spoken at all. "I'd love to join you. Thanks for asking."

"What are you doing here?"

"Buying my tobacco from the newsagent over there, along with a paper and a lottery ticket. I usually get a big mug of tea and a bacon roll from the Cosy Café on the other corner before taking a slow wander around the market stalls, meeting a few old pals along the way, if I'm lucky. After that, depending on the time, I sometimes pop into the Wheatsheaf for a swift half before heading home. Can I interest you in a G&T?"

"Certainly not. I have a small sherry, strictly for medicinal purposes, after my Sunday lunch. Apart from that, I'm teetotal."

"You've changed a bit, then. I seem to remember your favourite tipple was a glass or two of Babycham back in the day."

"I really don't remember that. How strange that *you* do!"

"Oh, elephants never forget, and neither do I. Plain crisps with one of those blue packets of salt inside, as I recall. And you were also rather partial to fig rolls. I remember buying you a packet once."

"You're making this up."

"Really? What flavour crisps do you like, then?"

She hesitated for a few moments, but in the end she couldn't help smiling just a little. "Plain crisps, but they come ready salted these days."

His chuckle was deep and throaty as he sat down beside her. "There you go!"

She tipped her head to one side as she hesitated for another moment, then reached down into her shopping bag and pulled out a long packet.

"Would you like a fig roll?"

He threw his head back and laughed again. "I don't mind if I do."

She opened the packet and they each munched a couple of

biscuits as they gazed around at what was happening in the square.

"Busy here today," said Percy.

"Christmas shopping, I suppose," she replied. "I always used to do my shopping really early. I'd have all the presents bought, wrapped and stored away in the wardrobe by the end of September."

"Now why doesn't that surprise me about you? I bet you were a Girl Guide, always prepared for everything."

"Actually, I was. But I've always liked being organized. I can't bear clutter and last-minute panic. I like to get things just right."

There was affection in his eyes as he looked directly at her. "Yes, I've noticed that. Is that why you're so sharp, and quick to tell other people off if they do or say anything that doesn't meet with your approval?"

"I can't bear bad manners."

"Oh, I think we've got that message loud and clear."

"I'm never sharp, though."

"My dear Ida, your tongue could cut through ice. I should know, given that most of your comments are directed at me!"

"Well, you need to be told. You're a very cheeky man, Percy Wilson."

He laughed again. "Oh, I hope so! I really do hope so. How boring life would be if we couldn't have a bit of fun now and then. What happened to you, Ida? You always used to have such a great sense of humour. You seem to have very little interest in having a good laugh these days."

She sighed while she considered her answer. "My Ernie wasn't a man who laughed often. His mother was a very dominating woman, and I think she knocked the humour out of him when he was a youngster. There were so many rules and regulations she insisted on, he had a permanent dread of getting things wrong. I suppose it became a habit for him in the end."

"Did you realize that when you married him?"

"A bit, I suppose, but I thought things would change after we were wed. And he was quite a catch. He had that good job with the gas board, you know, and he ended up being the manager of the parts department. He was good at making sure everything was in its place. I suppose that rubbed off on me after a while."

"But you were a giggler once – I do remember that. I'd have thought Ernie would have liked that about you."

"Not really. Ernie liked routine. His dinner had to be on the table at six o'clock sharp, his shirts ironed and folded in a particular way, and his socks tucked together in pairs so they could be laid in the drawer in flat, neat lines. In fact, he wanted me to do things exactly as his mother had before me. He got very flustered if things weren't as they should be, almost going into a panic just at the thought of it. So I soon learned that the secret of a quiet and happy married life was to keep everything neat and tidy, on time and according to routine. He felt safe that way, which made me feel secure and settled too."

"You two never had children, then?"

Ida's eyes clouded over in response to this question. "We did, yes. Our son, Stephen. He joined the civil service and did very well there. He'd already had a promotion when his father had that heart attack. He was a good boy back then, helped me a lot."

"Where is he now? I can't remember ever hearing you mention him."

"He was hit by a car one evening while he was walking home from work. It was dark, and apparently the driver had been drinking. Stephen didn't even make it to the hospital. He never stood a chance."

Percy was genuinely shocked. "Ida, I'm so sorry. I had no idea."

She shrugged. "It was a long time ago… fifteen years now. And he'd moved away from here by then, so there's no reason why people around here should know."

"And you've been living alone ever since?"

"In the same house, keeping up the same old routines with just my memories of Ernie and our boy."

"But you seem to get out and about quite a bit."

Her expression was blank as she looked across at him. "That's why I'm sitting on this bench, watching the world go by. The prospect of going back to sit in that house isn't very appealing. Oh, it's my home, and I'm so fortunate in many ways to have my health and a group of lady friends. And Ernie was a good provider. He left me very comfortably off, so that's a relief."

"No substitute for your son, though, and the life you might have enjoyed if he were still around today."

She looked down at her lap, avoiding his gaze. "No. But it is what it is."

"Well," he said at last. "Why don't I nip over to the Cosy Café and bring us back a nice cup of tea?"

He expected her to decline, but she nodded her agreement.

"And a bacon roll?"

"Certainly not!" she snapped back in her usual disapproving tone.

"Please yourself," he said, getting to his feet. "Sugar?"

"No, thank you."

He started walking away.

"A cheese and tomato sandwich on brown bread with a touch of mayonnaise would be nice."

"And a packet of plain salted crisps?" he replied, without even turning around to look at her.

"Of course," she said. "Is there any other way?"

Maggie was always at her happiest when she was in the kitchen, but when she glanced up at Phil, who was sitting on a stool at her breakfast bar, smacking his lips with appreciation at the aroma of the casserole she had just pulled out of the oven, she thought that having his company in the kitchen while she cooked made her favourite place happier than ever. In fact, happiness was a way of life for her these days, and Phil was the reason for it. He made

161

everything fun, and she wondered if she'd ever laughed as much as she had in the few months since she had been back in contact with him.

It wasn't that they couldn't chat about serious matters; it was just that being together seemed to bring out the best in her. She felt braver and brighter in his company. He did make her laugh, but he also made her listen and share and sing and dance and giggle and cuddle up like a teenager. He encouraged her to try new things. Whoever would have thought she would enjoy a bike ride after all those years of being horrified about what she would look like on a bike? Or that she would allow him to drag her along to a salsa class, where, to her surprise, she found the steps much easier than she had anticipated? Most encouraging of all was the look in his eye when she was courageous enough to follow the teacher's instructions and sidle up to him with her hips swaying like an exotic Cuban beauty. He wasn't horrified. He didn't laugh. He just pulled a pen out of his jacket pocket and clenched it between his teeth as if it were a long-stemmed red rose, before clicking his heels together and striking a pose like a famous matador. What fun it had been! How they had laughed! How they always enjoyed each other's company.

They had decided to eat at the breakfast bar because it was easy and comfortable, and they chatted about this and that while Phil devoured two bowls of casserole, along with several slices of her freshly made olive bread. As she dished up his favourite hot lemon pudding with a fruity citrus sauce, she saw that he was lost in his thoughts.

"Where are you?" she smiled. Then she realized with a start that his expression was quite serious. His usual good-natured smile was lacking. "Are you okay?" Suddenly anxious, she took a seat on the stool beside him.

He reached out to take her hand, pausing for a moment before eventually answering. "I've been wondering about asking you something. Say no if you need to. I just felt that I'd like to ask."

Maggie held her breath, dreading what might be coming. She noticed the way he cleared his throat before speaking, a sure sign that he was nervous.

"As you know, I was married to Sandra for many years before our divorce."

Maggie nodded.

"And remember that I told you our marriage had faded away more than anything else? We were leading parallel lives; wanting to do different things, but still committed to our family life together – until the family didn't need us any more. David's going to be twenty-four in a couple of weeks' time, and he's very happily settled in his job, with his own flat in Chichester. Everybody likes David. He's got a great personality. He gets on well with the lads he's grown up with and the girls seem to be queuing up for him too."

Maggie remained silent, uncertain where this might be leading.

"And as you know, Melanie married Simon nearly a year ago now and they've got a lovely home up in Bromsgrove. Being in the estate agency business, I think he managed to pick up a bargain that suits them perfectly."

"That's all you really want, isn't it?" she ventured. "To know that your children are happy and settled. You must be very proud of them."

"Oh, I am. Sandra and I both are."

Maggie felt her stomach churn itself into a tight knot.

"I've told you before that Sandra and I still get on very well – but then we've been friends for all these years. We've often said that perhaps we should have just stayed that way and never married, but then look what that marriage brought us. We have Dave and Mel, and our life together was contented, even if it never set the world on fire."

Maggie was finding it hard to breathe. This was it, then. She had always known it would come eventually. She knew he would start comparing her to other women, especially the wife he plainly still

163

loved in his own way. Right from the start she had been waiting for him to discover and acknowledge that she, good old Maggie, would never quite come up to scratch. Of course this wonderful man would find her lacking in comparison to any other woman – especially the wife who was still so dear to him.

"Anyway, we've got a big family occasion coming up at the end of November."

"Of course. I understand. You must go. Naturally, you'll want to be with all your family and they'll want you there, back where you belong. That's where you should be."

He looked relieved. "Oh, I knew you'd get the picture. I hoped you'd react like that."

"Well, you know how busy I'm going to be at Hope Hall in the run-up to Christmas. I wouldn't have had much spare time to see you anyway. Please do whatever's right for you, your ex-wife and your family. That's fine by me."

He looked at her quizzically. "Hang on a minute. Are you breaking up with me?"

Maggie smiled as warmly as her broken heart could manage. "That's what you want, isn't it? You're going back to be the decent, principled family man I know you to be. I would never stand in the way of that, and I truly wish you well. You know I'd always wish you well…" To her horror, a hot tear rolled down the side of her nose and plopped unceremoniously on to the breakfast bar between them.

Appalled at her obvious distress, Phil quickly dragged his stool up close to hers and gently cupped her face in his hands. Maggie kept her eyes tightly shut. She didn't want to look up. She couldn't look at him. She didn't want to see the pity in his eyes.

"Maggie, you've got this all wrong. It's my fault. I've been clumsy in what I said and it's all come out the wrong way. I don't want to break up with you. How could you ever imagine that I would? We're great together, aren't we? I think so, anyway."

She did look up then, peering through her tear-filled eyes to read his expression. He said nothing further for a moment, but instead leaned forward to plant a gentle kiss on her cheek.

"What I'm trying to say in my stupid, cack-handed way," he continued, "is that my family would like to meet you. They've been nagging me about it since we first started seeing each other. I think they want to make sure you know what you're taking on, so you can run away in horror when they've given you the lowdown on all my shortcomings."

"*Meet* them?" repeated Maggie, as she considered the idea for the first time. "They want to *meet* me?"

"Well, I've met your family… and as I'm not planning to disappear from your life any time soon, it makes sense. I'm aware that Steph and Darren have been giving me the once over, checking that I'm not an axe murderer – or a Southampton fan!"

Maggie couldn't resist a weak smile at that thought. "So you want me to meet your son and daughter?"

"I want you to meet Sandra, most of all. It's her fiftieth birthday a week on Sunday, the 22nd of November. She doesn't want a big 'do' – that's not her scene at all – so she's asked if the family can get together for a nice Sunday lunch in a rather swish hotel in Chichester, and she'd like me to bring you along, if you feel able to accept the invitation."

"Wow!" breathed Maggie. "The ex-wife wants to meet the new lady in your life. That's very modern and civilized."

"But that's Sandra. She really is a nice person, and she couldn't be more pleased at the thought of meeting the woman I talk about all the time. She's happy for us. She has her own very contented life. She's comfortable and settled, and she'd like the same thing for me. We don't want to be married any more; not to each other, that's for certain. And because there was never any animosity in our break-up, there's no bad feeling now. She just wants me to find my own happiness – and I've found that in you."

"What about your children, though? I doubt they were very happy to see their parents' marriage break up. That must have been devastating for them. And to see you with someone else now, especially at such a special occasion for their mother… It doesn't seem right."

"Look, I'm putting this badly. Let Sandra explain herself. She's sent a note that she asked me to give you."

Phil got up to find his coat, which was hanging on the back of the kitchen door. Drawing out a white envelope from his inside pocket, he handed it to her as he sat down beside her again.

Maggie's fingers shook as she carefully opened the envelope to draw out a single, folded piece of paper.

> *Dear Maggie,*
>
> *I'm very much hoping that you will feel able to join me and the family at my 50th birthday lunch at the Mews restaurant at one o'clock on Sunday 22nd November. David, Melanie, Simon and I have heard so much about you from Phil since the two of you met up again after all these years. You've certainly put a smile on his face, and we're all grateful for that. Please say you'll come. We look forward to meeting you then.*
>
> *Kind regards,*
> *Sandra Coleman*

Maggie let out a slow breath as she digested the contents of the letter.

"So?" he asked. "What do you think?"

"I think I might be working at the hall that day. Or I might need to babysit Bobbie, because I'm sure Steph and Dale mentioned they're going out somewhere special around then."

Phil smiled at her. "What do you *really* think?"

Her eyes locked with his. "I think I've got nothing to wear. And

166

I've got nothing to say that would interest them one bit. I think I'd need to lose a stone, or maybe two, so they don't think you've completely lost your marbles when they see me. And I think it might be better if they didn't see me just yet – or perhaps at all – until I've got my act together, so I don't let you down."

Phil took both of Maggie's hands firmly in his. "You *never* let me down! How could you even think that? You're kind, clever, talented and a great organizer, and you have the biggest heart I've ever known. I'm proud to be with you, to spend time with you, to be allowed to get to know you better. And I'd like you to meet the other people who are very important to me. They'll love you – I just know they will."

She was lost for words.

"Please say you'll come," Phil added.

Maggie noted the anxiety in his eyes as he gazed at her. She took a big breath to calm her thumping heart. "You're sure they won't see me as a man-hungry divorcee trying to get my clutches into you – because I'm not, you know? I was fine on my own, and I'd be fine again if you changed your mind."

"I know that." His voice was soft, but with a note of determination as he continued. "I know you don't need a man to make your life complete. But I hope you need a friend to brighten up your day. Someone who loves your company and considers you to be a very special person."

She searched his face as she tried to process her thoughts.

"Look, Maggie, I know them, and I know you. I have no doubt that you'll get on like a house on fire. Just promise me you won't get up in the middle of the Sunday roast to tell the kitchen staff what they're doing wrong."

Maggie chuckled at that. "Oh, believe me, there's nothing I like more than the sheer pleasure of eating a meal I haven't cooked for myself. I'll enjoy every mouthful."

Chapter 9

The members of the Know-it-All team, captained by Ida, were among the first people through the door of Hope Hall on the evening of the Rotary quiz. Betty and Flora hurried through the foyer, tickets in hand, ready to nab the table they considered to be the best and most convenient in the room: well lit, close to the serving hatch and the nearest possible to the ladies' cloakroom.

Percy's team wasn't far behind, and with a mischievous twinkle in his eye that only Ida could see, Percy took his seat at the next table to set up camp for the Conquerors. Joining him, John and Robert looked a bit bemused by the whole affair. Connie bustled in a few minutes later and immediately pulled a flask of hot coffee out of her shopping bag, along with two packets of chocolate hobnobs and another of custard creams.

"I just want to make sure our team has all the energy it needs to triumph this evening," she explained.

"Oh look, there are James and Ellie," cooed Betty, waving enthusiastically in the vicar's direction as he held out a seat for his wife.

The other couple in their team also took their places at the table. Flora turned to look, then huffed at the sight of Gregory Palmer and his wife, Fiona. Earlier in the year, when Gregory had been taken on as the new musical director at St Mark's Church, he had made many enemies by sacking every single member of the existing church choir, including several who had been stalwarts in the stalls for decades. He instantly renamed the choir, without a by-your-leave to any of the congregation. Once it had been given the rather ostentatious title of the St Mark's Choral Choir, he had insisted on auditioning all potential members. Singers came from far and wide, ready to impress with their sight-reading, and their ability to hit high notes and hold their harmony lines.

The end result was that only one person from the original choir had been invited to continue. Keith Turner was a young man with a lovely tenor voice who liked to gossip as much as he liked to sing. He had happily offered to become a spy in the new choir, reporting back whenever he met up with his old friends from the original church choir – people like Flora and her friend Pauline Owen, who were both highly indignant at the way they had been turfed out of their singing duties after turning up every Sunday for as long as either of them could remember.

With Keith's encouragement, they had decided to set up their own choir, and once they'd discovered a terrific musical director in Ronnie Andrews, the pianist for Hope Hall's ballet classes, a new singing group had been formed by nearly all the former members of the St Mark's Church choir. The singers were a little uncertain when Ronnie made his decision about their new name. Whoever would want to come and listen to a group called the Can't Sing Singers? But their first performance at the Easter Centenary Fayre had drawn cheers of delight (or possibly tears of laughter caused by disbelief), and from that moment on, the Can't Sing Singers were on their way. Who cared if their singing was terrible, when it made people laugh? They promised out-of-tune singing, and that's exactly what they delivered. And they were loving every minute of their new-found fame and popularity.

"I don't suppose that awful man Gregory Palmer managed to get a starring role for *his* singers in the Hope Hall panto!" Flora announced. "The Can't Sing Singers are already in rehearsal for their Christmas performance and have also been approached to consider other future bookings."

Around the hall, latecomers were hurrying in to claim their

choice of table. Once settled, each team was required to write its chosen name on a piece of white card, which had been set up in the middle of each table. The playgroup girls had chosen Small But Mighty. The Money Advice Service members had called themselves the Tycoons. Shirley had made up a team called The Clean-up Crew, with her husband, Mick, their son, Tyler, and Hope Hall caretaker Ray. Shirley's sister, Barbara, sitting at a table with Della and their partners, was representing the Hope Hall dance school by calling their team On Your Toes.

"Hey, Maggie. I reckon there are more than thirty teams here," commented Liz as she leaned across the serving hatch to take a closer look.

Stepping away from the buffet she was preparing for later in the evening, Maggie came across to see for herself. "Well, hopefully the event will make lots of money. I had a feeling it might be popular, so I over-catered to be sure that everyone could have a really nice supper tonight."

Roger Beck, the town's popular and jovial Rotary head, had volunteered to be quizmaster for the evening. At exactly seven thirty, he rang what sounded like a really loud bell on his table, which immediately stopped the buzz of conversation around the hall.

"Good!" he smiled. "That's the sound you need to recognize tonight, because each question I ask will have a time limit, during which your team can agree on an answer. I hope you've all assembled a group with a broad general knowledge, because these questions cover music, science, food, geography, maths and puzzles – with a lot of questions thrown in just for a bit of fun. The best news is that the winning team will receive four front-row tickets to the Hope Hall pantomime, as well as a hamper filled with the very best goodies from Maggie's kitchen – and you know what a treat that will be. So, eyes down, everyone, and may the best team win!"

There was an excited murmur among the teams, along with the sound of chairs being scraped across the wooden floor as they huddled around each table.

"Question number one," announced Roger. "True or false? Was *From Russia with Love* the first James Bond film?"

"Yes!" declared Robert on the Conquerors' table.

"Oh, I'm not so sure," said Connie thoughtfully. "I remember Sean Connery looking very young in *Goldfinger*."

All eyes turned towards Percy, who rubbed his chin as he looked first at Roger, then at Connie.

"I think it's true," he decided. "I remember taking an extremely nice young lady to see *From Russia with Love* at the Gaumont cinema. All she wanted to do was drool over Sean Connery, and I didn't get as much as a cuddle all evening. What a waste of a ticket! She didn't last long."

"Oh, Percy, you really are a *terrible* man," giggled Connie as she wrote "True" on their form.

"I heard Percy say it's true," squealed Doris on the next table.

"It's not," said Betty, leaning in to make sure she couldn't be heard beyond their table. "I know this one. I've never missed a Bond film, and I know without a shadow of doubt that the very first one was *Dr No*. So the answer is false."

The bell rang, then Roger continued with the next question: "What is the highest number visible on a dartboard?"

The Know-It-All ladies all looked at each other, hoping at least one of them knew the answer. No one did.

With a whoop of triumph, Percy dug his elbow into Robert's side. "It was a bit daft of those girlies to call themselves the Know-It-Alls. Ha! They won't know this one, will they?" Then he leaned over until his chin was almost touching the table as he hissed in a stage whisper across to Connie: "It's twenty. Write that down."

The bell rang and Roger spoke again. "What is Ringo Starr's real name?"

"Richard Starkey!" called out each of the women on those two tables, pens scribbling furiously on the answer sheet.

"I loved the Beatles," sighed Doris. "I would have married that Paul if he'd ever asked me. I gave up in the end and married Bert. I wonder if I should have waited a little longer…"

"Next question," announced Roger. "What is tofu made of?"

There was total silence on Percy's table, where it seemed no one had the slightest idea.

"Does anyone know?" asked Doris, looking around at the other Know-It-Alls.

Ida sighed deeply. "It's made from soya beans," she declared. "I often include tofu in my diet because the beans are high in protein and are a rich source of beneficial vitamins, minerals and plant compounds. Plus it keeps me regular."

There was an unspoken agreement that no further information was needed, and Flora immediately started filling in the answer.

The bell rang, and Roger spoke again. "Who was voted European Footballer of the Year in 1964?"

This time it was the turn of the Know-It-All ladies to look questioningly at each other, while three members of the Conquerors urgently debated among themselves.

"Denis Law." Connie's voice was so commanding that the men all turned to stare at her. "I had a huge crush on him," she explained. "I had posters up all over my bedroom wall. It's definitely him."

"I was just about to say that," said Percy.

"You were just arguing that it was George Best," retorted Connie. "And you, Robert, thought it was Bobby Charlton. But you're both wrong. Denis Law was by far the best of that Manchester United trio, and it was Denis who was voted European Footballer of the Year."

She was so confident, Percy shrugged and agreed, along with Robert and John, that she might be right.

There were forty questions in all during the first half of the evening. Then the answer papers were exchanged between the teams, and marked.

"Let's see how you all got on," called Roger. "Put your hands up if you got more than twenty points out of forty."

All but two of the tables held their arms high in the air.

"More than twenty-five?"

Half a dozen teams dropped out at this point.

"More than thirty?" asked Roger.

This left just ten tables in the running.

Then the quizmaster counted up from thirty, watching as one set of hands after another fell.

"Have any of the remaining teams scored more than thirty-five?" he asked.

Three tables still had their hands in the air: James, and his High and Mighty team from St Mark's; the Conquerors and the Know-It-Alls.

"It's neck and neck for our last three teams," announced Roger. "Let's see which team is destined to win this first half of the evening. Please keep your hands in the air if you answered more than thirty-five questions correctly."

Percy and Ida stared defiantly at each other for a few seconds before Ida's ladies slowly began to lower their arms at exactly the same pace as the Conquerors.

"Oh, bad luck to those two teams. And congratulations to High and Mighty! How many questions did you get right?"

"Thirty-eight!" Gregory Palmer called out the figure haughtily, as if he alone had answered every question. A round of applause rang out as the audience congratulated the winning team.

"But there's still time to catch them up," added Roger, "because after our buffet supper, which is about to be served, we'll have the raffle, and then the other half of the quiz. Well done to all of you!"

"Come on, Doris!" commanded Betty. "Leave your bag, Flora.

We've already paid for the buffet with the ticket. Let's get to the front of the line. I'm starving."

"Oh, stuff my diet!" declared Connie. "I saw some lovely quiche up there. Are you coming, Percy?"

"I'm girding my loins and will join you in a tick," he replied.

Once Connie and the others had set off at speed towards the buffet queue, Percy looked across at Ida and grinned. "Well played, my dear. I thought the Conquerors would wipe the floor with your team, but the Know-It-Alls obviously had an excellent captain."

"As did the Conquerors," replied Ida graciously, her eyes sparkling back at him.

"May I accompany you to the buffet?"

Ida thought for a moment, then smiled. "You may. That would be a most gentlemanly gesture."

"Your wish is my command, madam," said Percy, getting to his feet with a movement that suggested he was taking off his hat and bowing courteously in her direction. But somehow it didn't quite work out like that. Perhaps his shoe became tangled around the leg of the table, or maybe he simply lost his footing – but, as if in slow motion, the smiles drained away from their faces as Percy embarked on his unstoppable journey towards the hard wooden floor. The crash had every set of eyes in the hall turn in his direction.

"Percy!" screamed Ida.

He didn't answer. His head had collided with the table on the way down, and blood began to trickle from a wound on one side of his temple. His face was deathly white, his eyes wide with shock.

"Stay there! Just stay still!" called Ida, struggling out of her chair to reach him.

His lips began to move as if he were trying to speak, but all that came out was a dreadful wail of pain.

Now on her knees, Ida grabbed his hand and squeezed it as she snapped out her command. "You hold tight, Percy Wilson. You just hold tight. I'm here. I'm here…"

His eyes turned to focus on hers for just a moment. Then he let out a shuddering breath as his head slumped to one side and his eyes closed.

Once the ambulance team had arrived, the crowd inside the main hall was no longer really interested in the quiz. It was difficult to see exactly what was happening, but it became clear from the serious expressions on the faces of the paramedic team that this was a real emergency. Within minutes, the team was racing out of the door with Percy clearly visible on the trolley, his body skilfully wedged to prevent any movement and an oxygen mask strapped to his face.

"He wasn't moving, was he? Do you think he's dead?" Betty had always loved a good drama, and being at the heart of such a dramatic turn of events had really made her evening.

"Well," said Flora, her face full of concern, "he was very pale. I remember seeing my dad when he dropped dead with a heart attack. He was pale like that."

"But did you see Ida's face?" interrupted Doris. "She looked as if she'd seen a ghost. And she was down on her knees holding his hand. Ida holding Percy Wilson's hand? She hates him."

The three women looked at each other in complete confusion.

"Perhaps it was the shock," suggested Flora. "That can do funny things to people and make them act out of character."

"But Ida holding Percy Wilson's hand?" Doris wondered, thinking that the most unlikely sight they could ever have imagined.

"Perhaps she pushed him," suggested Betty, who had obviously seen too many Miss Marple episodes. "She saw the chance to get rid of the man who has long been the bane of her life – and she pushed him!"

"Or," began Doris thoughtfully, "they do say that love and hate can be very close companions."

"Oh, Ida *definitely* hates Percy," retorted Betty.

"Exactly," replied Doris. "That's just what I mean."

The junior doctor swung through double doors that instantly closed behind her, separating the medical area from the waiting room in the accident and emergency department. It was nearly two in the morning, and only a handful of people were there, either hoping they would soon be called in for treatment or waiting to hear news of a patient who was already being attended to behind those forbidding doors. The doctor glanced around to work out who she might be looking for, then stepped over to the far corner, where an elderly lady sat, stiffly upright, gripping her handbag tightly on her lap.

"Excuse me. Are you Mr Wilson's wife?"

Ida looked up. "He's a widower. He has no relatives. I'm his neighbour and good friend; as near to family as you'll get."

The doctor eyed her with concern, seeing the lines of exhaustion and worry etched on her face. It belied the tension in her body, which gave the appearance of an animal poised to leap into action.

"How is he?"

"Well, Mr Wilson has taken a hefty knock to the right side of his body. There was a nasty cut on his forehead. We've stitched up the wound, but he's going to be heavily bruised. After such a substantial knock to the head we're naturally very concerned about the possibility of concussion, so we'll need to keep a close eye on that."

"He went down really heavily…"

"Yes, and that's clear from the injury to Mr Wilson's hip, which seems to have borne the brunt of his fall. He'll have to have a hip replacement. We're hoping to schedule him in for surgery sometime tomorrow, once the consultant has had a good look at the X-rays, which also show a fracture in the humerus."

Still trying to take in the news that Percy would need a hip replacement operation, she wasn't sure what this last piece of news meant.

"He landed on his right-hand side," continued the doctor,

"hitting his hip, his head and his shoulder, causing a fracture in the large bone in his upper arm, just below the shoulder joint. The consultant will advise on treatment for that in the morning – surgery might be needed for that too. But it may just be that he'll need to wear a special sling for several weeks."

Ida let out a long breath as she took in the details of his injuries. "He passed out. What might that mean? Could that suggest any other kind of damage?"

"We don't think so, but it's too early to be sure. We'll need to arrange further tests in the morning."

"Is he awake? Can I see him?"

"He's not very coherent, but then he's had a serious shock, so that's to be expected. I think it might help him to see a familiar face while we're waiting for a bed. Would you like to follow me?"

Hastily scooping up her coat, Ida followed the doctor through those awful double doors into a different world, where the rest of the medical team were too busy caring for the urgent needs of their patients to take any notice of a newcomer. The doctor led Ida towards a curtain, which she drew back to reveal Percy stretched out on the bed, apparently asleep.

While the doctor busied herself with a few immediate checks, taking his pulse and updating his notes, Ida looked on from just outside the curtain, thinking that this larger-than-life character with whom she both clashed and clicked looked oddly vulnerable without his glasses, and probably some of his front teeth, judging by the puckered shape of his lips as he slept.

"Do come in. There's a seat over here," said the doctor with a smile. "I think he's nodded off for a bit, which will do him no harm at all. But you're welcome to stay, if you'd like to. It'll be good for him to see a friendly face when he comes round."

Ida was too overwhelmed to reply, so she simply slid into the hard plastic chair by the bed and reached out rather nervously to take his left hand, with its protruding blue veins and hot, dry skin. Stroking his hand gently with her thumb, she looked down at Percy's face. A large dressing stretched across his right eyebrow and up to the top of his forehead. It had been quite a gash, gaping and gushing blood when she had seen it last. He would have a scar. She chuckled to herself. He would look even more rakish then. Percy would like that. Then her gaze took in his right arm, which was encased in a severe-looking sling, and the right-hand side of the bed, where there was a structure beneath the blankets to keep the covers off his broken hip.

"Now what did you want to go and do *that* for, you silly man?" Her voice was low as she chastised him, her thumb still stroking his hand. "It's typical of you," she continued. "Just because you didn't win the quiz, you had to get everyone's attention in a suitably dramatic way."

His expression didn't change, and she fell silent for a while.

"You're going to have to change your ways now, aren't you? No more swaggering about wherever you go. It'll be a Zimmer frame for you from now on."

"Over my dead body!"

She jumped at the sound of his croaky voice. "Percy? Percy! It's Ida. How are you feeling?"

With a huge effort, he slowly turned his head towards her. His eyes were barely open as he struggled to peer in confusion at the scene – and the woman – in front of him. "Have I had a nip too many? Am I drunk or dreaming?"

"You're in hospital. You took a tumble at the Hope Hall quiz night. Do you remember that?"

A slow smile turned up the corner of his dry lips. "The Know-It-Alls. We beat you, I think."

"That proves you're not thinking straight. We were joint second with your Conquerors."

"We went easy on you—"

"Which is more than I can say for your fall. You hit the floor

178

so hard I reckon you made a dent in it!"

His eyes closed, as if he were trying to make sense of what he remembered. "It's all a bit foggy," he said at last. "Did I put on a bit of a show?"

"You can say that again. Emergency ambulance, flashing blue lights, the lot. I don't think Betty's ever going to recover from the excitement of it all."

He almost chuckled at the thought, but the slight movement made him grimace. It was then he noticed that his arm was encased in a sling. When he tried to move a little so he could take a proper look, all he could manage was a deep-throated groan of pain. "Is it bad?" he asked.

"You fell hard on your right-hand side," Ida explained. "Your hip's broken. They say you'll have to have a replacement operation, probably tomorrow. And you've got a fracture in the top part of your arm."

He swallowed, and Ida wondered if she was seeing tears shining in his unnaturally bloodshot eyes. "No dancing for a while, then."

"You've got a nasty gash above your eyebrow. I'm afraid it'll be a long time before you regain your natural good looks."

He attempted a cheeky grin, revealing that the denture which accounted for several of his front teeth had been removed.

Ida glanced across to see that it had been placed in a dish on the cabinet beside the bed.

"Oh, the girls like a chap with a bit of character. They'll think I look dashing."

"I don't think you're going to be out flirting with the girls for quite a while, Percy Wilson. You'll need a lot of care to get back on your feet again."

The smile on his face faded. "I'm not going into a home. I refuse to go anywhere near one of those places where all those old people sit around in a trance waiting for the Grim Reaper. I won't go there, Ida. I won't!"

She pulled her chair a little closer and squeezed the hand she had never stopped stroking. "Quite right! Nothing like that'll happen while I'm in charge. You just concentrate on getting better. I'll take on the world to make sure we have you fit, well and back in your own home again before you know it."

There was no mistaking the fat tear that coursed down his face this time, followed by another and another as his body began to shudder with quiet sobs.

Ida delved into her handbag to draw out a neatly ironed linen handkerchief. "Now that's enough, Percy. I'm going to be right here. I'll stay tonight until I know you're settled on the ward, and I'll be ringing first thing in the morning to find out when I can visit. If you want me to collect any particular items from your home, you can let me have your key and I'll bring them back with me tomorrow evening."

"How will you get here? You don't drive."

"I'll get the number 93, of course. I'll be here in no time. Don't you worry about that."

His eyes filled up again. "Ida, I—"

"I know," she interrupted, tapping his hand gently, a warmth in her eyes as she carefully dabbed his wet cheeks with her hankie. "I know."

The feeling of privilege overwhelmed her as she walked into the plush office with its smell of rich leather and beeswax polish, and the thick soft carpet into which her high-heeled shoes sank quietly and comfortably. Celia took her time looking around the large office suite with double-aspect window on the corner of the smart Apex Finance building, which stood in a prime position on the outskirts of the town. From this level, ten floors up, the eye was drawn towards the horizon of gentle hills and green fields. Inside, the decor and atmosphere of the elegant office spoke of the luxurious style across the whole top floor, reserved solely for directors of the international corporation. And now that was her.

As soon as Uncle Joe officially retired just before Christmas, the polished walnut sign bearing her name and new title would appear on the door. She had made it! After many years of hard slog and dedication to the organization, her efforts and talent were finally being rewarded. Celia Ainsworth, UK Finance Director for one of the biggest and most influential corporations in the world. She almost hugged herself as she thought of how much that title would have meant to her father. If only he could have been there to see his daughter's achievements. He would have been so proud – but nowhere near as proud as she herself felt at that moment.

"Good, you're here!" Uncle Joe walked into the office with a broad smile. "I see you're keen to move in and get on with the job."

Celia walked into the welcome of his open arms and hugged him. "Oh, I'm aware that I have a lot to learn before I take over here," she said. "I'm so glad we've been able to organize this month of handover time so I'm absolutely certain I know the ropes before I settle into that seat all by myself."

"Well, now we know Jenny Williams has been selected to take over your present role in pensions, things can really move ahead."

"Jenny's a great choice," agreed Celia. "She's been in the department long enough to know it inside out. There'll be no steep learning curve for her. That'll give me a chance to get to grips with the much wider area of UK and world finance, so I can reward the trust the board has placed in me by giving me this role."

Joe smiled, heading for the beautiful mahogany drinks cabinet over on the left side of the room. "Brandy?"

"Not this early in the morning," she replied, "and definitely not if I want to keep a clear head for all the facts and figures I need to get to grips with in record time. Lead on, Uncle Joe. I am your most devoted student. Teach me all I need to know!"

Banjo seemed to have developed a sixth sense for when Wednesday rolled around, knowing it was the evening when Ray would be taking him along to the Waggy Tail Club. Banjo thoroughly enjoyed the classes. He loved the company of the other dogs. He also loved the discipline of the obedience exercises, which he wanted to race through to show how much he had learned and how efficient he was – except that the teacher, Ali, would then come and tell Ray off for not keeping his overexcited dog under firmer control.

He especially liked the agility games later in the session, when he had to navigate his way around posts, through tunnels and over jump bars and along raised platforms. It was great. He couldn't resist leaping up and down and barking for joy at the end of each exercise, which once again brought a disapproving Ali to his side to tell Ray off for his lack of control. This meant his master was sometimes grumpy with him for the rest of the lesson. But Banjo didn't mind a bit. He knew Ray would forgive him, and that he was secretly quite impressed with his little dog's performance. Ray would give him an extra chew when they got home, and that made Banjo pretty excited too.

"Pay attention, everybody!" called Ali as the lesson drew to a close. "Don't forget that we need your support at the Christmas Charity Fayre here in the hall on Saturday morning. Several voluntary organizations and clubs from the town will be taking part. We'll each have our own stall and display area in the hall, but we've also been given special permission to set up an agility course in the playground outside so we can show everyone how wonderfully talented our dogs – and their owners – are.

"If you have any donations for the raffle we're organizing on our stall, we would welcome all contributions. Just make sure they're suitable to go straight on to our table, and that they look good enough to entice people to buy loads of tickets.

"Finally, if your dog is taking part in the agility display, don't forget to come and pick up your instructions and the performance schedule before you leave this evening."

Ray's friend John tugged on Bertie's lead to bring him to heel. Bertie looked up at John with a bored expression, then promptly plonked down on his haunches, completely disregarding the instructions his owner was trying to give him. John couldn't help but laugh at his laid-back pet. "No performance for Bertie on Saturday. I can't imagine why Ali didn't invite him to take part!"

"Whereas Banjo is beside himself at the chance to show off," said Ray wearily. "He's exhausting. He never stops bouncing about like an excited toddler from the moment he's awake until last thing at night, when he curls up in his basket."

"Yep," agreed John. "My Bertie's not built for speed."

"Are you coming on Saturday?"

"I might pop in just to show willing and buy some raffle tickets, but I think I'll leave Bertie at home so he doesn't let the class down by stretching out for a nap in the middle of the agility area. He's not a good advert for the Waggy Tail Club, where dogs are supposed to learn obedience, is he?"

Ray laughed. "Perhaps not. Will I see you both in the morning? Seven thirty at the park gate, as usual?"

John shrugged. "Depends on the weather. Bertie doesn't like rain, and I don't like frost and ice. Look out of the window and you'll know whether to expect us or not." With a cheery wave, John pulled the reluctant Bertie up on to his feet and the pair ambled amiably out of the hall.

Banjo barked and looked up at his master with intense devotion.

"I know," smiled Ray. "You want your chew and I want my hot chocolate and biscuits. Let's go home and put our feet up, shall we?"

With another bark and a couple of twirls in the air, Banjo led the way towards the main door as they headed for home.

"Well, what do you think?" Richard slipped his arm around Kath's shoulders as they stood at the front of the aisle in the small chapel nestled within the grounds of Ainsworth Hall.

"It's beautiful," breathed Kath.

"Apparently, this family chapel was built as part of the original design of the house back at the start of the eighteenth century, when it was the manor house for a farming estate three times larger than the one the Ainsworth family owns now."

"How long has it been in the family?"

"Ever since my great-grandfather, Reginald Ainsworth, picked it up for a song in 1919 and changed the old name to Ainsworth Hall. He was already a very successful farmer and landowner when he married Beatrice at the turn of the century, but it wasn't until many years later, just after the First World War, that she managed to have their first and only child, Neville. Neville Ainsworth had two children: my mother Nancy, and James, who was father to Celia and Douglas. As the son and heir, Douglas now lives with his family at the hall. So this chapel has been in the family for many years, and it's still consecrated. This is where most of the family's marriages have begun."

"So you married Elizabeth here."

"Yes," he replied, watching her expression carefully. "Does that worry you?"

She smiled back at him. "No, it really doesn't. You enjoyed a happy marriage with a woman you loved dearly, and I know how sad the last few years have been without her. How do you think Elizabeth would feel about you remarrying?"

"It's what she hoped would happen. She told me that herself when she knew the end was soon to come. In life, she never wanted anything but my happiness. And now she's gone, that wish remains."

Kath looked around the walls of the small chapel, taking in the plaques that had been erected down the years to mark the baptisms, weddings and funeral services that had been held there.

Those old stones had seen so many poignant, pivotal moments in local family life – happiness and tears, hope and despair, endings and beginnings.

"Then I think our life together should start here too."

Richard drew her closer to him, then whispered, "Thank you. It feels right that I should make my vows to you here."

"With just a few friends. The ones that matter."

He smiled. "There's no choice on that front. You couldn't possibly squeeze in more than about thirty people, and that's if they're all breathing in."

"And I would only ever want a small wedding, intimate and personal. My inclination is to keep things simple. Our wedding is just one day. Our marriage is for a lifetime, and that's what I'm really looking forward to."

"Agreed," he said, searching her face, then kissing her tenderly. "We'll get married here the day before Christmas Eve, enjoy our wedding breakfast at Ainsworth Hall that afternoon, and start our life as husband and wife that evening in a lovely hotel not too far away."

"That sounds perfect."

"Have you decided who's going to give you away?"

"Well, as you know, the only living member of my immediate family is my sister, Jane, and she's really disappointed that she and her family simply can't get across from Australia at this time of year, which is always especially busy for her and her husband's business. They're planning a visit around Easter, they say, which I'm really looking forward to. Seeing as there's no relative of any generation I can ask, I'd like to ask Trevor if he'll do the honours. He's been so incredibly kind and supportive since I came to Hope Hall, and I consider him and Mary to be very dear friends."

"I'm sure he'll feel deeply honoured to be asked."

"And you? Who will choose as your best man?"

Richard laughed. "The very best man I know – William, of

course. I know it seems odd for a son to be involved in this way, but he has been very supportive of my decision to ask you to marry me. He just wanted to know what took me so long!"

"We'll go and talk to James at St Mark's, shall we? Do you think he'll be able to fit in a marriage ceremony so close to Christmas?"

"I've already had a word. He's put it in his diary in big red letters, because he said it'll be his favourite service of the year."

"That's it, then. We're on our way…"

"We are, my love. On our way to very happy times ahead." And he sealed that thought with a kiss.

Chapter 10

"Trevor, you've got to help me!" wailed Mary as she walked into their lounge waving a pad of papers.

Trevor looked up from the newspaper he was reading with a sigh, then folded it and placed it beside him on the sofa. Years of experience had taught him that when his wife approached with that panicked look in her eyes, she expected nothing less than his full attention. "Help with what?"

"The panto script. There's so much of it. I had no idea the Fairy Godmother would have so many lines to learn."

"But she just flits on and off the stage every now and then, doesn't she? I don't remember her saying a lot, but then I haven't been to a panto since Andrew was in short trousers, and he's just had his thirty-fifth birthday!"

"I thought the same thing," she replied, plonking herself down right on top of his newspaper. "I mean, I was really pleased when they asked me to play this part. I thought I'd be sure to have the prettiest costumes, and I've been practising my wand control with the washing-up brush, and saying words like 'abracadabra' and 'bibbity, bobbity, boo'!"

"It sounds like you'll be fine."

"That's what I thought until I took a look at the script and saw how much I've got to learn. Look!" She shoved the papers into his hand, pointing repeatedly at the top of the page. "Read it out loud," she ordered. "Then you'll see what I mean. You're going to have to help me with this, Trevor. You really are."

Trevor pushed his glasses back up on to the bridge of his nose and started to recite:

"*Well, here I am; that's a surprise*
That I've appeared before your eyes,
My wand gave me a bit of bother –
Awkward for a Fairy Godmother!

I like to change things for the better,
A lazy boy into a go-getter.
A prince changed to a pussy cat?
I reckon I could cope with that!

I gave a wave and made a wish,
And turned a cat into a fish,
I changed the spell and tried again,
And whoosh! The fish became a hen.

So now I'm stuck with this darned chicken!
But who's there, kindling sticks a-picking?
Why, Cinderella's in the wood,
Finding firewood as she should.

Her shoes have holes, her clothes are rags,
She's often dressed in dustbin bags.
And that's because her Ugly Sisters
Are a pair of scheming twisters.

Cinderella's good and kind,
Not a bad thought in her mind,

> *They are selfish, cruel and vain,*
> *I'd like to stop their little game.*
>
> *I think that it would serve them right*
> *If they had a nasty fright.*
> *How they'd hate if Cinderella*
> *Found herself a handsome fella.*
>
> *And it would truly make them wince*
> *If Cinderella found a prince.*
> *I'm off to see what I can do,*
> *See you later – toodle-oo!"*

"Oh, I like it," grinned Trevor. "I can just see you in your fairy costume reciting that. You'll be brilliant."

"But how will I ever be able to remember all those words?"

"They rhyme. That should help."

"But suppose I get the verses in the wrong order – or my mind goes completely blank? I'm terrified I'll let everyone down."

"But isn't that half the fun of panto – that people forget their lines or just make it up as they go along? Whatever you do, everyone will love it. People fight to get tickets for the Hope Hall panto because it's so popular."

"You're right. I'd forgotten about all those people in the audience that I probably know. Oh, I think I've made a dreadful mistake here. I'm going to have to tell Maurice I have a pressing family engagement that day, which I simply can't miss. You can back me up. He'll believe you."

"No."

"Oh, for heaven's sake, Trevor, this is important to me. I don't want to make a fool of myself or find that people are gossiping

189

about *you* because the esteemed accountant of Hope Hall has such a featherbrain for a wife."

Trevor took his wife's hand patiently. "No, Mary. You agreed to do this. You're perfectly capable of doing a wonderful job, and I know that in the end you'll love every minute of it. You're nervous about learning the words, but you've got a few weeks to go, and I'll test you any time you need me to."

Her expression was dramatically forlorn as she got to her feet and glared down at him. "You know that if you make me do this, I'll be hell to live with the next few weeks, don't you?"

"No change there then!" Trevor laughed. And when she picked up a cushion to throw it in his direction and missed him completely, he laughed even louder, until Mary found herself laughing too.

In the end, Ida wasn't allowed to visit Percy the day after his accident. He spent the day being examined, X-rayed, discussed, observed and generally prodded about until the late afternoon, when he was finally wheeled down to theatre to have his hip replaced. By that time, it was decided that the break at the top of his arm was likely to heal naturally if it was kept in a sling for several weeks, and Percy was left lying helplessly on his bed wondering how he would ever be able to take his pyjamas off, put his clothes on or tie up his shoelaces again. He was right-handed. How would he clean his teeth, shave or have a shower?

Since Margaret died, he had taken pride in his independence and his ability to cope on his own. How would he manage that now? And how could he convince the busybodies at the hospital that he would be able to cope alone – especially that teenager of a social worker who had just "popped in" to say hello and find out how he was? "I'm aware you may need help with your accommodation as soon as you're well enough to be discharged from hospital," she had said. He shuddered at the thought. He was not going into a home. He would *not* go into a home.

For the first time since Margaret died, he suddenly felt helpless and overwhelmed by fear. The pain was dreadful, and he had a thumping headache. The blow to his head might account for that, he reasoned, as well as the fact that the hospital ward was unbearably hot. And then there was the throbbing soreness in his arm and the sharp discomfort down the whole length of his right side, especially around his hip. More than that, it felt as if every sinew in his body had been stretched to breaking point. He was horrified to realize he was crying again. A great big fella like him, and there he was, crying like a baby. It was a good job no one was there to see him. He couldn't bear the thought of being caught like that.

He thought of Ida at that moment. Either he had been hallucinating because of the pain the night before, or she had really been there at the hospital, sitting in the seat beside him, stroking his hand and telling him it would all be okay. He couldn't quite remember the details, so perhaps he had been dreaming. He hoped not. He needed someone in his corner right now, and he felt sorry for anyone who dared to go against Ida's wishes. She was a force to be reckoned with, and he seemed to remember her saying that she would sort things out.

At that thought, Percy felt the tension ease from the knot of muscles in his neck and shoulders. Maybe he was just being a silly old fool and she hadn't been there at all last night, but he took comfort from the possibility that Ida Miller, that formidable enigma of a woman, had cared enough to be there for him, far more than she cared about what anyone else might think. And with that in mind, he closed his eyes and drifted off into an exhausted sleep.

Kath had put a call through to the hospital the morning after Percy's fall, explaining to the ward sister that the accident had happened at Hope Hall, and that as the administrator of the well-known Good

Neighbours scheme which was much appreciated and often used by professionals at the hospital, she was in a position to help with any ongoing care Percy might require following his injuries. The result of this conversation was that Jasmine Grainger, the social worker who had spoken to Percy earlier that day, rang back to give Kath the rundown on everything she knew about Percy's injuries, as well as her concerns for his future care.

"It's very early days, of course," Jasmine explained. "The ward sister asked me to talk to him this morning, just to get some idea of what difficulties he'd have looking after himself in his own home. I believe he lives alone, but I'm not completely aware of his family situation. Are you?"

"From my records, Percy has no family. His wife died some years ago, and they never had children. He's a very popular character in the community, though, with plenty of friends, so there may be other options available to him."

"That's something I might need to explore with you in more detail in due course. In the meantime, we need to think about his immediate care when he leaves the hospital."

"What possibilities are you considering?" Kath asked.

"Well, we think that, initially at least, he'll need a spell at the Abbotsbury Nursing Home, if they have space available. They can start his physiotherapy and carry out a proper assessment of how his injuries are likely to affect his ongoing mobility, or lack of it – in both the short and the long term. If we don't feel he can adequately look after himself in his home for any length of time in the future, we might have to consider alternative accommodation."

"Such as?"

"The Beaumont Residential Care Home on the outskirts of the town has a good reputation. As you know, it's a very grand and graceful old house, and is surrounded by lovely countryside."

"I have a feeling Percy wouldn't be very interested in beautiful countryside. He's an independent man – the life and soul of the

192

party much of the time. Take him out of the community that's been his home all his life and there's a danger you'll take the life out of the man."

"Well, Miss Sutton, I would certainly appreciate your help in finding the best solution we can for Mr Wilson. We'll try, of course, but the system is a blunt instrument, as you know. In the end, it might be a case of him having to accept whatever arrangements we're able to make for him."

"I'll be going in to see him as soon as the ward sister gives me permission to do so," replied Kath. "Let me talk to him then. I have a feeling he'd be more likely to open up to someone familiar from Hope Hall. Can I report back to you then, once we know how he's faring after his operation?"

"Of course. And in the meantime, I'll make enquiries about any accommodation, either temporary or permanent, that might be available to suit him. Goodbye, Miss Sutton."

Maggie had volunteered to drive herself down to Chichester on the morning of Sandra's fiftieth birthday party. Phil had accepted her decision without question, tactfully recognizing that Maggie was rather nervous about meeting his ex-wife and family at such an important gathering of the clan. His heart went out to Maggie as he pictured her running around like a headless chicken that morning, trying on various outfits again because her decision on what to wear had changed at least a dozen times in the past twenty-four hours.

As it happened, his idea of the turmoil she might be going through was spot on. In fact, Maggie had been awake most of the night, with her thoughts going round and round in circles. Should she wear something voluminous that would hide the shape of her overgenerous curves? Or should she look casual, as if this meeting meant nothing at all to her and she'd dressed as she usually would on a relaxed Sunday morning? And what would the other ladies choose to wear that day? Would Sandra and her daughter dress up to the nines because it was such a special birthday celebration?

This *would* be the morning her flyaway hair decided to conduct more electricity than ever, so that when she caught sight of herself in the bathroom mirror she looked as if she had got her finger stuck in a wall socket. And what's more, she'd bought a new pair of shoes that she'd decided to wear around the house the day before so they would soften up a little, only to discover within a couple of hours that they had rubbed a blister and were killing her. What on earth was she going to wear now? The trainers she wore for work because they were comfy and practical? That would make a great impression on Phil's family, wouldn't it?! They would think he had completely lost the plot if his new lady friend turned up in scruffy old trainers with her hair sticking out at right angles all over her head!

She was just about to burst into tears of frustration when Phil rang. Later on, she couldn't quite remember what he had said. Perhaps it wasn't his words but his tone that had lowered her panic levels – along with her shoulders, which had felt as if they were stuck to her ears, they were so high. In the end she had sent him pictures of the three outfits she was thinking of wearing. He had chosen one immediately, and she was relieved to realize it was the one she actually liked best.

His last words were so caring, funny and reassuring that she stuck a plaster over the blister on her foot, donned her new shoes, smothered her wayward hair with spray and squirted on her oldest perfume, which she always resorted to in situations like this because it felt like her. Then she grabbed her satnav and car keys, and set off before she could change her mind.

Maggie panicked again when she arrived a little earlier than she had intended to, but when she saw that Phil was already sitting on a low garden wall near the entrance of the hotel waiting for her, she breathed a sigh of relief. He was by her side in an instant, helping her out of the car, reassuring her that she looked lovely and following her instruction to draw an interesting-looking box out of the back seat of the car.

"That's for later," she whispered. "A little present I hope Sandra might like."

"I'm sure she will," he replied as he leaned across to plant a kiss on her cheek. And taking her hand in his, he led the way towards the hotel restaurant.

"Dad!"

The young man who approached them to give Phil a hug took Maggie's breath away. Suddenly, in her mind's eye, she pictured Phil on those long-ago mornings when they had walked to school together in the same group of friends. She knew this must be David, who had clearly inherited his father's strong, broad frame and his pale grey eyes, which lit up with warmth when he smiled.

"I'm David, and you must be Maggie," he said, holding out his hand in her direction. "I've heard so much about you."

She couldn't help but match the friendliness of his greeting. "I've heard a lot about you too. It's nice to meet you, David."

"Come on in. We've all gathered in the bar while we wait for our table. Everyone's here now, I think."

Taking a breath, Maggie felt Phil's fingers link with hers, and their eyes locked for just a moment before they turned to follow David into a homely but stylish bar, with a huge window overlooking the cathedral mews. A young couple immediately got up from the sofa they had been sitting on to say hello.

"You're looking good, Dad!" beamed Melanie as she wrapped her father in a bear hug.

As her husband, Simon, greeted Phil, Melanie turned her attention to Maggie. There was no hesitation at all as she came over to give her father's new partner a quick hug, which felt genuine and affectionate. "So, you're the lady who's been putting a smile on the old man's face!" she quipped. "I'm so glad you came today, Maggie. Come and meet Mum."

And before she knew it, Maggie had to loosen her grip on Phil's hand as Melanie propelled her in the direction of a slightly built woman who was sitting in an elegant winged armchair. Maggie's first thought was that Sandra looked really nice, with her short, neat haircut, her soft pastel-blue jumper decorated with small white pearls, and neat navy trousers teamed with comfortable flat shoes.

"Maggie, it's so good to meet you at last," she smiled, reaching out to shake Maggie's hand. "Forgive me if I don't get up, but they bought me a G&T as a bit of a treat. I only ever drink on high days and holidays, so one glass is definitely enough for me!"

Maggie chuckled. "I know what you mean. I'm cooking lots of Christmas puddings and fruit cakes at the moment, and it's tempting to keep licking the spoon when I'm feeding them all with brandy. Just a little bit makes my head spin."

"Oh, I like to make my own Christmas puddings too," replied Sandra. "I've even managed to rustle up a fruit cake once in a while, but I have to admit I'm terrible at icing."

Before she knew it, Maggie was lowering herself into the seat beside Sandra. "I'm so glad to have a couple of really brilliant assistants at Hope Hall who are much better at royal icing than I ever was. And although I love fruit cake, I've never been keen on marzipan."

"Nor me," laughed Sandra, unaware that Phil was watching anxiously from across the coffee table to check that Maggie was okay. He grinned to himself as he saw that he needn't have worried. The two women were nattering away as if they were old friends.

The party stayed in the bar for ten minutes before the waiter called them through to take their places for lunch. With just six in the group, conversation was easy around the table, and although Maggie was only able to listen and observe during discussions about family memories, or how Mel, Simon and David were getting on in their lives and careers, she felt comfortable and welcome in their circle.

At one point, when Simon was talking at length about some extra qualifications he was taking in order to move up through the ranks at the estate agency business where he worked, Maggie felt Phil's fingers intertwine with hers. Barely moving, she glanced over at him with a small smile as he gently stroked her hand beneath the table.

The meal was delicious – and when, just before dessert was served, the waiter came in carrying a gorgeous chocolate cake bearing birthday greetings and a discreet number of sparkling candles, Sandra was plainly delighted. They all joined in to sing "Happy Birthday".

Soon after that, Maggie slipped away to powder her nose, only to find herself quite literally bumping into Sandra just outside the door of the ladies' room on the way back.

Laughing as they almost collided, Sandra's face became more serious as she said, "Actually, I'm glad to see you away from the rest of the family for a moment. I just want you to know how much I appreciate you coming today. It can't have been easy meeting the ex-wife and the family, but you've fitted in so well, as I had a feeling you would."

Wondering whether this conversation might be heading somewhere, Maggie simply replied, "It was so kind of you to ask me."

"Well, we had an ulterior motive. Phil is a dear man, and we all love him very much. He and I have been separated for quite a while now, and none of us has any problem with that. We're both much happier now that we're not married, but the bond of friendship between us is as strong as it ever was. And when Phil suddenly began talking about this wonderful old friend he'd met again, and he was plainly so smitten, the kids and I thought we ought to check you out. Oh, I'm sorry, that doesn't sound quite right. I'm not putting this well…"

Maggie smiled. "I understand entirely. My son and daughter reacted in much the same protective way, but Phil has really won them over. When he worked his magic on Steph's utility room to create a brilliant hairdressing area so she could start having customers at home now she's got her son, Bobbie, to care for, that did the trick for her! He's not pushy, he's not showy – he's just good, comfortable company – and I feel so lucky to have crossed paths with him again after all these years."

"Well, after today, I can assure you that our family feels much the same way about you. Who knows what the future will hold for you, or how this renewed friendship with Phil will progress? We just want you to know that you're welcome, and that perhaps we can all count ourselves as friends from now on."

Flustered to find that her eyes were pricking with tears, Maggie simply said, "Thank you. Thank you so much for that."

A few minutes later, when Sandra returned to the restaurant area, Maggie had placed a cream-coloured box tied with a dusky-pink ribbon on the table in front of the birthday girl's seat. Her face full of curiosity, she untied the ribbon and peeled back the leaves of the box to reveal a tempting display of small cakes and biscuits, all in different shapes, designs, colours, flavours and decoration, which just demanded to be eaten.

"Mum, they're beautiful!" exclaimed Mel. "Maggie, how did you know Mum has a sweet tooth?"

Sandra was too busy to comment as she studied the cakes in great detail, trying to decide which one to taste first.

"Now this is what I call the perfect birthday present," she said at last, her face beaming as she looked across at Maggie. "I'll have a wonderful time working my way through these – and if you lot are really good, I might even let you dip in too!"

As coffee was served, Maggie kicked her new shoes off under

the table with relief and sat back in her seat, feeling quite at home in this delightful company.

When Kath called in to the hospital to see Percy the next morning, she was taken aback to find that she was not his only visitor. To her surprise, Ida was sitting beside the bed, holding Percy's hand as she perched on an upright faux-leather chair that was definitely designed for easy cleaning rather than comfort. Ida's hand shot back into her lap the moment she saw Kath approaching.

Hiding her curiosity with a broad smile, Kath took a seat on the other side of Percy's bed. "It's lovely to see you both. How are you feeling, Percy? That was quite a dramatic show you put on the other evening!"

He shifted his position slightly in an attempt to get more comfortable. "We didn't win the quiz, though, did we? I had to do something to cheer my team up."

"I bet you're regretting that now. Can you tell what hurts the most?"

"Did they tell you I've got a new hip?" he asked. "I only had the operation yesterday, and this morning a physiotherapist came along wanting me to get out of bed and go for a walk!"

"And did you?"

"I really didn't want to try, because I've got more aches in my body than I realized could be possible. But she did get me on my feet, and I even walked a step or two with the help of that awful Zimmer frame. I always swore I'd never use one of those. They're for old men! And now here I am, reduced to this."

"Well, you've got to keep moving, Percy Wilson," retorted Ida, "or you'll seize up altogether, and you wouldn't want that now, would you?"

"Ida's right, Percy. The doctors need you to get that new joint of yours moving as soon as possible so you can start getting up and about again, doing all the things you need to do to look after yourself at home."

"Ah well, they might manage to get me back on my feet, but I'm still a bit useless with this," he said, looking down at the sling that encased his right arm and shoulder. "I've got a complete fracture across the bone right up here by my shoulder joint – and did you know they don't plaster something like that these days? The doctor reckons the bone will just heal itself. I can't say I'm convinced."

"This silly old man nearly knocked his brains out when he decided to throw himself on the floor," added Ida. "They're still keeping an eye on him for the effects of concussion."

"I suppose they will do," agreed Kath. "That can be very nasty indeed. Are you feeling light-headed, Percy? How's your vision?"

"Oh, he's as daft as ever," smiled Ida, "so he must be getting better."

"I, er…" Kath began, choosing her words carefully. "I didn't realize you two were such good friends."

"We've been friends for years," guffawed Percy, tapping Ida's hand affectionately.

"But it never seemed that way when you were at the hall. In fact, I thought you really hated each other at times."

"Really?" asked Ida, her face the picture of innocence. "I can't imagine why you thought that. Percy and I have been friends and neighbours since we were teenagers. Naturally, as soon as I realized my old friend was in need of a bit of company and an occasional helping hand, I was happy to step in."

"That's why I'm here too," replied Kath. "Obviously, you need to stay in hospital until the doctors are really sure you're on the mend, but there has been some discussion about what might be the best option for you after that."

"He can come and stay with me," stated Ida with a steely gleam in her eye. "I have a spare room on the ground floor with a divan that's never been used. I've looked after many people over the years who've needed care along the same lines as Percy, and I passed my

St John's Ambulance first-aid exams with flying colours."

Percy beamed at her. "When did you do that?"

Ida looked slightly uncomfortable. "Oh, a few years ago now, but the elements of my training remain the same."

"How long was the course?"

"Six weeks, but it was very thorough."

"That's really useful information for us to know, Ida," said Kath, "because Percy has already been allocated a social worker who will be making decisions and arrangements for his further care."

"I'm not going into a home!" he declared.

"Well, there may be a need for you to spend a short time in Abbotsbury Nursing Home, just while your hip heals and your physiotherapy treatment gets properly under way."

"How long is a short time?" Percy demanded to know. "I'm *not* going into a home."

"Not a residential home where you go and live, but a nursing home just for a week or two, where you'll be given the medical and therapeutic support you need to get back on your feet, and hopefully back into your own home."

Ida nodded at that news. "Abbotsbury is very nice. My neighbour stayed there after she had a stroke, and I went to visit her several times. She was in a hospital ward, but the atmosphere was more relaxed, with lots of help to get patients eating, sleeping, moving or speaking again, depending on what had taken them into hospital in the first place."

"How long was she there?" Percy asked.

Ida's face was thoughtful as she tried to remember. "About three weeks, I think."

"And then she went home?"

Ida hesitated before she answered. "She did for a while."

"And then?" he asked.

"Then she had a very severe stroke about a month later. I'm afraid she didn't make it through that."

Percy fell silent.

"There's no reason to think that you won't recover well from these injuries, Percy," continued Kath, "but you have been through the trauma of a serious accident. You need proper treatment and time to recover, with the appropriate care in place."

"It'll be good for Percy if he has to stay at Abbotsbury for a while," stated Ida. "After that, he can stay with me. You can organize whatever bed or equipment he needs, but I can provide a downstairs room with a loo nearby and regular meals, and I can get his laundry done. He can have visitors and potter out to the park, because I'll make sure he takes regular exercise, following professional guidance. And he'll receive genuine care. I will *care* for Percy, and make sure he's able to recover in a safe, organized environment."

"Is that what you want, Percy?" Kath asked.

Percy's eyes were glued to Ida's. "That's exactly what I want. If this brave woman is prepared to take me on, I will be nothing but grateful. I will promise to behave and to eat everything she puts in front of me – except greens, that is. I never eat *anything* green. I will clean my teeth, say my prayers before bedtime and watch my language. And…" His gaze softened as he continued to look at her. "I will be very, very grateful. More than you can possibly know."

No one spoke for a while, until eventually Kath opened her organizer to make some notes. "I've got your address and contact details, Ida. If the medical team and social worker are prepared to consider this arrangement, I imagine the occupational therapist will want to pay you a visit to see if any equipment needs to be installed – handrails, raised toilet seats, that sort of thing. In the meantime, would you mind if I popped round to your house in the next day or two so we can chat about how feasible this might be?"

There was just the slightest glimmer of triumph in Ida's eyes as she answered. "You're very welcome. Just let me know a time and I'll be glad to show you around."

As Kath got to her feet, she asked, "Is there anything you need, Percy? Perhaps some essentials from home – a toothbrush, night or day clothes, anything that might be helpful?"

"I've already organized all that," replied Ida. "I'm keeping an eye on everything Percy might need."

"Except she's brought me *green* grapes," he sighed. "Now if she'd brought me red ones, I'd have scoffed the lot."

"That's okay," chuckled Ida. "I like the green ones."

With a smile, Kath said goodbye to them both, and when she turned back to wave as she left the ward, she smiled again to see that the two of them were already engrossed in their own conversation.

Chapter 11

All her adult life, Celia had woken early in the morning, filled with enthusiasm to get out of the house and into work – and now, with the prospect of taking over her new role, that urge to get cracking every day felt overwhelming. She was gloriously happy, even when faced with completely new areas of business, where there was so much to learn and know. Uncle Joe seemed to have complete faith in her ability to pick up most of what she needed as she established herself in the job, so his explanations were sometimes a bit too superficial for her liking. He made sweeping assumptions that she was experienced in areas of international accounting that she had never needed to know in her previous roles.

She found herself remembering the old saying, "Those who can, do; those who can't, teach." Uncle Joe had been a master in this role for decades, and had probably forgotten more than she would ever know. But he wasn't a good teacher – mainly, she realized, because it bored him. He hadn't the patience to answer her detailed questions about the minutiae of the business. He knew it inside out, so it seemed perfectly easy and logical to him. He simply couldn't imagine that his brilliant god-daughter, with her analytical mind and flair for figures, might be struggling with the mountain of information she was trying to get to grips with in a very short space of time.

Celia was of a generation that had grown up with technology, so every document, fact or agreement she had ever come across was neatly stored on her desktop computer, her laptop and on the cloud. It soon became clear that Uncle Joe dealt in broad brush strokes rather than nitty-gritty detail. More than that, he obviously wasn't keen on keeping precise records on his computer, but preferred agreements to be printed out on paper, with copies signed by all relevant parties in their own handwriting.

Celia also discovered that Uncle Joe had a habit of doing business with some of his closest and most important clients as if they were all members of a gentlemen's club, where deals were agreed over a meal that finished with a bottle or two of champagne to celebrate, and the contract was sealed on the basis of nothing more than a handshake. Paperwork might follow, at the insistence of Valerie Goddard – who had been Joe's highly efficient personal assistant for years – but as Celia began to delve into some of the ongoing relationships she would be taking over responsibility for, she started to realize that the paperwork she was able to find didn't always match up with the service being provided. When she asked Uncle Joe about specific clients for whom she couldn't find a record of an ongoing contract at all, he was frustratingly vague. With a patient tone in his voice, as though she were a five-year-old unable to grasp the basics, he explained that he came from the era of the gentleman's agreement. With his oldest clients his word was his bond, based on years of personal friendship in both business and private life.

"That gives each side the benefit of flexibility," he said. "With a certain class of client, if tweaks or slight changes are needed during the ups and downs of their business, we can agree to short-term arrangements that don't need to be on record in a formal way that might reflect on their worth or viability in a fluctuating financial market. With this kind of client, I never agree to any new arrangement, temporary or otherwise, unless I know enough about their business to be able to rely on and agree with their judgment and assessment of their ability to pay it back. But it works both ways. This is a two-way street."

"I scratch your back, you scratch mine." Celia's voice hardened as she took in the irregularity of what he was explaining.

"You've got it in one."

"But surely that breaks all the accepted regulations? How can a major financial corporation like Apex allow that?"

He shrugged, looking directly at her. "The books balance. My results are excellent. I'm considered to be an experienced and instinctive investor who knows the business inside out, and who reads our clients with a great deal of skill. I'm their golden boy."

"But I can't see myself being able to work that way," she replied, her eyes not leaving his. "I've always done things by the book. You know that."

"And that's why, my darling girl, you still have a lot to learn. You'll make this job your own in time, but I'll admit that I enjoy being a bit of a maverick, doing deals my way. They work. I've established my own style, and you will too. If you're wise, as I know you are, you'll decide for yourself what needs to be done 'by the book', and what simply needs to be left alone. If it ain't broke, don't fix it."

Those words often echoed through Celia's mind during the first weeks of the handover period when Joe was supposed to be working alongside her. Most of the time he wasn't there. In his mind, he was easing himself into retirement in a very enjoyable way, which meant that he never appeared before eleven and then frequently went out to lunch to say farewell to one or other of his favourite clients, with no intention of returning to the office afterwards.

On several occasions, Celia was invited along so she could meet those clients for herself. At other times no invitation was extended, and she got the distinct impression he felt that her doubts surrounding his business technique might cause offence, and damage the easy relationships he had built up over the years. He had no doubt that she would come round in time. It was early days. She was very bright, and it wouldn't take her long to recognize how the biggest financial rewards didn't always come from doing things by the book.

In the middle of one particularly difficult afternoon, as she was ploughing through a large pile of her uncle's files, trying to tie up the arrangements recorded on paper with the corresponding records on the Apex IT system, she was surprised to see Douglas's name flash up on the screen when her mobile rang.

He came straight to the point. "I'm having to go to the Berkshire estate again. Lord Harry needs my help."

"Oh, I hope he isn't ill again. How's he doing?"

"Well, Diana will tell you he's at death's door, but he seems very coherent during our regular phone calls. He likes to keep family business strictly within the family – hence his wish for my input while he's not able to take charge as usual."

"What about David? Shouldn't he be the one learning the ropes from Harry at the moment?"

"Huh!" snorted Douglas. "Dave, as he prefers to be known, is apparently living in an artists' commune in Cornwall. He says he's too busy to get away at the moment."

"But David is next in line. He'll inherit the title and the estate. Surely, if Lord Harry's health is a cause for concern, it's David who should be there to learn all he can about the running of the business."

"Well, that's what we all assumed. But when Lord Harry's health first took a turn for the worse, he decided he'd have to delay the training of his successor. He said that when David is able to get away in a few months or so, the business of training him to take over the reins of the estate can start in earnest. In the meantime, he seems very grateful that I, with my experience of animal husbandry and the running of a large estate, am able to step up and help when it's needed."

Celia grimaced, grateful that her brother couldn't see her expression from his end of the phone. "But you *haven't* had much experience of running a large estate."

She sensed Douglas bristle at her comment. "Ainsworth Hall is a very substantial property with farming responsibilities as well as a thriving international business producing breakfast and other cereal products. Of course I have the relevant experience. Lord Harry recognizes that, even if you don't."

Changing tack in a bid to diffuse a brewing argument, Celia asked, "Is Diana going with you?"

"She is. I keep telling her she's just fussing, but she's worried about her mother. I've always found Eleanor to be a very nervous, impractical sort of woman, so it's no surprise that she's panicking about Lord Harry and taking everything the doctors say to heart."

"What *are* the doctors saying?"

"Nothing too worrying. He seems to have recovered from that bout of what Diana keeps saying was pneumonia. Harry said it was just a bit of a chest cold. He was complaining about his heart beating irregularly, which has alarmed him a bit, but the test results don't appear to be concerning the doctors unduly. And that TIA he had a few weeks back seems to have been a one-off. They said it wasn't a stroke, just a little blip, probably caused by overwork. They've put him on medication to thin his blood, and apparently that's working."

"But he's still poorly enough for you and Diana to be racing up there to support her parents."

"Naturally. We don't want them worrying. Diana is the best possible companion for her mother, and Lord Harry clearly appreciates my company too."

"I'm sure he does," replied Celia through clenched teeth. "Do you know how long you'll be away?"

"Well, we have to be back by the 15th of December, when the boys return from school. And then there's Richard and Kath's wedding to organize for the 23rd of the month."

"I know Richard has been working hard to get all the arrangements for the wedding finalized in good time. James, the vicar from St Mark's, will be taking the service in the chapel. Richard's booked some excellent caterers to provide everything

208

that's needed for the wedding breakfast. It's lovely to think it will be held in the Ainsworth Hall dining room. It's such a spacious, elegant room, with all that beautiful oak panelling. It's the perfect place for a small wedding reception, and it's so kind of you and Diana to invite them to use it."

"He's family. We're pleased to help, although we haven't the time or inclination to get very involved beyond that offer. We'll be there on the day, of course, but the rest is up to him."

"Richard has it all in hand. It promises to be a lovely occasion. It's so good to see him happy again after the sadness of the last few years."

"Yes. I just hope William shares that sentiment."

"He most certainly does."

"Well, I must go. We're leaving for Berkshire in the morning. I'll be on my mobile if you need to contact me for anything, but Mike is our estate manager, so he should be your first port of call if you want to check wedding arrangements or anything else."

And before Celia had chance to say thank you and goodbye, the line had gone dead.

Kevin was waiting on the steps of Hope Hall so he would be sure to see Chloe the moment she arrived. She had been so kind. It had been obvious from the first panto rehearsal that taking on the role of Buttons was a real challenge for him. He wanted to curl up and die whenever he thought of his second rehearsal, when he had had to learn dance steps, along with a full chorus of villagers, for a big production number that would close the first half of the show. It seemed to him that everyone there, even the five-year-olds, must have had some sort of proper dance training, because although he'd always been able to create a stir with his eye-catching moves when he went clubbing, he knew nothing about this style of stage dancing, and he couldn't get the steps right at all.

At one point, all the performers on stage were singing and

moving together in long rows, almost like line dancing. The most embarrassing moment had come when everyone on stage turned to the right and he had ended up turning to his left. He realized his mistake the moment he found himself face to face with the whole of the rest of the cast, who were all pointing in his direction.

Worst of all, he had ended up eyeball to eyeball with Jason, who completely dropped his act of being Prince Charming and exploded into derisive laughter about how they'd definitely got the right person to play the village idiot this year, and that Kev was well cast as Buttons. Chloe had looked furious, and once the dance rehearsal was over she had made a point of finding Kevin and telling him she thought he was doing really well, especially when he had so much to learn.

"I don't think I'm right for this, Chloe. They've made a mistake. I'm going to tell Maurice he'll have to find someone else to play Buttons."

"Oh no you don't!" she smiled. "Don't let Jason put you off. You've never done this before, but it's clear to Maurice, and to me too, that you have real talent. I have a feeling that once you get on the stage with a proper audience you'll realize just how good you can be."

"Maybe," he sighed. "When we're rehearsing I feel as if everyone's looking at me and wondering why on earth I was chosen, when I'm obviously struggling to learn it all. And then I make even more mistakes. I can't remember my lines. I can't remember the moves. I can't remember my own name half the time."

"Can I help? You and I have quite a few scenes together. Why don't we practise them ourselves? That might help you feel more confident about them. We could find a quiet time here at the hall, and we might even be able to rehearse on the stage."

"Oh, I could ask Kath about that." Kev's face lit up at the possibility. "I'm sure she wouldn't mind us using the stage for half an hour if we need to."

And sure enough, when he asked Kath the following day, she

immediately agreed. "Of course you can, Kevin. You know the timetable for each day. Just make sure you don't get in the way of any of the clubs or activities that are booked, and let me have a note of any times you have in mind. How are the rehearsals going?"

He let out a long breath. "To be honest, I feel really out of my depth. I've never done anything like this before and I'm terrified of letting everyone down."

Kath smiled. "I've seen you in action, singing and dancing at the Grown-ups' Lunch Club, mucking around and making them all laugh. You come across as a natural entertainer. You may not realize it yet – and I can imagine that having to become a character, stick to a script, learn lines and make all the right moves on cue is a tough challenge – but honestly, I think that by the time the panto comes around you'll be loving every minute of it."

He looked doubtful. "Well, promise me you won't come and watch any of the rehearsals until then, because I'm terrible at the minute."

"Practice makes perfect," Kath replied. "Break a leg, Kev!"

So there he was, later that day, standing at the main door of Hope Hall, when he spotted Chloe hurrying towards him. She looked absolutely gorgeous.

"Sorry I'm late. I got held up at school. Is the stage still free?"

"At least for the next half an hour," he replied, suddenly feeling tongue-tied in her company.

"Come on, then," she grinned, grabbing his hand as she pulled him through the foyer and into the main hall. "Your Cinderella awaits!"

Ever since Richard's proposal, Kath had felt as though her feet weren't quite touching the ground. In all honesty, she hadn't expected him to make such a grand gesture, and certainly not so soon – but the moment he had asked, she knew the prospect of sharing her life with this kind, clever, caring man felt as natural as taking her next breath. They seemed to be like two parts of a jigsaw that fitted together perfectly to make each of them complete. What had started as an easy comfortable friendship and an exciting attraction had quickly and effortlessly grown into a deep and enduring love.

She had said yes without a shadow of doubt about the wisdom of her decision – and from the second that decision was made, it had been action stations to get everything arranged and their new life together planned. Kath would be moving in to live with Richard at the lovely house that had been in his family for many years, meaning that after the wedding she would sell the apartment that had been her home since her mother's death. She had enjoyed living there, and had filled the apartment with items she'd chosen with care. That had to be balanced against the fact that she would be moving into the house Richard had lived in with his first wife until her death. Kath wondered if he would feel sensitive about her bringing her own possessions and perhaps giving a slightly different feel to the house once she was living there, but he anticipated her worry. Before she even had a chance to bring up the subject, he made it clear that their house was to be her home, and he longed for the two of them to start making new and very happy memories there together.

"I will always feel love for Elizabeth and carry the gift of those years we spent together in my heart," he explained. "She made it very clear she hoped that in time I would move on – and now I am, with you. I think she'd be very happy to know that this house will be filled with love and laughter again."

It had been an easy decision for them to keep their wedding a small, intimate affair, with only their closest friends there to see them take their vows and share their day. When Richard took Kath over to Ainsworth Hall – where Diana hugged them both in warm congratulations before showing Kath the elegant old dining room in which many family occasions had been celebrated down

212

the years – Kath could just imagine how wonderful their wedding breakfast would be in such lovely surroundings.

She decided against having any bridesmaids or a maid of honour. At the age of fifty, and certainly not a young and blushing bride, it didn't feel appropriate. She simply wanted a quiet, sincere and heartfelt service – and although she was certain that the day itself would be perfect, what she was looking forward to most of all was *being* married, rather than *getting* married.

She had asked Maggie if she could spare the time to help her look for a wedding dress, but with an apologetic smile Maggie had said she would rather not. This wasn't for any lack of friendship or a genuine desire for Kath's marriage to bring her great happiness. She explained that, first of all, having recently gone through the breakdown of her own marriage she still felt rather raw about the whole subject. And then she had grinned broadly and added that she didn't think anyone should trust her opinion when it came to dress sense.

"I'm hardly the shape of a mannequin," she had laughed. "For as long as I can remember, I've only ever looked in the plus-size department when it comes to clothes of any sort!"

In the end, it was the vicar's wife, Ellie, who travelled up to London with Kath so they could visit a whole range of shops in the shortest possible time. It was at the third place on their list, a little shop down at the other end of the road from Harrods, that she stepped into a creation in cream silk that scooped across her shoulders in flattering lines of lace dotted with tiny pearls, before falling in soft, elegant folds to the floor.

"Oh, Kath," breathed Ellie. "You look absolutely beautiful. That's the one!"

Glancing at her image in the long mirror, Kath let out a long breath. "It doesn't look too young for me?"

"No. It's grown up, elegant and totally gorgeous. You'll make a lovely bride."

Much later that evening, after she had carried home the large box containing the precious garment, Kath drew out the dress to hang it up on her bedroom wardrobe. A ripple of excitement and anticipation flashed through her as she thought about her wedding day, which was only a matter of weeks away now. *Perhaps I should feel nervous*, she thought. *Or maybe I should feel less organized and in a complete panic about all the arrangements.*

The truth was, she felt nothing but a warm feeling that this was right, and that finally, after years of waiting, she had found a beloved partner who would be right for her for ever.

Doris, Betty and Flora hadn't expected to see Ida at the Grown-ups' Lunch Club the following Tuesday, but to their surprise she arrived as promptly as always and joined them just inside the room.

"Ida! You're here!" exclaimed Betty.

"Why shouldn't I be?" asked Ida, frowning as she took off her coat and scarf.

"Well," said Flora, "you've been so busy lately—"

"Visiting Percy Wilson," finished Doris.

"And your point is?" asked Ida.

"You *hate* Percy Wilson," said Betty. "You've *always* hated him."

"Ah well, that's where you're wrong." And with that enigmatic reply, Ida strode off towards their table, leaving her friends open-mouthed and speechless.

Once they had scuttled over to join her, Ida became aware that all eyes around the room seemed to be focused in her direction, including those belonging to the three other members of Percy's usual table, who had drawn their chairs closer so they could hear every word she had to say.

"Well?" demanded Doris.

Ida took her time to reply, placing her handbag neatly by her feet and rearranging the cutlery in front of her before she began. "We're neighbours. I would always help a neighbour."

"But you're not even friends!" retorted Flora.

Ida smiled. "Percy and I have been friends for years."

Her three table companions looked at each other in confusion.

"In that case," demanded Betty at last, "why do you always talk to him, and *about* him, as if he's a bad smell you can't bear?"

"Oh, that's just a game we play."

"What do you mean?" asked Flora. "Are you saying that you don't disapprove of him after all?"

"Oh, he's a terrible man," sighed Ida. "And of course I disapprove of his total disregard for manners, not to mention his lack of care for his own health and safety. But that doesn't stop us being friends."

Doris's eyes narrowed as she tried to weigh up whether Ida was still playing a game – this time with them. "From the way you reacted when he took that tumble," she said at last, "plus the fact that you've been rushing over to the hospital to see him every day, it seems to us that you're actually quite fond of Mr Percy Wilson."

Ida shrugged. "I consider that to be rather an impertinent statement. As to whether or not it's true, that's for me to know and you to wonder. Is there any sign of our lunch yet?"

"You're changing the subject."

"I'm extremely hungry. I've ordered the steak and kidney pie. I hope they've remembered to put the kidney in this time."

And with that, the subject was closed, leaving all the regulars on Ida and Percy's tables filled with an infuriating mix of curiosity and frustration.

"Sit up straight, ladies and gents!" called Kevin from the door of the kitchen as he swaggered through with a trolley of hot meals. "I've got *a lorra lorra* lunches here!"

And after that, they were all too busy to give much thought to the puzzle of straight-laced Ida and her "friend", poorly Percy.

Ali arrived at Hope Hall before eight o'clock on the Saturday morning of the Christmas Charity Fayre, anxious to get first dibs on a good site for their stall in the main hall so she could have their raffle prizes on display as early as possible. The doors were to open at ten sharp, and she was well aware how quickly time could fly when there were too many people rushing around trying to do their own thing in the same area.

She was still smarting at the fact that she had been forced to bring seven-year-old Emily with her when she had arranged weeks before that Clive would take Emily along to Zachary's football training that morning.

"I'm sorry, Al," he had said at 7 a.m., when she took him up a cup of tea and let him know that the twins had both had breakfast and would be happily occupied in the living room until he went down and organized them for the football outing. "Apparently, the ref can't make the practice today, so they've asked me to stand in."

"But Clive, you promised! You know how important this morning is to me. Can't someone else be ref? How difficult can it be?"

He bristled. "It's a *very* important role, and it needs someone who's been trained to do it. You know I used to ref when I was at uni. Of course I should step up to help when the team needs my training and expertise."

"And what about the Waggy Tail Club, for which I have a very high level of training and expertise? This is an important income stream for us, as well as an outlet for me that recognizes my skills in a way that fits in with our family life. Come on, Clive. Don't let me down on this!"

"Sorry, Ali," he sighed, reaching out to take her hand. "I realize this has come at a very bad time, but I can't help it. You'll just have to take Emily with you. She'll love it. You know she will. And she'd be bored to tears having to stand out in the cold watching football for a couple of hours. She'd get up to no end of mischief."

"There's a lot more scope for her to get up to mischief at Hope Hall this morning, especially when I'm going to be so busy supervising the agility demonstration." To her great annoyance, she felt tears pricking her eyes, and she batted off Clive's attempts to pull her into his arms. "Look, just don't! Leave me alone. I'm going to be late now, because I'll have to sort Emily out before we can leave."

"I'm so sorry, Al," he said, his face suitably forlorn.

Resisting a strong impulse to throw something at him in an attempt to knock that stupid expression off his face, she turned on her heel and marched out of the room.

"Mummy! Mummy!" Back at Hope Hall, Emily's voice broke across Ali's thoughts as she struggled to set up their trestle table. "I need a wee, Mummy. Can you take me?"

"Em, the toilets are just over there. Can you see the sign on the door? I'll watch you go in, and you can just come straight back over here when you've finished."

The little girl's face puckered, as if she were about to cry. "There's no need to cry, Emily. You're seven years old, a big girl now – and you can do this on your own. I'll be here to watch you. I'm not going anywhere."

Two minutes later, after Emily's flat refusal to comply and her heartfelt wailing had turned all eyes towards Ali in disapproval, she gave up what she was doing and took Emily to the loo. Her daughter immediately brightened up, chatting and smiling as if nothing had happened. By the time they returned to the stall, having had to take a detour to the serving hatch to buy a packet of biscuits and a hot chocolate to persuade Emily to sit down quietly to have her snack, Ali glanced at her watch to see that it was nearly nine o'clock.

"Can I help with anything?"

Ali knew the voice must belong to Ray, because a sandy-coloured, wire-haired ball of energy had thrown himself at her legs at speed.

"Banjo, sit!" she commanded.

217

Banjo obediently did as he was told, looking up at her with a lop-sided grin.

"What he's trying to ask," grinned Ray, "is can *we* help? Would you like me to lay out the agility course? I've got the plan of what you have in mind."

"Oh Ray, would you? I'm so far behind with everything. I've had to bring Emily with me this morning, and she's not keen on being ignored. She's driving me crackers."

"It looks as if she's found a friend," Ray smiled, nodding towards the little girl, who was on her knees being enthusiastically greeted by Banjo. "He'll keep an eye on her, won't you, boy? Don't you let Emily out of your sight. Have you got that?"

Banjo had turned his attention to his owner and seemed to be listening to every word, with his ear comically tilted to one side. Then he barked, as if understanding and agreeing to this command.

"Right, I'll go and get started outside," said Ray. "Come out when you're ready to make the final adjustments."

Because of Ray's help, Ali had been able to get the stall laid out by opening time at half past nine with an impressive array of raffle prizes donated by members and supporters of the club. She also had a rota in place to ensure that the stall was manned throughout the morning. Ali had taken Emily outside with her, along with her new canine companion, who was dutifully staying by Emily's side so her mother could oversee the start of the agility display, which would last for most of the morning. Time flew past, especially once the hall started filling up with people willing to part with their money for the range of excellent local causes that had set up their own fundraising stalls.

It was at just gone eleven when Ali glanced over, for the umpteenth time, to where Emily had been playing in a sandpit in the old school playground, with Banjo keeping watch alongside. They had gone! Ali frantically looked around, searching for Emily's distinctive red coat, but there was no sign of her or Banjo.

"Ray!" Ali yelled in panic. "Ray, Emily's disappeared! Did you see them leave? Where are they?"

His face full of concern, Ray told her he would take a good look around as they couldn't have gone far.

"But the road is right there!" Ali cried, anxiously scanning the street that ran alongside the playground wall in case her daughter had wandered off in that direction. "You don't think she'd have gone that way, do you?"

Ray touched her arm reassuringly. "Banjo's with her. He knows not to go near that road. They're probably in the main hall. I'll find them and bring them back here. Don't worry."

But ten minutes of urgent searching produced nothing. Ray had an announcement made over the tannoy system, asking if anyone had seen a seven-year-old girl in a red coat, but it brought no response. Most worryingly of all, Banjo had disappeared too. Ray felt a shudder of fear shoot down his backbone as he made his way back to where Ali was anxiously waiting. "I can't find her."

Ali's hand shot to her mouth as her eyes filled with fear.

"I've got everyone looking, but it's possible that the two of them have made their way off the premises."

"This is all my fault," stammered Ali, her hands shaking as she spoke. "I should have kept a closer eye on her."

"Look, why don't I go to the office and phone the police? They may have already found her, or at least they can make sure they keep an eye out for her."

"I'll come with you."

The two of them raced across the playground to the side entrance of the old school building. Ray's storeroom wasn't far from the administrator's office, and to his surprise, Ray found that the door was ajar. Pushing it open, he and Ali were greeted by the sight of Emily, sound asleep on a pile of rubber mats, with her arms around Banjo, whose eyes were bright as he looked up at them without moving so as not to disturb the sleeping girl. To one side of the pair was Ray's biscuit tin, which had been opened and apparently shared by the two friends.

Sighing with relief, Ali dropped to her knees, stroking Emily's forehead gently as she woke her daughter up. "Hello, my darling. Were you taking a nap?"

Emily nodded groggily. "I was cold. Banjo knew that, so he brought me in here. We had a snack."

Ali wasn't sure if she was crying or laughing when she heard that. "So I see. Well, thank you, Banjo, for taking such good care of our girl."

Banjo happily accepted Ali's stroke on the head with what looked like an enormous smile on his face.

"Do you need to get back to the agility display?" Ray asked.

"No, Jim's taken over now, but I'll go and explain what's happened. Gail's on hand too, so I'm sure they can manage. It's only a case of timing each dog's performance and keeping a record of the results now that we've got everything set up. I'm sure they won't mind holding the fort until everyone's had a go."

"Okay. Then how about Emily, Banjo and I go and grab a table in the foyer so we can all have a cup of hot chocolate to warm us up?" suggested Ray.

Ali smiled to see that Emily was almost out of the door before she could answer. Mouthing the words "thank you" to Ray, she watched them leave before heading back out to the playground.

Soon after the fayre finished at half past twelve just as Ali and Ray were packing away the final props from the agility course, Clive arrived with Zachary, who looked suitably muddy from his football game.

"How did it go?" he asked.

Before Ali could say a word, Ray stepped in. "Your wife has done a tremendous job here this morning, running a highly successful raffle as well as organizing a display of agility tests that were the highlight of the whole event. However, she still hasn't perfected the art of being in two places at once. More importantly, she doesn't have eyes in the back of her head, which any parent knows you need when you have a bored seven-year-old to look after on top of everything else."

Unsure of how to respond, Clive glanced at Ali with a smile. "Oh, she's great. I'm glad it's all been such a success."

"In the middle of it all, Emily disappeared. Everyone in the hall was searching for her, and we were on the point of calling the police when we found her safe and sound asleep in one of the side rooms."

"Oh, no harm done then, thank goodness!" Clive replied. "You gave everyone a scare, did you, Em?"

"Mummy was very upset," the little girl replied. "She thought she'd lost me."

"But you were there all the time, pumpkin," said Clive soothingly, ruffling her hair.

"I believe," continued Ray, "that you agreed to have Emily with you on what was a very important occasion for your wife. Because you changed the arrangements at the last minute, you caused Ali and everyone here a great deal of worry and concern."

"Oh well, I'm sorry to hear that. But I'm afraid it couldn't be avoided."

"Do you know, Clive, I was married for more than forty years to a wonderful woman who died just a few months ago. I probably took her for granted too. Now she's gone, I keep thinking of all the times when perhaps I let her down, or when I could have helped or reassured her, but didn't. I sincerely hope you don't look around one day to find that your wife is no longer with you – not for the same reason, of course, but because marriage is a partnership where you have to be able to rely on one another. Ali can't trust you to do what you say you'll do. Marriages have fallen apart for less than that. If you value your family, and in particular your remarkable wife, I suggest you take a long, hard look at how well

221

you're doing as a husband before it's too late." And with that, Ray whistled to Banjo, and the pair walked off towards his storeroom.

Chapter 12

Phil had sounded so excited on the phone. "Can you come down to Chichester tomorrow?" he had asked. "That's your day off this week, isn't it?"

"It is, but I'd planned a hot date with the washing machine and ironing board," Maggie replied. "Whatever could you offer to drag me away from that?"

"A surprise?"

"Really? You know how impatient I am. You'll have to tell me."

"Well, perhaps it's more of a suggestion."

"Now I'm even more curious. You've got to tell me now!"

His chuckle was warm and deep. "If you want to know more, you're just going to have to come. Could you get here by ten, do you think?"

So there she was, turning into his driveway with five minutes to spare.

"Great, you're here!" he said when he opened the door, giving her a quick hug as he grabbed his coat from the stand in the hallway. "Let's go in my car. Hop in!"

"Where are we going?"

"Just get in and I'll show you."

He drove towards the centre of the town, parking not far away from the hotel where they had celebrated Sandra's birthday a couple of weeks earlier. Intrigued, Maggie climbed out of the car, at which point he took her hand and walked her, at quite a pace, towards Priory Park.

Not sure what she should be looking for, she almost tripped

223

when he suddenly stopped in front of an empty shop. But what a sight it was! It was the perfect setting for an olde worlde teashop, with huge, latticed bay windows. There was a short pathway leading up from the pavement through a tiny cottage garden that wasn't looking its best during those winter months.

"What do you think?" he asked earnestly.

She looked at him in confusion. "It's beautiful. The perfect teashop location."

"Right answer. You've always wanted your own teashop and this one is up for sale."

Her expression was puzzled. "But I can't afford it."

"I can."

She laughed. "But you can't bake cakes."

"You can."

"What are you saying? That you're interested in buying this?"

"Only if you're interested in running it."

"But it wouldn't be mine."

"It would be if it were our joint business. If we owned it together."

"As business partners, do you mean?"

"Or something more? We're something more than that, aren't we?"

Maggie opened her mouth to answer, then closed it again because she couldn't quite get her head around what he seemed to be asking.

"Oh look, Steve's here. He's the estate agent and an old friend of mine. He can show us around. You can take a good look before either of us says anything more. See how you feel once you've had a chance to take a look around inside."

The moment Maggie walked up the garden path and through the open door, there was no doubting what she thought. It felt as though she'd stepped back in time as she pictured the past elegance of white tablecloths, patterned china and sugar cubes served with tongs. Round tables of various sizes had been positioned across the large room, which had presumably been the two main downstairs rooms in the original, rather large, cottage. On one side, at the back of the room, a staircase led up to another wide seating area.

There were chintzy curtains at all the windows, and at the rear of the building a set of French doors opened out on to a courtyard garden, where more tables were neatly stacked, ready for the summer months. To one side, in the middle of the downstairs room, was a long display cabinet, on which Maggie could just imagine cakes of every kind tempting customers to try a special treat. Most impressive of all was the kitchen, which was bigger than she'd imagined, and very well equipped for the kind of baking that would be done in a vintage teashop like this. Maggie barely heard a word the estate agent said. She was too busy imagining how the shop would look if it were hers.

Then she zoned in as Steve continued. "I think I mentioned, Phil, that Mrs Claxton, who's owned this shop for nearly twenty years, has just retired, but she feels very strongly that she wants to sell it to the right person. Someone who will understand what a treasure it is and love every minute of being here, as she has."

"What sort of trade did she do here? Did she have a lot of customers?" asked Maggie.

"This place was always full. She didn't take bookings, as a rule, so it was first come, first served. I've often seen a queue stretching right around the corner."

Maggie took a deep breath as she leaned back against the display counter.

"Look," continued Steve, "I've got another appointment in ten minutes, so let me leave you here with the details and you can give me a ring when you've had time to think about it. You can drop the keys back to me later, Phil. I must tell you, there's already been quite a bit of interest in the property, because of its location, from people who want to buy the shop for a different kind of business, but I know Mrs Claxton isn't keen on it changing. I doubt it'll stay on the market for long, though, so let me know as soon as possible if you're seriously interested."

The two men shook hands and Steve disappeared as Phil pulled two chairs out at a nearby table. He offered one to Maggie before sitting down beside her. "Well? What do you think?"

"I agree with you. It's everything a proper teashop should be – and it's so well equipped and laid out. I love it."

"Enough to want to make it happen – with me?"

She turned to look properly at him. "It's not that easy, though, is it? I've just bought my new apartment and I've got a great job at Hope Hall. After all the upheaval of the past year I'm finally settled." She sensed his shoulders drop with disappointment and reached out to take his hand. "It's a great idea, Phil, but I just can't see how it could work."

"We make *us* happen!" he replied. "Maggie, I haven't got this all wrong, have I? I can't ever remember being as happy as I've been since we've been spending time together. I think we make a great team."

"As business partners?"

He hesitated before answering. "If that's what you want, yes. We could go into business together, with me putting up the money for the shop and you providing the expertise to make it a huge success."

"But I'd have to live here."

"Yes."

"But my family aren't here. I have a son, daughter and grandson that I adore."

"And they'd be just up the road. How long did it take you to drive here this morning? Twenty minutes?"

"But where would I live?"

His eyes bore into hers. "With me?"

She withdrew her hand from his. "I can't do that."

He ran frustrated fingers through what remained of his hair.

"This is all coming out wrong. I practised and practised how I would put this, and I've made such a mess of it. The most important thing, which I haven't had the courage to tell you before, is that I love you. I can't help it, I just do. And I can't think of anything better than sharing a future with you."

"A future?"

"I'd like to marry you, if you'll have me!"

"Phil, I'm obviously not very good at marriage. I've just got divorced."

"Through no fault of your own. That wasn't your choice. But this would be, Mags. I'm an old-fashioned guy who wants to be married to the woman he loves. And I love you very much indeed." He looked as if he hoped she might say the same thing in return, but she didn't.

He sighed, feeling as if she were slipping away from him. "I've said this too soon, haven't I? I meant to bide my time and give you a chance to find yourself again after all those years with Dave. Then I heard about this shop and I felt I had to tell you. But I'm putting pressure on you, and that's a mistake. Forget what I said. I'm sorry."

She slowly stretched out to take his hand in both of hers. "Honestly, Phil, I don't know what to say. I know what you mean about how right and comfortable it feels when we're together. You've brought fun, warmth, care and real friendship. You've changed everything, as if you've made the sun shine on my face, warming me right through after the coldness of the last year and a half."

"But…"

"But I don't really know how to put my feelings into words. I still can't believe someone as wonderful as you should care about me, and I'm constantly waiting for you to walk away when you realize how very ordinary I am. I'm frightened to put a name to this and terrified at you using the word 'love', because for me that means absolute commitment. If I get to the point where I feel sure enough

227

to tell you I love you, then I would be saying yes to everything else – to leaving Hope Hall, moving away from my family, selling my apartment, taking on the shop and walking down the aisle with you, if that's what you really want. But I just can't imagine that happening to me, because what on earth do you see in me? I'm plain and dumpy, and I made a mess of my marriage, and I'm full of doubt and fear and worry about all sorts of things. Why on earth would you want to share your life with someone like me?"

"Because I love you," was his simple reply.

She leaned in closer until their heads were touching. "I think I need to go now, so I can sort my thoughts out a bit."

"Of course. You will ring me, though, won't you? You're not thinking about ending this or anything terrible like that? I remember you doing that before, when I first asked if we could actually meet up at last. You practically put the phone down on me, and that was it. You shut me out. I was in an awful state. I had to come and dig you out of your garden shed in the end."

Maggie smiled at the memory, but she could hear a note of despair in his voice. "Of course I'll ring," she assured him, kissing him lightly on the cheek. "Nothing will change the way we are now, but I do need to think through our plans for the future."

He nodded, bringing her hand to his lips and kissing it for several long seconds. "I'll drive you back to your car."

He rose and headed out, while Maggie took one last look around the shop before closing the door behind her and following him down the path.

The panto was due to take place in less than two weeks' time, on the last Saturday before Christmas, and tickets for the matinee and evening performances were almost sold out. As the big day drew nearer, panic was beginning to set in – not just for Kevin, but for some of the other characters too.

Mary Barrett was a bag of nerves. "I'm even practising my

lines in my dreams," she wailed to a long-suffering Trevor. "I woke myself up the other morning because I suddenly shouted out: 'My fairy magic will make sure/That wicked stepmother is shown the door!'"

"That's all right, then," sighed Trevor. "You know the words so well you can say them in your sleep. Actually, I've heard you say them so many times that I could probably say them in *my* sleep too!"

"I'll dry up, I know I will. And you know they're using some sort of firework to go *poof* when I appear on stage?"

"*Poof?*" he grinned. "A firework that goes *poof?*"

"Oh, Trevor, stop it! You know exactly what I mean. But my fairy costume is made of nylon net. What happens if they get it wrong? I could go up in smoke."

"*Poof!*" he chuckled.

She tapped him smartly on the arm. "That's not funny. I can't bear you when you're like this, all smug and clever. Well, you've done it now. I'm not cooking your dinner. You can get your own."

"Takeaway?" he suggested, suddenly bright with interest. "That works for me."

A few streets away in the Wells household, Tyler walked into the living room just as his mum, Shirley, perched on a stool, was having her final costume fitting for her role as the wicked stepmother, Lady Devilia Hardup. Her sister, Barbara, was on her knees with pins gripped between her lips as she fixed the length of the hem.

"What do you think, Tyler?" asked Shirley. "Do I make a good wicked stepmother?"

He shrugged. "Well, Mother, you've always been 'wicked' – but not necessarily in a good way."

"What do you mean by that?" mumbled Barbara through clenched lips. "You've got a great mum."

"She's bossy, always sure she's right, illogical, infuriating and so *loud!*" he grumbled, although there was a definite gleam in his eye.

"Yes," agreed Barbara, pulling the last pin free to slide it into the hem. "And aren't you lucky she is? How many times has your mum had to go down to the school, or your employer or your girlfriend of the time, to sort out some mess or other that you've created? Your mum's a lioness. She fights for her cub. You should thank your lucky stars that you've always had her in your corner."

"In my *face*, more like!" he retorted. "*Why have you done this? What haven't you don't that?* Nag, nag, nag—"

"Listen!" Shirley's voice bellowed around the small room. "If you don't like it, leave! If you want to stay, you'd better say something nice about this frock I've squashed myself into. Does it make me look evil enough?"

Tyler suppressed a laugh. "Mum, you don't need a frock to look evil. Just give them one of your stares. That always did the trick with me – *and* my headteacher *and* my boss *and* half a dozen of my girlfriends. Just turn to the audience and give them a full blast of that look, and they'll behave like angels."

"Oh no they won't!" laughed Barbara.

"Oh yes they bloomin' well will!" boomed Shirley, causing the best crystal tumblers in the glass cabinet to rattle in alarm. "And don't you forget it!"

On the other side of the park, a dozen members of the Can't Sing Singers had gathered in what Ronnie flamboyantly referred to as his "music studio". It was, in fact, a large ramshackle shed at the bottom of his garden that let in the rain at one end and a gale-force wind at the other, but it was kitted out with a piano and an electric keyboard, shelves of sheet music and enough room for all of them to fit in, providing no one intended to throw their arms about as they sang.

"We can work on the movements when we're at the hall," he explained, "but this is where we can get the singing right."

"You mean *wrong*, don't you?" piped up a man's voice from the back row. "I wouldn't be here if I had any chance of getting the notes right."

"But you have to get the notes wrong in the right way," stated Ronnie, raising his voice above the chorus of complete agreement from the rest of the choir. "In order to sing badly, the Can't Sing Singers actually need to sing very well. So let's get down to it, shall we?"

At the same time, some of the younger members of the cast were gathering beside the low wall at the front of Broad Street Upper School so they could walk to Hope Hall together in time for the extra rehearsal at four o'clock that day. Jason was holding court, with dancers Gina and Chelsey hanging on to his every word.

"I reckon old Guilford is past it," Jason declared. "How many years has he been producing shows at the school? Can anyone remember anything about them? He's just so old-fashioned. And he's been producing the town's panto for ever, hasn't he? I reckon he should move over and let the younger generation produce something people *really* want to see."

"I hear the tickets for the panto are practically sold out, and the box office only opened three days ago." Chloe's voice was cool as she joined the group. "It seems people like the shows he produces. And anyway, panto's supposed to be traditional. Audiences don't want it to change all that much. They want to come every year and see more or less the same thing with a new title: Aladdin last year, Cinderella this time and probably Jack and the Beanstalk or Sleeping Beauty next Christmas."

"Oh, here she is," drawled Jason, "the love of my life, my wife-to-be..."

Chloe neatly sidestepped his outstretched arm.

"I'm taking my Cinderella to the cinema on Friday," announced Jason to the group in general. "She's coming to see the latest Marvel film with me. Her very own superhero will be holding her hand during the scary bits."

"I'm busy on Friday," replied Chloe.

"I'll come," said Gina hopefully.

"Saturday, then," continued Jason. "Chloe and I will go on Saturday."

"I'm busy then too."

"I'm not. And I'd really like to see that Marvel film," said Gina, who seemed to think it was worth trying again.

"I'll take you," said Sean. "You can come with me, Gina."

Gina barely looked at him as she retorted, "Thanks, but no thanks."

"If you really want to see the film, Sean, I'll keep you company."

Sean turned towards Chelsey in surprise. "You will?"

"Yeah."

"Right! Okay then," he agreed, pleased to know there was someone who wanted to go with him.

Jason hadn't taken his eyes off Chloe. "You will go out with me in the end, my dear Chloe. It's our destiny. But I can wait. I'm a patient man."

"You're an idiot."

"Oh no, my beloved, the only idiot we know is that Kev, who's making such a mess of playing Buttons. What a mistake old Guilford's made with him. He's hopeless."

"He's not, actually," snapped Chloe. "He's nervous, but that's not surprising when you lot are glaring at him all the time, trying to make him feel uncomfortable. I reckon he might just surprise us all."

"And pigs might fly!" answered Jason. "*Oink, oink, oink…*"

Chloe turned on her heel. "I'll see you there."

And without a backward glance, she strode off towards Hope Hall, followed by several of the girls in the group who gathered up their bags and hurried to catch up with her.

Celia had been systematically working her way through the tall wooden cupboards in Uncle Joe's office, trying to line up paperwork with the agreements she could see listed on the computer. With Joe rarely coming into the office now that his retirement was just over a week away, Celia had found a sympathetic ally in his long-time PA, Valerie Goddard.

"He's always been a nightmare with paperwork," Valerie explained with an expression that was more indulgently sympathetic than businesslike. "Whenever he throws papers on my desk, I have to work through them line by line to get everything on the system correctly. Often I've had to ring up the PA of the client he was talking to so the two of us could make sure all the details were present and correct on both sides."

And then that day, completely by chance, Celia discovered a bulky old metal document box. It was locked and firmly tucked away at the back of the top shelf of the far-end cupboard, and she'd only found it once she had clambered up a set of steps to check that she hadn't missed any paperwork in her uncle's haphazard filing system. With great care, she'd pulled the box down and on to the floor. Then she had dug around in the desk drawer, where she had previously noticed a couple of stray keys. Neither had fitted the lock.

"Valerie," she asked, as she walked through to the PA's office, "have you got any idea what's in here?"

Valerie looked up from her keyboard. "Oh, I haven't seen that for a while," she said with a smile. "Those are Joe's personal papers. He told me there's nothing in there that I need to know about – just family bits and pieces, I think."

"Do you have the key?"

"I think he keeps it with him. I've only ever seen him open it a couple of times in all the years I've been working with him. Because it's so personal, he's never gone into detail about the contents, and I've never asked."

Deep in thought, Celia made her way back inside the office. Why would Uncle Joe keep family papers there when Aunt Trish was known for being great at keeping all documents, photos and memorabilia relating to the family in apple-pie order at home? And whatever they were, why did Joe keep them locked up and stashed away in such an inaccessible corner? These thoughts niggled away at her all day.

She had already discovered how hit and miss Joe's records seemed to be, but she began to wonder what she *hadn't* been able to find, and to dread what the mystery box might contain. She knew she should just take it around to Uncle Joe's that evening so he could open it for her. No doubt they would laugh together at the family memories it contained. And that was exactly what she *had* decided to do – until she heard Valerie call goodbye as she left for the evening and Celia found herself staring at the box on the floor in front of her. Without a second thought, she snatched it up, grabbed her coat and briefcase, and left the office.

Once she was home, she placed the box on the kitchen worktop while she went out to the garage to find a large flat-headed screwdriver and a hammer. Five minutes later, after several failed attempts to break the lock, she managed to prise the box open.

It was full of files – probably about twenty in all, she guessed. Taking a quick look through the first few she pulled out, she didn't immediately recognize what they were. So she grabbed a bottle of white wine and a glass, popped a ready meal in the microwave and made herself comfortable at the large kitchen table in the middle of the room. Placing her reading glasses firmly on her nose, she started to read.

Kath walked up the garden path to Ida's door and rang the doorbell. She had promised the social worker that she would visit Ida as soon as Percy had had time to settle in. An ambulance had brought him from Abbotsbury Nursing Home the morning before, and Kath was keen to see how Ida was coping with her new lodger – and how *he* was coping with his rather bossy new nurse. Because Kath was the organizer of the town's Good Neighbours scheme, the social worker had been happy for her to keep a regular eye on the pair and report back with any problems she felt they were having.

Kath hardly recognized Ida when she opened the door. She was smiling, and Kath had never seen Ida smile before.

"Come in," she said. "He's just having breakfast. He'll be pleased to see you."

Kath glanced inside the first door on the right-hand side, where a bedroom had been kitted out for Percy while he recovered. A hospital bed had been delivered, which enabled him to get in and out or sit up quite easily. The sheets were neatly tucked in and the pillow case had been crisply ironed. There was a bedside cabinet on which his pills, a pair of glasses, and a water jug and tumbler stood. Discreetly placed in one corner was a commode, presumably to save Percy having to wander through the house in the dead of night. There was a jug of fresh flowers on the sideboard, a radio on the shelf above the bed and a television set in the far corner, operated by a handset that lay close at hand by the bedside.

"That looks great, Ida. Well done!"

"It seems to work," the older woman agreed, plainly pleased at the compliment.

Percy was sitting in the lounge with a folding breakfast table laid out in front of his high-backed armchair. On it was a bowl of muesli, a selection of fruit, a glass of orange juice, a boiled egg and some wholemeal toasted soldiers. After greeting Kath, he looked at the breakfast tray with disdain. "No bacon. No black pudding. Not even a fried slice!"

"That's right," smiled Kath. "I see Ida is looking after you exactly as she should. Everything on that tray will do you good, Percy. She'll have you fighting fit again in no time."

"And another thing!" he grumbled. "I would have thought I'd need lots of rest after all I've been through, but this woman has had me walking up and down the garden path. Whatever will the neighbours think if they see me tottering along behind that

235

Zimmer frame? They'll think I'm an old fella who's completely past it. And she seems to have forgotten that I've broken my hip. She should have a bit more compassion."

"You *are* old, and you've got a brand new hip that needs some decent exercise," retorted Ida, her eyes warm as she looked at him. "I know it hurts, but it's got to be done. You're going to come out of this even more of a spring chicken than you were before."

"Will I be able to tap dance?"

"Of course. You'll be a regular Fred Astaire."

"That's good," grinned Percy, "because I've never been able to tap dance before!"

Kath laughed, taking a seat on the settee beside him. "I see you two are getting along famously."

"She's a bully."

"He's like a naughty little kid."

"Do you think, Percy," asked Kath, "that you could manage in your own home at the moment?"

"Probably not." He shrugged.

"And if you're honest, is your every need being taken care of by your highly efficient, if a little bossy, nurse here?"

His chin dropped towards his chest as he considered the question. "I like Marmite on my soldiers!" he declared at last.

"I can do that," agreed Ida.

"And I like a glass of beer every afternoon."

"I've got Guinness in. It's full of iron, so it'll give you energy. That's better for you than beer."

He grunted, but a smile was beginning to creep across his face. "And I like two sugars, not one, in my tea."

"You'll have one sugar, or you can make your tea yourself."

"You're a hard woman, Ida Miller!"

"Well, thank goodness I am. I might just save you from yourself."

Kath sat back with relief. These two were going to be just fine.

Who would have thought it? They were chalk and cheese, but somehow it worked!

Hope Hall was almost empty, with the afternoon clubs over and the evening meetings yet to begin, as Maggie walked out of the kitchen to head home one evening. – so it was a surprise to see an elderly lady standing on her own in the main hall. She was staring at the display boards put up to celebrate the centenary of the building with photos and memorabilia that had been collected to show the role the hall had played in the town throughout its one hundred years.

"Are you okay?" Maggie asked. "Do you need any help?"

"That's my Colin," the lady replied, pointing to a picture that had been taken in 1967. "I remember that night here at the hall. It was a Valentine's dance, and I came with my friend Gloria. She disappeared, because she knew someone in the band. They were local but quite famous at the time, because they'd had a record in the charts. Simon Dupree and the Big Sound, they were called. So I was left on my own.

"I got fed up with being a wallflower while everyone else was dancing, so I got up and joined in all by myself. It was really crowded, and the bloke behind me kept bumping into me, so I lost my rhythm. He made me so mad that I turned around to tell him to back off, and there he was! My Colin – blue eyes, a nice smile, not the best of fashion sense, but I liked the look of him straight away.

"We decided to dance together, then a year later we danced down the aisle, and we never stopped dancing to exactly the same beat. We got on well, Colin and me. He was a very, very nice man."

"*Was?*" asked Maggie gently.

The woman's face puckered. "I lost him ten days ago. Oh, he'd been ill for a long time, poor love. He was so brave. Cancer's a devil, isn't it? How many times did I tell him he should give up smoking? But he couldn't quite manage it, and it got him in the end. Lung cancer. Very painful. It's hard to see the man you love go through that."

Maggie reached out to touch the woman's arm, unsure what to say.

"I wouldn't let them take him away from me, though. I nursed him till the end. He did ask if I'd prefer him to go into a home or a hospice, because he was worried it was too much for me, but I'd spent more than fifty years looking after that man of mine, and I intended to do my best until the very end. I wanted every last second with my Colin. I wasn't going to miss a moment."

"That must have been so painful for you," said Maggie.

The woman's eyes misted over with tears, which she quickly brushed away. "Yes, but I'd promised to love him in sickness and in health. I'd had the good days, and I wasn't going to run away when the going got tough."

"And how are you doing? Have you got family around you? All the help you need?"

"Oh yes, we've got a couple of brilliant daughters who are still local. I'm all right. It's just the night times when we always used to cuddle up to watch TV, or the mornings when he'd bring me up a cup of tea before he went off to work. I especially miss him then. And I talk to him. You might think I'm mad, but I still talk to him like I always did, as if he's right there beside me. He'd probably laugh out loud if he knew I was doing that."

"It sounds like he was a lovely man."

"Oh, he was," sighed the woman, looking longingly at the old photo. "We did a lot of laughing together. We had the same sense of humour, but then whatever we did I just enjoyed being with him. I hated heights, but he got me climbing up mountains in Scotland. I'm scared of flying, but he persuaded me to board a plane to Spain one year, and we ended up flying off for our summer holidays every year after that. I can't swim, and I'm scared of water, but he got me on a cruise for our golden wedding anniversary. He gave me courage. I'd always thought of myself as mousy, not wanting to stretch beyond what felt completely safe, but he brought me out of myself. He even persuaded me to join him on a parachute jump for charity once. Never again – but I did it! He was there, and we did it together. Having a partner like that who truly loves you just as you are, and encourages you to be more than you ever thought you could be – well, that's a wonderful thing."

Before Maggie could think of how to respond, the woman looked up at the clock above the foyer's double doors. "Goodness, I should go. My daughter will panic if I'm not where she thinks I should be. But this has been nice. It's a good memory. Thank you for listening. Colin would be pleased that I wasn't talking to myself in a public place! Bye now."

For several minutes after she'd gone, Maggie stayed where she was, gazing at the photo but not really looking at it.

Chapter 13

Celia was in turmoil, unable to get the contents of the secret box out of her mind. At first it had been difficult to work out exactly what the papers revealed. She knew she still didn't have the complete picture, but a series of discoveries had brought her to the conclusion that her kindly uncle Joe Munro was most definitely a wolf in sheep's clothing.

The first shocking discovery had been a pile of bank statements dating back more than fifteen years in the name of Munro Holdings. A quick check showed that while this company looked official, there was no mention of it at Companies House, which immediately aroused her suspicions. It took her a while to find out about the nature of the bank in which the Munro account was held, but a bit of detailed searching told her it was an old and established private bank – the sort that worked with the old boy network, where questions weren't asked and secrets were discreetly kept.

She drew in a sharp breath when she saw that the balance on all the annual statements in the box had never fallen below five million pounds. She decided to find out where the money had come from, and was very quickly able to trace it back to huge one-off payments made by clients whose folders were all inside the metal document tin. The few details she managed to find told her that they mostly belonged to elderly women, many of whom had never married, the others apparently widowed.

Given her natural instinct to follow the money, Celia decided to check on any payments made by Munro Holdings over the years. As each new payment came in, Munro Holdings had apparently invested large sums quite wisely on the money market in ways that wouldn't draw much attention to the transactions. Joe's expertise was evident in the direction and the means by which he had invested – some here, some there, some safe, some risky – but his skill on the money market had doubled and sometimes tripled the investments he had made.

However, none of the interest from those investments ever came back to Munro Holdings. Instead, it was paid into two separate bank accounts held at the same private bank. And when she saw that these two bank accounts had names she recognized – Ventus, Joe's beloved first racehorse, and Optimus, the horse that had replaced him – her blood ran cold. Each account had more than four million pounds in it, and the only signatory on both accounts was Joseph Munro.

Added to that, a will had been drawn up at the same time as each investment, in which the client's assets were listed. Looking closely at the small print, Celia could see that none of them made mention of the client's investment in Munro Holdings, which meant it wouldn't be flagged up as part of their estate when they died. And Joseph Munro was listed as the witness for each will.

Eventually, after a night of tossing and turning, Celia got up in the morning knowing what she had to do. She placed all the papers back in the tin, but instead of going straight to work, she headed for her uncle's house.

Aunt Trish answered the door. She looked surprised to see Celia, but welcomed her warmly. "You'll be wanting Joe, I expect. Not long now before you take over his job completely. Honestly, Celia, it can't happen soon enough for me. It'll be lovely to see him relax a bit after all these years. When I think back over the number of meals and nights that have been spoiled because Joe was on the phone to investors all over the world. Go on through. He's in his study. I'll bring you both some coffee."

Joe's face lit up as she opened the study door and walked in, but the moment he recognized the folders she was carrying, his expression changed. "Oh, so you've found them. I knew you would. The contents of that box are extremely good news for both of us."

"How can you say that?" she hissed, slamming the folders down on his polished mahogany desk. "You've been taking money for investments from vulnerable clients, and you've never paid them any dividends. And for years you've been creaming off all the interest for yourself! At best, it's dishonest. At worst, you should be locked up!"

"For heaven's sake, Celia, stop being so melodramatic. I haven't hurt anybody. My clients were perfectly happy that their investments were safe, and they were far too rich to notice whether any interest was paid or not. What's more, they had all begged me to help them. They were elderly ladies living alone, with no family around, mostly because they'd outlived them all. A few of them were spinsters, never married, and the rest were widows who'd inherited estates and far too much money from their husbands. They simply wanted advice on how to invest their funds, and I provided that help."

"And that help included persuading them to draw up a new will that didn't mention these investments at all, which you signed as the witness!"

"Of course I'd advise them to make a new will when there were no longer any family members around to take into consideration. I was doing them a favour."

"And were those wills made available when the ladies died?"

"Sadly not," he said, his eyes locked on hers. "They apparently died intestate. Occasionally a distant relative came sniffing around to see if there was anything left to them, and often there was – houses and land, and so on. And if those investments had been discovered, their contribution could simply have been paid with a modest amount of interest, and no suspicions would have been aroused."

"How often did that happen?"

242

"Never, as far as I can recall."

"So you just invested their money yourself for years and kept huge sums of interest that should have been theirs."

"No one knew. No one wondered. No one got hurt. And I'd done my duty in making sure their investments were safe. In fact, they couldn't have been safer than with me looking after them."

"How did you meet these women?"

"Oh, a few I'd known for years because their families or husbands were part of the county scene. Others I knew from one of my clubs. Mostly I came across them through their banking investments. I just followed up anything that seemed interesting, and every now and then I hit the jackpot."

"Are you saying that those ladies who met you through your role at Apex Finance thought it was the company that was working on their behalf?"

"Some of them did. Others were so wealthy, and totally inept at keeping track of their money, they just accepted that I was helping to organize things in a more efficient way. They didn't really care whether it was me or Apex sorting the details out for them."

"All the better for you!"

"And for you, my darling. You noticed, of course, the names of the two accounts into which the proceeds have been paid."

"Optimus, your most successful racehorse to date—"

"And Ventus, my first horse, and the one you adored from the day you were born. Well, my dear Celia, everything in that account is for you – my gift to you as your doting godfather. It's all set up so the money in Munro Holdings is constantly invested and the profits are automatically transferred into the Ventus and Optimus accounts every month. Thanks to my careful investment, each of those accounts has been paid in excess of a half million pounds a year for some time. Congratulations, my dear. You are a very rich woman, and you're getting richer every day. Best of all, you have nothing to do but enjoy it, with my love!"

Extra rehearsals were called for the whole cast on both weekend days before the show began. It was utter chaos on the Saturday, as Jan's husband, Keith worked with his team, who were mainly Rotary members, to build the sets and get the staging and lights working. That task might have been easier if Barbara and Della had not been trying to hold rehearsals for the big dance numbers at the same time – the ones for the ball, in the woods and at the wedding – as well as the opening scenes of both acts. Cast members arrived late, tempers were frayed, characters forgot their lines, harmonies were cringeworthy and Maurice felt as though he had steam coming out of his ears.

Towards the end of the afternoon, after several failed attempts by Maurice to make himself heard over the general babble, one voice brought everyone to silence.

"Shut up, all of you!" yelled Shirley. "We can't hear ourselves think. Maurice has notes to give you before we try a full run-through. Just belt up and listen."

But in the end there was no chance of a run-through that evening. A couple of the characters had to go to work, while others had to get home to cook dinner for the family. So with a heavy sigh, Maurice declared that there would be a full rehearsal without costumes the next morning, then another with costumes in the afternoon.

By the end of the following day, everyone was exhausted and very disheartened at the way the rehearsals had gone. It had taken them until three o'clock to complete the first run-through, and it was five o'clock before they had donned their costumes, and the dress rehearsal started. It was eight o'clock by the time they called it a night without even starting the second half. Cinderella hadn't met up with her glass slipper. The Ugly Sisters hadn't practised their encounter with the giant spiders in the deep, dark wood. Buttons's voice couldn't be heard at the back of the hall, and Prince Charming kept disappearing outside for a cigarette and a can of lager, missing all but one of his entrances.

"Oh well," said Liz from the side of the stage, where she was in charge of props, "you know what they say about a bad rehearsal."

"Give up?" suggested Roger.

Nobody within earshot had an answer to that.

With the wedding just a week and a half away, Kath decided to take a few days off. This meant that her last appearance at Hope Hall before becoming Mrs Richard Carlisle would be the Saturday evening of the panto. The two of them had seats far enough back in the crowd to avoid the usual danger of being too near the front on such occasions! The build-up to Christmas at the hall was always frantically busy, with seasonal gatherings and parties of all sorts every day and some evenings too, and there was a general sense of anticipation in the air as Christmas Day approached. Two days before that special day, she would walk down the aisle to say her vows to Richard.

"Are you nervous?" asked Liz when Kath popped into the kitchen to grab a coffee.

"I keep thinking I should be, but honestly I'm not. With such a small chapel it'll be a nice, quiet wedding, which suits us fine. I'm just thinking of it as one wonderful day at the start of the rest of my life full of happy days."

Without thinking, Liz leaned forward to give Kath a hug. "I'm really pleased for you, love. You deserve that sort of happiness."

As the two friends chatted away, Jan and Kevin were working in tandem at the back of the kitchen preparing lunches, with Kevin spooning the chicken, mushroom and tarragon mixture into individual pastry cases and Jan popping the lids on and expertly crimping the edges.

"I was terrible," Kevin groaned. "I told Maurice before we started that me singing little ditties for the old ladies here is not the same as belting out a big number to a large audience. They couldn't even hear me."

245

"But there wasn't a proper audience there, Kev, and the acoustics will be quite different when the hall is full and the microphones are set up properly. I can see your confidence has been knocked by that horrible Jason and his cronies. Take no notice of them."

"They're on my case all the time. They're whispering and laughing about me whenever I try to rehearse. They think I'm no good, and they're probably right."

"I think," said Jan, turning to look at him properly, "that once you have a real audience in front of you – one that is determined to enjoy every minute – you will come into your own. Believe in yourself, Kev. *We* all do. We know you'll be absolutely fine."

Still unconvinced, Kevin huffed out a big sigh before digging his spoon into the chicken mix to fill another pie.

Richard could tell from Celia's voice on the phone that something was dreadfully wrong. She said she was on her way over, and she made it in record time. Just fifteen minutes later she was walking into the kitchen, where he already had her favourite coffee waiting for her. Half an hour after that, Richard's face was duly sombre as the two of them sat together at the table with the documents from the metal case spread out before them.

"You and I have known Joe all our lives," said Richard at last. "He's always been our cuddly, loving uncle. But this shows a really mean streak that has totally shocked me."

"Now I've had a few days to think about all this," Celia replied, "I find myself remembering occasions when I've heard him be quite brutal to the lads at the stable or to waiting staff in restaurants. And we both know how spiteful and rude he can be about anyone he disagrees with. He's a man who always expects to have his own way."

"What's he like at work? Is he as ruthless there?"

"He's good at his job, and he gets results. Apex is an American corporation, and the top management is into strategies, deadlines, goals and bonuses. But Joe has always managed to do his own thing his own way, and because he makes money for them, they indulge him. They think he's quaint but good."

"And don't you have to have a ruthless streak to be that good? If so, do you feel you have that character streak in you?"

"In business, yes, I think I do, but I hope I have a sense of morality about the way I work. I believe that good ethics and a reputation for fair practice make me someone people can trust with their money."

Richard's gaze ranged across the papers laid out before them. "And is this just an ethical misdemeanour or a crime?"

"Joe says that if any of these ladies or their beneficiaries wanted their investment money back, he would simply give it to them. And he would also argue that the interest that has found its way into those two private bank accounts would never have been earned without his input and expertise on the money market, so it's money he's created and therefore has a right to keep. So in that respect, it's ethical."

"But?" Richard prompted.

"But," Celia continued, "I think it's a crime."

"Then you have a painful decision ahead of you, and it's one that only you can make. I'm here, though, and I'll back you in every way I can."

She smiled. "Except that you're getting married and going away on honeymoon in just a few days' time."

"You'd better make a decision fairly quickly, then."

"How are *you*? You're making a big decision too. Are you feeling okay about it all?"

His face lit up with warmth and love. "I've never been more certain about anything."

Celia nodded approvingly. "I must make sure that I'm certain about my decision too."

A queue stretched along the low wall at the front of Hope Hall long before the doors opened for the matinee panto performance. Free seats had been given to all members of the Grown-ups' Lunch Club and many other elderly and vulnerable people in the community. As the audience took their seats, the hall seemed to be half filled with silver-haired pensioners and the other half with chattering young children and their parents.

With Betty, Flora and Doris all backstage as members of the chorus, Robert, John and Connie eagerly found their places amid a block of seats reserved for the Grown-ups. Connie dug out her flask of coffee and the packets of biscuits she had brought along as usual to stave off afternoon hunger for members of her group.

Robert glanced towards the back of the hall to see that the clock was ticking down to "curtain up" time at two. It was then that his face lit up with delight. "Percy!" he cried out. "You're here. Welcome back, old man!"

Leaning heavily on one crutch, Percy looked triumphant as he slowly made his way down the middle aisle. One by one, people turned to look around at him, and because so many had either been at the quiz night when he had fallen or heard about it since, a round of delighted applause broke out to greet him. Percy beamed at them all, even managing to wave at the welcoming crowd.

"Come along, Percy!" commanded Ida, who was following in his wake. "Keep going and get properly settled in your seat before the lights go down and the curtains come up. Look, I've organized a couple of places over there next to Connie. You've got a proper high-backed padded chair, so you should be comfortable."

She was right to chivvy him along, because they had only just made it to their seats when the hall was plunged into darkness. A flash of light and a puff of smoke announced the arrival of Mary Barrett, a vision of fairy loveliness in a frothy costume that sparkled in different shades of purple.

"My name is Fairy Pollyetta,
My aim is just to make life better
For people who are kind and good,
Whom others don't treat as they should.

I've come to tell you a sad tale
About a beautiful young girl.
She is a poor lass, Cinderella,
Who spends her days in the kitchen cellar
Because she has a cruel stepmother,
Who causes her a lot of bother.

Lady Devilia is never kind,
She has a calculating mind,
She married Cinderella's dad –
That's when Cinders's life turned bad.

Lady Devilia is very vain,
To be most beautiful is her aim,
She's furious when her mirror tells her,
"More beautiful is Cinderella."

And so, against the girl she plots,
And keeps her scrubbing at the pots,
She lives in rags, she works all day,
For Cinders, life is just that way.

But you and I know that's not right,
So I plan to change her path tonight.

However bad her life may seem,
It's time our Cinders found her dream!"

And they were off!

The curtains opened on to a stage that was filled with villagers and children welcoming in the day with singing and dancing. One by one, the main characters appeared: pretty Cinderella, who is loved by everyone; her father, Baron Hardup, who is generally pitied because of his new wife, Lady Devilia, who soon makes her evil intentions known – to the sound of boos and hisses from the audience. Her two daughters, Beryl and Cheryl, then appeared in enormous hooped dresses with huge hats, brightly coloured wigs and over-the-top make-up, cleverly hiding the fact that beneath the costumes Trevor and Derek were having great fun hamming up their parts to the delight of the audience.

Next came the romantic moment when the dashing Prince Charming was introduced. He had switched places with his groom, Dandini, just before meeting Cinderella as she collected firewood. They instantly fell in love, and the story was well and truly underway.

But the greatest applause of the afternoon was reserved for Kevin, who burst on to the stage as Buttons to a huge cheer from the Grown-ups' Lunch Club members, who instantly recognized and loved him before he'd even opened his mouth.

Jan watched from the wings as the nervous young man grew in stature and confidence before her eyes, quickly becoming the cheeky chap who sang and danced his way into their hearts as he served the Grown-ups' dinners every Tuesday. From that moment on, there was no stopping Kev. He was funny and endearing. He ad-libbed and joked with the audience. He was athletic as he raced on and off the stage and danced comically in all the big production numbers. The audience melted when he confided in them about his love for Cinderella. It would have been so much easier if they hadn't known the end of the story. Sadly, their Buttons was destined for heartache, but they loved him all the more for it.

Two hours later, with their sides aching from laughter, the enthusiastic audience cheered and stamped their feet as the cast took their bows. The volume of their applause rose even higher when the handsome prince took Cinderella in his arms and swept her off her feet, before kissing her passionately.

"That's not in the script!" hissed Chloe, quickly pulling away.

"True," agreed Jason, "but the earth moved for you, didn't it, sweetheart? There's plenty more where that came from."

Gritting her teeth, Chloe pinned a bright smile on her face as the curtain closed. Then, her eyes blazing with indignation, she headed for her dressing room, with the jeers of Jason and the other lads ringing in her ears.

The cast had a couple of hours' break between shows before they were gearing up once more for the evening performance, which was due to start at seven. Once again, every seat in the hall was occupied as the Fairy Godmother opened the show in a puff of light and smoke.

Flushed with success from the matinee performance, it was clear that the actors were thoroughly enjoying themselves as the fairy tale unfolded. The performance wasn't completely seamless, however. Trevor, playing Ugly Sister Cheryl, was sitting comfortably at the side of the stage waiting for his entrance while the stage and props teams were desperately searching for Cinderella's magic ball gown, which had disappeared. There was a five-minute delay, during which they pushed Buttons on stage to keep the audience entertained. It wasn't until Cheryl got up to stretch her legs that the ball gown was discovered on the seat beneath her enormous skirt.

There was also a sudden panic when it was discovered that Cinderella's abandoned glass slipper had been moved to the wrong side of the stage during the interval, so when the prince and

Dandini arrived at the Hardups' house to see who it might fit, it took some desperate searching to find out what had happened to the panto's most important prop. Jason stepped up to entertain the audience, asking if they thought he was handsome and whether his lost love might miss him so much she would return to claim him. Watching him from the wings, Chloe thought he was the smuggest, most vain person she had ever met.

Then there was the highlight of the ball scene, when the Can't Sing Singers, all dressed as courtiers, stepped forward to perform an ear-piercing rendition of "I Could Have Danced All Night". They looked beautiful, they sang with great sincerity and emotion – and yet every single note, even if it wasn't exactly wrong, was definitely not right. It was hilarious, and many in the audience were dabbing their eyes with laughter by the end of their number.

Once again, it was Kevin who really stole the show. He had the audience eating out of his hand, warning him when the giant spiders were trying to steal his lunch bag, getting them all singing along with the words, highlighted by a bouncing ball on the screen that was pulled down from the ceiling, persuading a group of small children to come up on stage as "helpers", and laughing out loud whenever he got the better of the Ugly Sisters. They loved him – and they felt his pain when he so obviously minded that the handsome prince was claiming the hand of the girl he loved.

They watched as the prince triumphantly led his princess on to the stage in her wedding dress. As the final song came to a spectacular end, the cast members took their bows and the audience got to their feet. But when the prince lunged at Cinderella to claim his kiss, they were surprised to see Cinderella firmly push him away. Then, turning to Buttons who was standing beside her, she put her arms around his neck for a kiss that seemed to last for ever. The audience cheered louder than ever at that. Buttons had got the girl! That felt like a *much* better ending.

Everyone was in high spirits at the end-of-panto party Maggie had organized for the cast and crew once the audience had left. They were all ravenous after such a long and exciting day, and they tucked into Maggie's buffet with great enthusiasm. Next came the thumping rhythm of favourite disco numbers, which soon got everyone up on their feet – especially Kevin and Chloe, who couldn't take their eyes or hands off each other as they boogied and bopped and smooched, according to whether the track was fast or slow.

As the crowd started to disperse, Maggie looked across at Phil, who had come up to watch the show, and had then, in his usual way, rolled up his sleeves to help with the clearing up. Her heart lurched at the sight of that kind, practical man. She noticed he was standing just under the board where Colin's picture was displayed. What was it Colin's wife had said? Something about how wonderful it is to have a partner who truly loves you just as you are and encourages you to be more than you ever thought you could be.

And suddenly, without thinking twice, Maggie went over to tap Phil on the shoulder, inviting him to join her for the last dance. And there, in full sight of everyone, she kissed him. Then she kissed him again. And if anyone was surprised to see their businesslike catering manager acting like a lovestruck teenager, neither of them cared a bit.

To the strains of "Canon in D" by Pachelbel, Kath laid her hand in Trevor's as he led her down the aisle of the small family chapel, which looked warm and welcoming. It was decorated with hanging ivy, branches of bright-red holly berries and flickering candles that sparkled on every window ledge and surface. Around her, she saw the smiling faces of people who were dear to her, and ahead her gaze was drawn to the look of love on the dearest face of all.

With a nod of thanks to his son and best man, William, who looked resplendent in his naval uniform, Richard stepped forward to greet his bride and take her hand, thinking she looked breathtakingly beautiful in her elegant cream gown with a sparkle of diamonds in her hair. She felt his hand tighten around hers, and, hardly bearing to take their eyes off each other, they turned towards James as he started the service by welcoming everyone to the joyful occasion. Then he turned his attention to the couple with the words: "God is love, and those who live in love live in God, and God lives in them."

Then he looked up towards the congregation as he said: "In the presence of God, Father, Son and Holy Spirit, we have come together to witness the marriage of Richard Neville Carlisle and Katharine Anne Sutton, to pray for God's blessing on them, to share their joy and to celebrate their love."

Sitting in the pews on one side of the chapel, Maggie turned to look at Phil in the seat next to her, only to find that he was already watching her. They gazed at each other for several seconds before the words of the minister came back into focus.

"Richard, will you take Katharine to be your wife? Will you love her, comfort her, honour and protect her, and, forsaking all others, be faithful to her as long as you both shall live?"

His eyes still on Maggie, Phil silently mouthed the words, "I will."

"And Katharine, will you take Richard to be your husband? Will you love him, comfort him, honour and protect him, and, forsaking all others, be faithful to him as long as you both shall live?"

Gazing at Phil, Maggie's eyes filled with tears as she whispered, "Yes, I will. I love you."

Phil looked as if he were near to tears himself as he tipped his head towards her so that only she could hear. "And I love you too, Mags, so very much."

At the front of the chapel, Kath turned so that Richard could take her hand in his. She knew she would never forget the depth of emotion she saw in his eyes as he made his vows to her.

"I, Richard, take you, Katharine, to be my wife,
To have and to hold from this day forward;
For better, for worse,
For richer, for poorer,
In sickness and in health,
To love and to cherish,
Till death us do part;
According to God's holy law.
In the presence of God I make this vow."

Then it was Kath's turn to make her vows, drawing confidence and calmness from the loving devotion she saw in Richard's expression as she spoke. Next came the wonderful moment when he placed the wedding ring on her finger, after which James made the announcement she had longed to hear:

"In the presence of God, and before this congregation,
Richard and Katharine have given their consent
and made their marriage vows to each other.
They have declared their marriage by the joining of hands
and by the giving and receiving of rings.
I therefore proclaim that they are husband and wife.
Those whom God has joined together let no one put asunder."

And at that moment, Richard's face beamed as he leaned forward to kiss his wife. A round of delighted applause echoed through the little chapel as the congregation congratulated the new Mr and Mrs Carlisle.

Celia was acutely aware of Joe's presence, especially after the ceremony, when he was obviously trying to catch her eye across the room as the first guests arrived to be greeted with either coffee or champagne in the Ainsworth Hall dining room. She turned away as casually as she could, and was glad to find that she had been placed at a table on the opposite side of the room when they were asked to take their seats for lunch. She had already made her decision. He didn't know it yet, but he soon would.

After much soul-searching, she had followed a course of action that she knew would have consequences as devastating for her as for Joe. She had written to the president of Apex Finance in the States, offering her resignation from the role of UK finance director before she had even had time to take up the post properly. She went on to say that her decision would best be explained by the information contained in the attached papers, which were copies of every document she had found in the metal box. She invited him to show these documents to the corporation's auditors so they could rectify the wrongs they found there and investigate any other irregularities in the way the previous finance director had done business in the past.

She finished by saying that because that man was a relative, she felt it would be inappropriate for her to accept the role, and she hoped they would go on to find just the right person to take Apex Finance to even greater heights in the UK.

In doing this, Celia knew she had left herself without a job and probably a questionable reputation among the old boys' network in the finance world, who would feel that she was not a team player, and was therefore not to be trusted. She had written off her own career in the higher echelons of finance and started a process that could possibly lead to herUncle Joe, dearly loved for as long as she could remember, ending up in jail. But if his future looked bleak, hers didn't look much better. Who would employ her now?

Her thoughts were interrupted by the chink of a spoon on glass to get the room's attention. She looked up with some surprise to see that it wasn't the best man who was rising to his feet, but her brother, Douglas.

"I just wanted to welcome you all to my family home here at Ainsworth Hall – a fitting place for the marriage of my cousin Richard and his new wife, Katharine. Before we move on to the formal speeches, I just wanted to take this opportunity to give you all an important piece of news. You will notice that my wife Diana is not here with me today. She is with her mother, Eleanor, for the tragic reason that my father-in-law, Lord Harry Buxton, had a very serious stroke last night. His condition is critical and the doctors are not expecting him to pull through, especially as he has already been significantly weakened by a long bout of illness over several months.

"During that period, Lord Harry asked me to spend as much time as possible with him, discussing the future of the estate following his demise. Diana is his only child, but the estate traditionally goes to the nearest male descendant. That is Diana's cousin David, or 'Dave' as he prefers to be known. But Dave is rather… how shall I put it? A weak, disorganized man is how he should be described, I think. He lives in an artists' commune in Cornwall, and has neither the inclination nor the intention to take up his place on the family seat.

"And so Lord Harry, who thinks of me not just as his son-in-law, but as his own son, has graciously offered to bestow that honour upon me. The legal papers are being drawn up as I speak, and I will shortly become lord of the family manor. For that reason, my family and I will be vacating our home here as soon as possible. You can imagine my excitement to be leaving here to take up such a prestigious role, and I just wanted to use this opportunity to say farewell to you all!"

Whatever reaction he was expecting, Douglas sat down to stunned silence. It was William who recovered first, rising to his feet to get the traditional wedding toasts underway. William's speech was touching, ringing with affection for his father. He related several funny dad-and-son stories that had all the guests laughing along with him. He also gave a very moving tribute to his mother, echoing her wish that his father would find love and happiness again.

Then he looked towards Kath with a warm smile as he said that he shared his father's feelings about her joining their family, and that she had brought nothing but love and happiness to them both.

Trevor stood up next to pay tribute to Kath, singing her praises as a wonderful person and dear friend, and regaling those present with all that she had brought in terms of experience, expertise and enthusiasm to her work at Hope Hall. He also read out several messages for the couple, including a funny and affectionate greeting from Jane, Kath's sister in Australia. Jane promised a family visit to England in the spring, and said that she couldn't wait to meet her new brother-in-law.

Then the couple began to circulate around the tables, hugging and laughing with their guests, all of whom told them that they were thrilled to see the pair so happy together.

Just as proceedings were beginning to wind down, Douglas came over to take the vacant seat beside Celia. "Well, Sis, what do you think of the news?"

Celia was careful to keep her expression neutral. "It's a wonderful opportunity for you, Douglas. I hope you, Diana and the boys will settle happily in Berkshire, and that you'll enjoy the new role that's been bestowed upon you."

"Your brother lord of the manor, eh? I wish Dad could have seen this come to pass. He never believed in me. He was always talking me down, belittling my achievements. It seems Lord Harry can see qualities in me that our own father couldn't."

Celia remained silent. There was nothing to say.

"So," he continued, "I get the advancement I deserve, and you get what you've always longed for."

She eyed him with curiosity.

"You've always wanted to run the mill, and now it's yours! Take it over. Make of it what you want. I don't care. I have more important work to do. I've already sent a letter of resignation to the board. They've been angling to make you the chief executive for years, so you might as well get on with it."

Clearly taking satisfaction in the way her mouth had fallen open with shock and pleasure, Douglas got up from his chair and walked away without a backward glance.

"Do you think, husband dear, that we could quickly drive past Hope Hall on our way to the hotel this evening?" asked Kath as she nestled in towards Richard. A few minutes earlier, they had driven away from their wedding reception in his car, which had a sign saying "Just Married" emblazoned across the back, as well as a string of jangling tin cans that rattled along behind them.

He smiled across at her. "I think I should probably stop for a minute anyway to take those tins off the back. I'm not sure what the police would make of them."

And so it was that Kath stepped out of the car, still in her wedding dress, and looked up at the familiar face of Hope Hall. And a face it most definitely was – kindly and inviting, with windows that gleamed like sparkling eyes, and bright red doors that seemed to smile a welcome.

"Thank you," whispered Kath. "Thank you for drawing me here, for making me feel so at home, for allowing me the chance to get to know such wonderful friends and for finding me this dear man I love so much. I'm leaving now, but I'll be back after our honeymoon, ready to get working on your next hundred years. Look after them all while I'm gone."

As she turned to climb back into the car, the clouds parted just far enough for a glimmer of late afternoon sun to catch the front windows so that they seemed to light up in response to her words.

With a grin, she gave the hall a cheery wave and climbed back in beside Richard.

"Are you ready, Mrs Carlisle?"

"Ready for anything!" she smiled as he started up the car and they pulled away.

If you haven't yet read the first two books in the *Hope Hall* series, catch up with Kath and friends in these heartwarming tales!

PAM RHODES

Summer's out
at Hope Hall

CASTING
the NET

Pam
Rhodes

The
Dunbridge
Chronicles

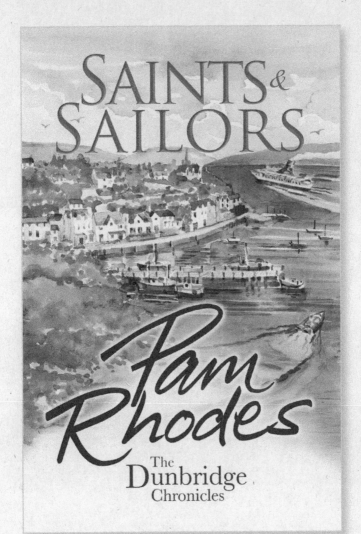

SAINTS & SAILORS

Pam Rhodes

The
Dunbridge
Chronicles